A Rogue to Watch Over Me

A Rogue of Her Own Series
Book 1

TARA KINGSTON

ARE YOU SIGNED UP FOR DRAGONBLADE'S BLOG?

You'll get the latest news and information on exclusive giveaways, exclusive excerpts, coming releases, sales, free books, cover reveals and more.

Check out our complete list of authors, too!

No spam, no junk. That's a promise!

Sign Up Here

www.dragonbladepublishing.com

Dearest Reader;

Thank you for your support of a small press. At Dragonblade Publishing, we strive to bring you the highest quality Historical Romance from some of the best authors in the business. Without your support, there is no 'us', so we sincerely hope you adore these stories and find some new favorite authors along the way.

Happy Reading!

CEO, Dragonblade Publishing

Chapter One

London, 1892

"THE MAN IS trouble, I tell you. I have it on good authority—Logan MacLain is an outlaw."

"On good authority?" Amelia Stewart scoffed at her friend's breathless pronouncement. Glancing up from cataloguing a recent addition to her lending library's collection, she met Beatrice's wide-eyed gaze. "I learned long ago to pay no heed to rumors."

After all, she'd inspired many a tongue-wagging biddy herself.

"What I've heard is not idle gossip. It's a warning." Beatrice lowered her voice as if she had revealed a solemn secret. "The man is a devil, I tell you. A born rogue."

"So, which is it, Bea?" Amelia bit back a grin. "Outlaw? Devil? Or rogue?"

"Well . . ." Beatrice nibbled her bottom lip. "I suppose it may be more accurate to say he's a gambler. But he's up to no good. There's no doubt about that. Heaven only knows how he filled his coffers."

Amelia cocked a skeptical brow. "Honestly, Bea, it's not like you to be drawn into empty-headed tales. Mr. MacLain is a tavern keeper, not a train robber fresh from a spree of pillaging."

"I wouldn't be so sure. I have heard talk of what goes on in his pub, tales not fit to be shared with a proper lady. The Rogue's

Lair, indeed." The excitement in Beatrice's voice betrayed her eagerness to repeat what she'd heard, indecent or not.

"I am not so very proper." Amelia gave a little shrug. "Surely you recall *the scandal.*"

"Not a scandal. Not really. Mere gossip, naught but hot air." Beatrice glanced away, a telltale sign she did not fully believe her own words. "Besides, that was a long time ago. At least the scoundrel had the good graces to make you a widow. Not a divorcee."

Widow.

The word echoed hollow in Amelia's thoughts. Somehow, it didn't quite fit. Even now, years after she'd cast aside her black mourning dress and ended what had seemed a hopeless charade, pinched-face shrews with little better to do twittered about her, their innuendo-laden whispers spoken in tones meant to reach her ears. Their cruel chatter no longer cut deeply, as it had in those days when she'd been torn between despair and relief. She had broken into sobs after the accident that ended her husband's life, but she had never admitted the bitter truth that her tears had not been born solely of grief. Blended with her sorrow, an elemental sense of solace had swept over her.

She no longer needed to fear the man she'd once loved.

Amelia sighed. "It seems a lifetime ago."

"I pray you know better than to let a man's handsome face blind you to his cold heart."

"That goes without saying."

Amelia glanced away, unwilling to reveal the unexpected ache in her chest to Beatrice's observant gaze. Her marriage had proven a bitter lesson, indeed. She'd seen the icy hardness in Edward's eyes from the start, but she'd believed her love could change him. How naive she had been. The man she'd wed had shown her no tenderness. No affection. If anything, he had looked upon her with a cynical contempt, his striking blue eyes viewing her innocent devotion to him as a fool's game.

He'd tried to break her spirit. It was as if Edward had wanted to leave her jaded. But she had known better than to give in. Known better than to surrender her hope.

Genuine love existed. Of that, she had no doubt. She'd seen the adoration in her mother's eyes whenever Mama had looked upon her father. And she'd heard the pure devotion in her father's voice whenever he'd uttered her mother's name, even in the moments before he took his last breath.

She wanted that kind of love.

She would not settle for less.

Never again.

"You're wiser now," Bea went on, pulling Amelia back from her thoughts. "But I do worry."

"Whatever about?" Amelia forced a lightness into her tone she didn't truly feel.

"You were a wedded woman, but you've no experience with the ways of rogues and seducers. With no want of a wife, they're the most dangerous of them all."

"And you believe Mr. MacLain is such a man—a scoundrel who would happily lure a woman like me into his bed?"

Beatrice nodded solemnly. "He's a wicked one, I tell you."

"How very exciting! I rather fancy the prospect of being ravished by a rogue, wicked or otherwise," Amelia teased, eager to watch Beatrice's face scrunch up into a little scowl.

"Do not go tempting fate. There's no telling what trouble a man like him might stir up."

"Oh, don't be a goose. It's not as if Blackbeard has purchased the pub around the corner."

"Not Blackbeard, my dear. Truth be told, this man might be even worse. Mr. MacLain spent years in America. In the wild west, no less. That's where he made his fortune. Ill-gotten gains, indeed."

Amelia set aside the book she'd been holding. No point in attempting to apply the Dewey Decimal system to the volume's classification while Beatrice rambled on about seducers and ne'er-do-wells.

"And now, the rogue has opened that den of sin," Bea went on. "Don't say I didn't warn you."

The tinkle of a small bell pulled Amelia's attention to the door of the reading room. A jaunty pup that looked to be a cross between a Cairn terrier and heaven-only-knew-what trotted across the rug, his head tilted as if he inspected the premises. Gazing up at her with unabashed mischief in his velvet brown eyes, the dog settled at her feet.

"Oh, Heathy, what did you get into this time?" Reaching down to pet the cocky ball of fluff, she smiled despite the nagging suspicion that the pup had been nibbling on something he shouldn't have. She'd learned soon enough after rescuing the abandoned puppy never to leave her shoes or anything else she held dear within his reach.

"He does look a wee bit guilty, doesn't he?" Bea observed with a chuckle.

"Unfortunately, I must agree." Not that his antics made one bit of difference to her affection for the dog she'd come upon in the park on a cold, dreary day nearly three years earlier. Huddled together with his littermates in a battered old crate, the tiny pup had tugged at her heart from the first. Amelia had taken in the lot of them, finding good homes for the wee pups, but she simply couldn't part with the affectionate little creature that bore a pointed resemblance to a chimney sweep's mop. Heathy had been at her side ever since.

Beatrice fixed her gaze on the silver-trimmed leather collar around the hound's neck, her brows knitting. "This little beast of yours wears more finery than you do."

"Heathy's collar was a present . . . from my brother."

"Quite lovely." Beatrice leaned closer to inspect the ebony and silver band. "Did Paul acquire it during his travels?"

"He commissioned it in London." Amelia gulped against a fresh wave of grief. Her brother's death had gouged a wound in her heart she doubted would ever heal.

"Whatever possessed him to purchase such an elegant piece

for a dog?"

"Paul was motivated by the bell on the collar, not the beauty of the piece. He was weary of the *bloody creature*, to use his words, sneaking up on him."

Beatrice's expression softened. "How long has it been, now?"

"Three months." Amelia brushed away a tear trickling down her cheek. "It still feels like a bad dream."

A nightmare.

In truth, no words could fully describe the heart-shattering news of her brother's death. The very thought that the authorities believed Paul had taken his own life was nearly too much to bear.

The detectives were wrong. Something had led Paul to that decrepit building. To that rooftop. He had been lured to his death. She felt that truth in her bones. If only she could prove it.

She wouldn't rest until she'd found justice.

Beatrice's eyes warmed with compassion. "I am so very sorry. I will not speak of it again," she said gently as the chimes at the entry door announced a guest.

The divided skirt of her teal walking suit swishing with each step, Edith Monroe strolled up to the desk. She uttered a few pleasantries before heading directly to the display of the lending library's latest acquisitions.

Taking quick advantage of the distraction, Heathy roamed over to a low shelf by Amelia's desk. As he reached up on his hind legs to sniff a bisque doll she'd placed there, she shooed him away.

"Naughty boy. That's not your plaything."

Her gaze danced over the beautifully garbed doll, and she traced a fingertip over its delicate painted features. A dull current of pain rippled through her, and she struggled to hold back tears. Her brother had given the French Fashion Lady to her following his last trip to Paris, but the memory was now bittersweet. Scarcely a week after she'd received the elegant keepsake as a birthday present, Paul's lifeless body had been discovered in an alley behind a bustling hotel.

Not an accident.

The circumstances of his death made no sense. None whatso-ever.

"I'm delighted you've acquired Miss Braddon's new work." Edith's animated voice tugged Amelia from her thoughts, a welcome intrusion.

"I quite enjoyed it," she said, placing the doll on a higher shelf before joining Edith at the circulation desk to complete the lending slip. As she penned a notation in her journal, the door latch jangled and the chimes sounded once again.

A man strode through the door, the solid *clunk* of his boots against the wooden floorboards jarring her from the task at hand. Tall, dark, and effortlessly imposing, he met her eyes as he headed directly to the desk behind which Amelia stood.

"Oh, dear," Beatrice murmured.

Oh, dear—indeed.

"It's him." Edith's not-quite-a-whisper brought a hint of a smile to his full mouth.

Amelia's breath caught.

Logan MacLain.

In the flesh.

Long-legged and lean-hipped, the sable-haired Scot possessed the look of a raider of old. Clad in an ebony coat that emphasized the breadth of his shoulders, black trousers, and polished leather boots, Mr. MacLain certainly would have made a most dashing outlaw.

Pity he was not a buccaneer at the helm of a ship, pistol at his side, spiriting her away to an oh-so-decadent fate.

Good heavens.

She gave her head a little shake to banish the scandalous notion. What had come over her? She might not be an entirely proper lady. But she was, if nothing else, a sensible one. Perhaps Bea's flights of fancy were contagious.

She fashioned a bland expression, even as her pulse sped, if only just a bit. She certainly was not expecting to see the man face to face—close enough to touch.

Close enough to detect the faint aroma of bergamot soap on his skin.

If not for the way he'd neglected to wear a tie around his neck—or to fasten the buttons at the collar of his pristine white shirt, for that matter—Mr. MacLain might have passed for a gentleman. Or perhaps not, she reasoned, even as her attention lingered over the vee of deep brown hair at his open collar. Decidedly improper.

Drawing her gaze like the glow of a flame lured a hapless moth.

With a little gulp of breath, Amelia forced her attention higher.

Ah, that might have been a mistake.

My, he was an appealing man. Logan MacLain's straight, dark hair brushed his collar. Perhaps too long to be in fashion, yet she longed to touch the rich brown strands. His classically carved features were undeniably rugged, while his dark brown gaze held hers in a most intriguing manner.

Mr. MacLain was undeniably handsome. Undeniably bold. And so very tempting.

Don't be a goose, Amelia.

Reining in her rebellious thoughts, she drummed her fingertips against the desk. Beatrice's talk of the rogue around the corner had taken its toll. It wasn't like her to be rendered nearly speechless by the mere sight of a man. A man who had no business crossing the threshold of her library, at that.

Amelia stepped away from her desk and squared her shoulders. She'd simply send him on his way. Of course, it was actually quite a simple task.

But when she spotted the gleam in his dark-as-midnight eyes, she sensed she'd made another mistake.

"Sir, this library serves an all-female clientele. Perhaps I might point you toward the establishment you seek."

Slowly, he shook his head. "I am in the right place, lass."

This was certainly unexpected. Undeterred, she held her tone steady. "It would seem you have been misinformed. I must ask you to leave."

He tilted his head, studying her. "Ye're Amelia Stewart, are ye not?"

"I am." Determined to project a look of confidence, she cocked her chin. "If you have business to discuss, I will provide you with the name of my solicitor."

"I've no need to speak with anyone but ye." He spoke in a rich, husky brogue, his tone quiet, yet firm and all too appealing.

He took a step toward her. Then another. One more stride, and he'd be close enough to touch her.

A wave of apprehension washed over her, but she steeled herself against it. She felt no fear of this man. But deep within, an instinctive warning sounded.

Something was wrong. Of that, she was quite certain.

"Please leave," she said. "Now."

Again, he shook his head. "I must refuse yer request."

She lifted her chin higher. By thunder, she was not about to let this stranger intimidate her. "In that case, I shall summon a constable."

"I would not do that if I were ye." He shot Beatrice and Edith a sly look. "I suspect these women already know who I am. The new scoundrel in town, purveyor of liquor and all manner of debauchery. Or so I've heard on the street. But for ye, lass, I will offer a more proper introduction. My name is Logan MacLain. I have come bearing a message from yer brother."

Chapter Two

CASTING A GLANCE about the cluttered space that looked to have once been a bookseller's shop, Logan MacLain questioned his resolve to take on a fool's errand. What in blazes was he doing in a library—a ladies' lending library, no less?

Surrounded by high-backed upholstered chairs, shelves brimming with well-used books, and the unmistakable aroma of rosewater in the air, Logan ruthlessly shoved aside his doubts. He had bloody little choice in the matter.

Years earlier, he'd incurred a debt. And he had given his word that when the time came, he would settle it. By God, he intended to honor that vow. Even if the woman at the heart of his quest regarded him as if he had gone mad. Or daft.

Or both.

From the moment he'd first stepped inside the place, Amelia Stewart and her companions had made clear their dismay that any man—much less a rogue like him—had dared to enter their domain. He'd seen no hint of fear in the lass's deep blue eyes, nor in the gawking countenances of her companions. Rather, he had spotted indignation that he'd had the gall to burst in and disturb their peace.

Now, he regretted the raw honesty of his too-blasted-blunt declaration. Amelia Stewart's lips had parted slightly, and she eyed him with ice in her gaze, seeming to search for a suitable rebuke.

Her sapphire eyes narrowed as she found her voice. "I know full well who you are. I'll ask you only once more to leave this establishment."

"I cannot do that." Damned if he would toss the promise he had made to her brother upon the rubbish heap. "I must speak with ye. Alone."

She threw her companions a sneaking glance. "Bea, please summon a constable."

"That would be a mistake." He spoke the truth. Any of the patrolmen in the vicinity could be allied with the schemer who'd led Amelia's brother to his death.

With a deliberate motion, he reached for the links of the watch fob dangling from his vest. Bringing the timepiece into her sight, he displayed its engraved gold back. *P.J.A.* A courier had delivered her brother's watch to Logan's doorstep, mere hours after a letter he'd never expected to receive made its way to him—a letter containing a desperate plea written in a dead man's hand.

For a long moment, she stared at the watch. The skin at her throat rippled slightly, as if she'd swallowed against an emotion she didn't want him to see. And then she set her keen-eyed gaze on him.

"Bea . . . wait." She threaded her fingers together, as if to steady them from trembling. "If the two of you would not mind staying a while longer, I would appreciate your presence. Perhaps you might peruse the periodicals that have recently arrived while I step into my office with our visitor."

One of the women, a dark-haired lass with a comely round face and a scattering of freckles over her nose, shot him a look of distrust. "If you need us, we'll be right here."

"Thank you, Edith." Amelia turned to him. "Very well, Mr. MacLain. Follow me. Please."

He trailed her into a cramped room filled with more books and shelves. She lit a lamp, closed the door behind them, then stepped behind a large desk.

Amelia Stewart was pretty. There was no denying that. Her golden hair bore hints of ginger, while her rosy mouth needed no assistance from lip rouge. But fine lines of tension feathered around her eyes, and the set of her mouth was taut. Unyielding. No wonder that. Her brother's demise had no doubt been hard for her to accept. The inquest had ruled his death a suicide.

But Logan knew better. And he suspected Amelia did as well.

Leaning forward, she pressed her hands against a small area on the desktop that was not covered with books or paper. Her knuckles whitened. Was he the cause of her distress? Or did something else trouble her?

"Mr. MacLain, you are not the first to claim to bear a message from my brother. And from beyond the grave, no less. Evidently, preying on those who've lost loved ones can prove quite lucrative. But you are the first who's dared to cross my threshold bearing stolen goods."

He drew the pad of his thumb over the back of the timepiece. "I take it ye recognize this."

"You knew I would." She reached for the pocket watch, but he closed his fingers around it.

"Not so fast."

Her eyes darkened. Hardened. "I'd dismissed the fanciful rumors that you were an outlaw. It would appear I was correct. You are merely a thief. But you are wasting your time. I will not offer payment for what is rightfully mine."

"I am no thief."

"Then tell me where in blazes you got your hands on my brother's watch?"

The fire in her voice appealed to him, even as she eyed him with cold daggers in her gaze. This woman had courage. Even when face to face with a stranger, a man she didn't think she could trust. Her brother had spoken of her intelligence. Of her gentleness. But never of her spirit.

"A courier brought it to the tavern this morning. The letter from Paul arrived last night."

"Ah, so that's it. The message from my brother's ghost, conveyed alongside stolen gold and Swiss-made gears."

"I assure ye he'd written the letter while he still walked this earth."

"Is that so?" A small sigh escaped her lips. "I must confess, I am surprised you would admit Paul did not communicate with you from another realm."

"I have no reason to mislead ye, lass. The messages I received appear genuine to my eyes, but ye can see for yerself." He reached into his jacket to retrieve the letter, but she stopped him with a curt wave of her hand.

"That will not be necessary. I have no desire to see another not-so-clever forgery." She folded her arms at the waist, as if to insulate herself from the fresh pain he had stirred. "The last *seer* to pass through this door also bore dubious proof of his communication with my brother. The conniver offered to lead me to a mysterious inheritance. For a generous fee, of course."

Meeting her eyes, he saw the distress she could not hide. Anger set his teeth on edge. Bloody bastards, harassing a woman in her grief. If he were to encounter one of their ilk, he'd set the villain on his arse.

"I am not here to seek monetary gain. Paul's letter will be yers to view when ye're ready. But in the meantime, I'm asking ye to trust that yer brother sent me to protect ye."

"Sent you? A man he had not spoken to in years?" Her lower lip trembled. "Yes, I know of you. Paul spoke of you when he was at university. Later, he said the two of you had parted ways. He wanted nothing to do with you."

Her words cut deeper than she might have imagined, but as he'd learned to do all those years ago, he paid the twinge of emotion no heed. If Amelia had known the truth, she'd have realized he was not the reason his friendship with Paul had splintered into a thousand sharp bits. But none of that mattered. Not now.

"The letter I received last night was penned a short time

before your brother died. He knew he'd made enemies. And he feared they would come after ye." He met her questioning gaze. "He asked me to protect ye when ye became their target."

"Enemies he'd made? Target?" She twisted her hands together, as if that might ease her pain. "How dare you! I have experienced cruel attempts at deception, but I believe this may be the most vile."

"I have no desire to mislead ye." Dangling the timepiece from its chain, he extended his hand. "Take the watch. Yer brother wanted ye to have it."

Curling her slender fingers around the watch, she snatched it out of his reach. Did she fear he would have a change of heart? She raised it to the light, the faintest of smiles lifting the corners of her mouth.

"Paul treasured this watch so very much. Our father gave it to him on his twentieth birthday." Her eyes brightened as she examined the engraved initials. "I'd believed it had been lost forever."

He allowed her to enjoy this moment of happiness before drawing her attention back to him with a purposeful clearing of his throat.

"Paul believed you were in danger. He wanted me to look after ye."

"Look after me?" she scoffed. "I do not need a protector, Mr. MacLain. Much less the likes of you."

"The likes of me, eh?" He pulled up a chair, sat down, and stretched out his legs. "So, what is it ye've learned about the Scoundrel MacLain?"

Her teeth grazed her plump lower lip, drawing his gaze. Bugger it. He forced himself to look away. By God, the woman's lush mouth could tempt a dead man to sin. Bloody shame her lips were pinched tight with disdain.

Disdain for him.

There was no changing it. Not that it mattered. He didn't need her to like him.

But he needed her to trust him. At least long enough for him to root out the vicious bastard who'd hurt her if given a chance.

"The Scoundrel MacLain?" She hiked her chin. "A bit dramatic, wouldn't you say?"

"Would ye expect anything less from a scoundrel?"

She pursed her lips into a bow. "In regard to your question," she began, keeping her tone crisp, "I am not about to discuss the salacious details with you. But I have heard enough to know you are no gentleman."

"Yer brother knew a *gentleman* could not defend ye."

Slowly, she shook her head. "You're worse than the charlatans who seek to profit from my grief."

"What do ye think I have to gain from this?"

"I do not know, Mr. MacLain. Nor do I care to find out. But I've heard enough—you need to leave."

"Not until you understand the danger ye're facing." He needed to choose his words carefully, but he could not turn away from the ugly truth. "Yer brother's death was no accident. Ye know that, just as well as I do."

Amelia went still. The color drained from her cheeks. "How cruel of you to twist the knife."

An invisible fist dug into Logan's gut. He hadn't intended to cause her pain. But at the moment, he had no choice. He had to convince her to accept his protection.

"We both know the truth. Paul was murdered. And I have good reason to believe ye're now a target."

"AGAIN, I MUST ask you to leave, Mr. MacLain."

Pulling in a low breath, Amelia steadied her racing pulse. If the arrogant rogue thought to frighten her, he was sorely mistaken. In those bleak days after her brother's death, she'd had quite enough experience with those who preyed upon the vulnerable. She'd learned to steel her spine and send the swindlers and cheats on their way. This was no different. She could not fathom Logan MacLain's true motives, but she had no tolerance for unsettling claims. Protector, indeed.

"I cannot do that." His gravel-edged words were firm with resolve.

"Please go." She bit the words between her teeth. "Now."

"Paul feared ye were in danger. He trusted someone— someone I do not know—to contact me when the threat became clear." Fierce determination blazed in his dark eyes. "Yer brother asked me to watch over ye."

"You speak of danger as if some dastardly villain lurks in the shadows. You must realize I have no reason to believe you."

"Aye, I do. When I received the first letter last night, I dismissed the message as so much rubbish, nothing more than a cruel prank. But when the courier brought Paul's watch to me, I took it as proof that he'd trusted someone to seek me out. I believe the message is genuine. And I will not cast aside my duty to watch over ye."

His gaze betrayed no hint of duplicity. Still, he had to realize that his claims were beyond belief.

"Tell me, Mr. MacLain, why would my brother send for you, of all people?"

"I owed Paul a debt, one I vowed to settle. I intend to see it through."

"Rather odd that he had not spoken to you in nearly a decade, wouldn't you say?"

"Our paths were different," he said. "But Paul knew I was a man of my word. He knew he could trust me, no matter what had gone before."

"You speak of paying a debt to my brother. That's quite the opposite of what I usually hear." Amelia let out a sigh. "If you lost to him at cards, I have no desire for your money."

"It has nothing to do with cards. Or money." MacLain plowed long fingers through his straight, dark hair. "I owe yer brother my life. Were it not for him, I'd have been long dead and buried."

Poppycock. Biting back the unladylike word, Amelia marveled at the gall of the man. Logan MacLain was not the first person who'd tried to deceive her since her brother's death. But Mr. MacLain's approach was far different from the rest. How dare he seek her trust with false claims of loyalty?

Did the rogue take her for an utter fool? She'd adored her brother, but Paul had never aspired to be a hero. Let alone one who'd saved a man's life. Even while they were children raised in a staid household, Paul had been wily and clever. He'd grown to be a schemer, a gambler, a man true to very few. Amelia might have been the only one Paul trusted. Even so, her brother had kept much of his life well concealed. Many of his activities remained a mystery, even to her.

But she certainly knew better than to believe the balderdash spewing from Logan MacLain's mouth.

Swallowing against a bitter lump in her throat, she glanced at the gold timepiece cradled against her palm. "I do want to thank you, Mr. MacLain. You have my gratitude for returning Paul's watch to me." She forced herself to meet MacLain's dark gaze. "But it is cruel for you to persist with this bizarre charade. Please do not disturb me again."

"I will leave ye. For now." He turned to the door. "If ye need me, send for me. Any time of the day. Or night."

"I assure you, Mr. MacLain, I will not be darkening your doorstep."

"Do not be so sure." He threw her a look over his shoulder as he walked away. "Trouble is coming. I sense it in my bones. When ye need me, ye know where I'll be."

Chapter Three

BEHIND THE BAR at the Rogue's Lair tavern, Logan poured good scotch into an amber glass and slugged it down. What in the name of Robbie Burns had he got himself into? God knew he was nobody's hero. He could cast aside the vow he had uttered as a foolish young man, the debt he'd never truly expected to settle. He had no one to answer to, and blast it all, honor had never been his stock in trade.

He could walk away before he was in too deep.

Too bloody late.

Now that he'd seen the fire in Amelia Stewart's dark blue eyes, he couldn't turn his back on her. If Paul was right—if Amelia was in danger—he had to protect her.

Blasted shame she'd looked at him as if he was a cheat and a conniver.

Kirk Murray's gruff voice pulled Logan out of his thoughts. The barkeep swiped a rag over the counter, making a show of cleaning it. "What the hell's got ye thinking so hard, lad?"

"Lad?" Logan deflected the question. "Ye forgetting I'm the one paying yer wages?"

Murray shrugged his bony shoulders. "Bollocks. I've known ye since ye were in nappies. What's troubling ye?"

Logan rubbed a nagging ache in the back of his neck. "Not a damned thing."

"Ye're a poor liar. Like yer da before ye." Murray scrubbed a hand over his gray beard. "A good man, he was. Ye're the spitting image of him."

The barkeep's words brought a smile, even as a sense of regret washed over Logan. His father had been a good man, an ambitious merchant who'd built his family a fine home in the city. But Da had worked himself into an early grave. He had not lived to see his son grow to manhood. The loss still cut like a dull blade to the gut.

"I had little time to know my father."

"He would be proud of ye."

"Ye've had too much whisky for one night."

"Ye doubt my words?" Murray went on.

"If he could see me now, Da would roll over in his grave. He wore his collar buttoned tight . . . respectability at all costs. That's not me."

"Ye're wrong. But ye always were headstrong. Like yer da."

Setting his glass upon the bar, Logan glanced at the clock. It'd be dark soon enough. The regulars would pile in, and thankfully, there'd be no more time for drivel he didn't want to hear.

Murray poured himself a drink. "Ye're going to check on the lass?"

Logan nodded. "What in hell was in her brother's head, sending the likes of me to watch over her?"

"He knew he could count on ye, MacLain. Whatever in hell is truly going on, whoever is behind the twisted riddle ye've received, ye will not let the woman face the threat alone."

As the door closed behind the day's last patron, Amelia slid the latch into place. At the end of an ordinary afternoon, she would relish this time, allowing the quiet to settle in around her, finding a sense of contentment in the simple tasks of shelving books and tidying up the library that was her haven.

But this evening felt different. Nightfall had filled her with a sense of wariness she couldn't cast aside. Logan MacLain's unexpected appearance at her doorstep had troubled her far more deeply than she'd let on. Even now, apprehension prickled her skin like a draft of icy air.

Had his claims been yet another attempt to frighten her into abandoning the building that housed her library? Since her brother's death, others had tried to convince her to leave. But why would Logan MacLain be interested in this place? Surely he'd have no use for a small shop that barely had room to house her collection.

Immersed in her thoughts, she took the watch from her skirt pocket and grazed her fingertips over the etched gold. The feel of her brother's carved initials offered a gentle, calming connection. Had a sense of integrity led Mr. MacLain to return it? Or had he intended to gain her trust with a gesture of goodwill?

The question gnawed at her, unraveling the momentary peace. MacLain's claims had been wild and utterly unexpected. But was it possible he was telling the truth?

Enough. She would not dwell on her nagging doubts. Before long, she'd go up to her flat, pour a cup of tea, grab a bite to eat, and hopefully she'd be able to put the events of the afternoon out of her mind.

She slipped the watch back into her pocket and turned her attention to a stack of recent acquisitions. Scooping up the books, she carried them to a table near the front of the library. Memories of her brother flashed through her thoughts. Paul had always supported her endeavors. When she'd set out to establish a lending library for the women of the community, he had never questioned the cost. For years, funding the library had posed no difficulty. Their father had spent his life building a minor fortune through hard work and shrewd investments. He'd left behind a substantial inheritance, trusting her brother to manage the funds to both their benefits.

The assets held in trust were hers now. Some believed her to be an heiress.

Heiress. The word rang hollow in her thoughts. After Paul's death, she'd discovered the truth. Much of their nest egg had vanished.

Fortunately, her brother had not left her destitute. If she managed what remained of the funds with an eye toward thrift, she could maintain a life of independence, lived on her own terms. Doing so would pose no hardship. She'd never aspired to luxury. Her flat above the library was quite comfortable.

Still, the revelation that Paul had squandered much of their inheritance—and in such a short time—had struck like a body blow. He'd drained a considerable amount from the accounts in the year before his death, money that had seemingly evaporated into thin air. What had gone wrong? Had he involved himself in some venture—legitimate or otherwise—that he'd concealed from her? Had he fallen into some sort of trouble?

Well, there was nothing to be done about it now. Amelia shoved a heavy volume onto the shelf, then another, taking some small release of tension from the exertion. As she reached for another book, a quiet thud against the floor reached her ears.

Startled, she turned. A thick tome lay on the floor near the shelves by the circulation desk. Heathy's collar bell jangled as he darted out of sight.

"Naughty boy," she said, more to herself than the wayward pup. "How on earth did you move such a heavy book?"

Her gaze trailed Heathy's path. He'd scurried toward the back of the library. Rather odd, that. It wasn't like the pup to run and hide. Usually, he was quite proud of his mischief. Had Heathy sensed something she had not?

A sudden chill danced over her skin. My, she was being a goose, wasn't she? Letting her nerves get the better of her. And all over her mischievous dog.

Perhaps Mr. MacLain's unwanted visit had gotten to her more than she'd realized. She'd put very little stock in his jarring words. She knew better than to take his claims or the bold promises of any of the others who'd tried to deceive her at face value.

Shaking off the way her skin had prickled ever so slightly, she determined to finish her tasks and be done for the night. Then, she could relax with a piping hot cup of tea and a good book.

She snatched up the book she needed put back in its place and headed to the proper shelf.

A quiet squawk of the floorboards cut through her resolve. She froze, her gaze pulled to the back of the library.

Definitely not Heathy.

Her breath caught.

She was not alone.

Fighting the instinct to flee, she calmed herself. *You are a logical woman, Amelia. Perhaps Mrs. Tidwell hasn't left after all.*

Yes, that was it, she reasoned. She doubted her elderly patron could hear the shriek of a teakettle, let alone Amelia's voice as she'd announced closing time.

"Mrs. Tidwell," she called, moving along the rows of bookcases. "Come along, dear. I'll see you home."

Behind her, the latch on the entry door rattled.

Her heart raced. *Someone is trying to get in.*

She spun around, her attention darting to the frosted glass.

No one there.

She let out a breath of relief. A patron had realized the place was closed for the day and gone along their way. Such a simple explanation.

Creak. One. Then another. And another, along the back shelves, betraying otherwise silent footsteps. The sounds seemed magnified by the utter quiet in the space.

She pulled in a low breath, as if that might slow her racing pulse. "Mrs. Tidwell," she called again as she canvassed the shelves. With each empty row, hope faded.

No sign of Mrs. Tidwell.

The old woman had not been the source of the floorboards' protest.

Another squeak of the floor, this time near the center of the collection shelves. This time, the steps were heavier, as though the intruder now made no effort to conceal their presence.

Amelia's thoughts raced.

No need to worry. You have a weapon.

And you know how to use it.

She rushed to her office and maneuvered around a pile of books in front of the cabinet. She'd stored the derringer she carried for the purpose of self-defense in the uppermost drawer. Taking the key from her pocket, she slid it into the lock.

As she turned the key, a man's large, heavy hand clamped over her shoulder. The intruder dragged her back against his towering frame. She cried out, her voice raw with instinctive fear.

"Quiet. Now." He caught her chin in one leather-gloved hand, his fingers digging brutally into her skin. Sliding his hand higher, he pressed his fingers over her mouth and nose.

Stifling her scream.

Cutting off her breath.

"Do as I say. Don't make a sound."

Frantic for air, she nodded her understanding.

"Good." He kept his fingers clamped tight over her mouth, even as he allowed her to take a breath. "He said you were a clever girl. Now just do as you're told, and I won't have to hurt you."

He. The word echoed in her brain like a thunderclap.

Someone had sent this man after her.

But who?

His hold unyielding, he tensed against her. He seemed nervous. On edge. Instinct warned her that he was unpredictable. And even more dangerous.

Do not trigger his anger. Or his fear.

Do not fight.

Not yet.

She couldn't see the man's face, but the feel of his wool jacket suggested the fabric was finely made. Expensive. A slight whiff of hair pomade mingled with the odor of spirits on his breath. The intruder was not an unwashed thug. Not a street thief or burglar.

Why would someone others might perceive as a gentleman come after her?

The door latch clattered. Muttering an epithet, he dug his fingers into her shoulder. "Expecting someone?"

She shook her head, desperate to keep him calm. To her relief, the jangling at the door stopped. As an uneasy silence fell over them, he roughly dragged her toward the back of the building.

"Lucky for you they went on their way," he murmured against her cheek. Keeping her back turned to him, he slid his hand from her mouth. "Where is it?"

She pulled in a breath. "I don't know what you're talking about."

He shook her. Hard. "Do not take me for a fool. He made that mistake."

"I don't know—"

"Tell me the truth. Where is the blasted diamond?" He curled his fingers around her hair and gave a rough yank. "Where is it?"

A cry escaped her as she braced herself against the sudden pain.

"I want the truth." He pulled her against him. This close, she could feel the gun beneath his jacket pressing into her back. "You were the only one—"

"You're mad." She gasped a breath, then another. "I know nothing . . . nothing about a jewel."

He coiled one arm roughly over her chest, threateningly close to her throat. "There's only one reason to keep you alive. Tell me what you know."

Or he will choke the life out of me.

Raw instinct flooded her veins. She had to fight. Had to get away.

"Perhaps I do remember something," she said, hoping the brute might believe her and let down his guard.

"That's better. Now start talking."

"He told me . . ." she said, leading him on as she shifted on her feet. With luck, he would not realize the subtle movement had a purpose. Years earlier, her brother had taught her a lesson in defending herself against an overly determined suitor. Or an attacker.

"Tell me," he demanded against her ear.

"There is a certain place . . ."

She pulled in a low breath. Summoning all the force she could muster, she stomped her foot down onto his boot. Her heel plowed into his instep.

As he let out a groan of pain, his hold eased. She jerked away, bolting for the door. Her fingers closed around the knob.

His large hands clamped down on her shoulders, holding her with a vise-like strength. Dragging her to him, he stared down at her. "That was a mistake." His tone was cold. "The diamond—I know it's here."

A bitter truth crashed over her. If this brute did not care that she saw his pale, broad features, he had no intention of letting her live. She clasped the skeleton key from the door in her hand. Carefully, she hid it against her palm. Not an ideal weapon, but it could inflict pain. And with that, she could buy time. She could find a way to escape.

"I have money," she murmured with a passiveness she did not feel. "I will give it to you."

An ugly laugh passed his thin lips. "Save yourself. Tell me where he hid it."

"I cannot tell you what I do not know."

"Where is the bloody treasure? Tell me." He bit the command between his teeth. "Before I choke the breath out of you and tear this place apart. Board by board."

The anger in his voice fueled the desperate fear deep within her.

Fight the cur!

She pulled in a breath and called upon a strength she'd never known she possessed. Wildly, she struggled against his hold. Still, it wasn't enough. His fingers dug into her upper arms, pinning her. She had to free herself. With a sharp twist of her body, she drove an elbow into his side. His low, pain-filled grunt told her she'd hit his ribs.

His breaths came fast and ragged. "You little shrew!"

With another sudden, violent motion, she wrenched her arm free. Careful to conceal the key in her hand, she eyed his face, steeling herself against a wave of revulsion.

"You will regret that." He reared back, raising his thick hand.

Now!

She struck his face, the slim metal key plunging into his left eye. Agony turned his voice raw as he cried out, instinctively releasing his hold on her other arm.

Run! Can't be trapped here!

Amelia darted to the door.

Heavy footfalls of pursuit sounded in her ears. Thick fingers grazed her back. Still, she evaded his grasp.

Suddenly, his hand clamped over her upper arm. Wild with fear, she searched the room for something—anything—to fend him off.

The bookends.

Fighting wildly against his hold, she strained to reach her desk. Her fingers brushed one of the sturdy metal braces.

Must reach it.

He yanked her nearly off her feet, but she coiled her fingers around the bookend's column-shaped base. His fingers coiled around her wrist, tight as a vise. With a vicious twist, he contorted her arm. She bit back a cry, but the small sound that escaped her only seemed to encourage his cruelty. Slowly, he increased the tension. More and more, nearly to the breaking point.

Pain rippled through her arm. Intense. Relentless.

She heard herself scream as the bookend tumbled to the floor.

Still, he did not ease the cruel pressure. Hauling her close, he stared down at her. His bloodied face sickened her. "I will wring your scrawny neck. Tell me where—"

Heathy's low growl cut through her captor's threat. The dog lunged.

With a roar of pain, the intruder staggered backward. "Blasted mongrel." Frantic to dislodge the dog's teeth from his shin, the brute let her go. Muttering a string of vile curses, he reached for the gun beneath his jacket. Gaslight gleamed off the barrel of his revolver.

Desperation surged through her. She eyed the bookend near her feet. Could she reach it before he pulled the trigger?

Dear God. She couldn't take that chance.

"No!" Dragging Heathy into her arms, she put herself between the dog and the gun.

"Move away," the intruder ordered. "Or I'll kill—"

A sudden, guttural groan cut through his threat as his knees buckled. He crumpled like a puppet untethered from its strings.

Amelia lifted her gaze to the man who'd claimed he had been sent to protect her. Standing over the assailant, a leather cudgel in his hand, Logan MacLain regarded her with an expression that bore no hint of triumph. Rather, his full mouth betrayed a look of resignation, as if even he had not quite believed the threat was real. Until now.

Her pulse raced as he came to her.

"Are ye well, lass?" His words were a husky brogue.

She nodded, meeting his dark eyes. "How did you know . . . I needed you?" She asked the first words that came to mind.

"I'd a notion ye might need some help." His voice was quiet and matter-of-fact as his attention shifted to her unconscious attacker. "From the looks of this bastard, I was right."

Chapter Four

A PECULIAR CALM fell over Amelia as she retrieved the intruder's gun from the spot where it had fallen from his grip. The weapon felt heavy, strangely so. If Logan MacLain had not arrived when he did, everything would have turned out quite differently. The brute who now lay unconscious on the floor might have used the weapon to kill Heathy. A sickening wave of fear washed over her. God only knew what the cruel heathen would have done after that. Likely, he'd have turned the gun on her. She may have died without even knowing why the intruder had come after her.

Pulling in long, steadying breaths, she shored up her courage as best she could. Despite the rapid cadence of her breathing, her hands remained steady as she held the revolver. Rather a miracle, that.

She studied MacLain beneath the veil of her lashes. He'd charged in, ready to play her champion. And in the very nick of time.

She should be grateful. After all, he had likely saved her life.

Pity his well-timed arrival was rather too convenient.

Seeming to sense her apprehension, Heathy stayed by her side. The dog's attention fixed on her defender with an unwavering stare.

MacLain cast the pup a narrow-eyed glance. "Bloody protective little beast, isn't he?"

"Heathy doesn't know if you are a hero or a villain. Truth be told, neither do I."

"Ye'll figure it out soon enough." He went to the window and calmly removed the braided tiebacks from the curtains. "Ye know this man?"

"I've never seen him before in my life."

Turning from the window, MacLain crouched down to secure the attacker's arms behind his back. He fastened the makeshift bindings with swift, efficient movements. "Not a callus on his hands. He's not a common ruffian. But ye already knew that, didn't ye?"

"I had worked that part out."

"I've seen this man lingering about the pub, deep in his cups. Goes by Jack." MacLain glanced up, meeting her eyes. "So tell me, lass. Why in hell did he come after ye?"

"I don't know." The words seemed not quite truth, not quite a lie. But she couldn't tell MacLain what the intruder had demanded of her. The very notion of a precious gem concealed somewhere within her library was madness. Even so, she couldn't chance putting ideas in anyone's head about hidden treasure.

He looped a curtain tie around the intruder's legs. "Ye think I'm fool enough to believe that, do ye?"

"Perhaps it's you who could shed some light on the man's motives," she countered. "After all, you confess to at least a passing acquaintance."

MacLain shrugged. "Most nights, he speaks only a few words, and those are to the barkeep. He keeps whisky flowing down his gullet."

"Yet tonight, you knew to follow him here."

"Now that's where ye're wrong." A dark expression fell over his features. "I didn't know the bastard was here until I heard ye scream."

"Just in time for you to charge to the rescue."

"But not to a hero's welcome, I see."

"I do appreciate your help." She weighed her next words

carefully. "Provided, of course, this was not a planned performance."

"Performance?" He fastened the binding into a stout knot around the intruder's ankles. "What in Hades are ye trying to say?"

She pointed to the door. "I cannot help but wonder how you gained entry. As you can see, the bolt is still in place."

"Aye, that it is."

"Yet you did not break it down."

"Only a fool would go to such trouble." Rising to his full height, he threw her attacker a look of contempt. "I gained entry the same way he did—through the alley."

"A door that was also secured," she countered.

"The puny lock on that rotted hunk of wood was no match for his pry bar." MacLain eyed the weapon in her hand. "Now, I'll ask ye to set that gun down before ye blow off one of my toes."

"I would not waste a perfectly good bullet on your toe. I am quite a good shot."

"Are ye now?"

"My aim is true to twenty paces."

"Good to know." The corners of his full mouth lifted, the merest hint of a smile. "Between yer dog eyeing my leg like a tasty bone and that gun ye're gripping for dear life, I'm starting to take issue with the welcome I've received. I am not used to playing the noble knight. Matter of fact, I'm of a mind that I'd have been better off if I had stayed at the pub and poured myself another draught of whisky."

"Until now, I had no need of a knight, noble or otherwise." Squaring her shoulders, she met his arrogant gaze. "Odd that the situation arose only after I'd laid eyes on you."

"If ye do not trust me, see for yerself," MacLain said as the trussed-up man on the floor began to stir. "Look at the back door. Then you can summon the authorities. Unless you'd prefer to keep this bloke here on your rug. In the morning, the ladies who frequent this place could step over him."

"Very well. Please, lead the way." She turned to whistle softly to her dog. "Come along, Heathy. I might be in need of your services."

She followed MacLain past the rows of shelves to a dimly lit hallway. She lit a gas lamp on the wall.

"Ye see how the latch is dangling off the frame?" he said as they approached the door that opened to the alley. "He forced the lock."

Amelia spotted a small iron rod stowed nearby, not quite out of sight. "He left his pry bar here, on this shelf." She sighed. "But when could he have done this? Surely someone in the library would've noticed."

"From the looks of it, he knew what he was doing. He'd be quick."

Had the chatter of her patrons' conversation and the ordinary sounds of the crowded, shop-lined street obscured the noise? "You may be right."

"The coward put some thought into this. He knew when to show himself." Mr. MacLain leaned closer, studying her in the hazy light. His eyes narrowed. "He left a mark on ye—on yer cheek."

"I am not injured. Not truly."

"He hurt ye." MacLain's jaw set in a hardened line. "I should have killed him."

A look of pure protectiveness flashed over his features. Suddenly, the weapon in her hand felt heavy. Unneeded.

"I had a fright. Nothing more serious than that."

Boldly, he brushed the pad of his thumb against the curve of her face, his touch infinitely more gentle than the intruder's rough hold. "He'll pay for what he did to ye. I will see to that."

"The authorities will see justice done," she said, asserting a confidence she didn't entirely feel.

Lamplight danced over the chiseled planes of his face, highlighting the dark growth of new beard shadowing his cheeks. Slowly, he shook his head. "I would not count on that."

"Nothing about this makes sense." She took a step back, then another, putting a bit of much-needed distance between her and this man who was still in truth a stranger to her. "From the moment you first spoke to me, the world feels as if it's somehow shifted."

"I sense it, too." His eyes seemed to drink her in. "Yer brother knew this day would come. That's why he sent for me. Now, I need yer trust."

SEATED ON AN intensely uncomfortable spindle chair in the spartan office of a weary-eyed police detective, Amelia glanced at the clock. She allowed herself a small sigh. In the hours that had passed since Mr. MacLain had subdued the violent intruder, she had explained what transpired in the library that evening to a series of constables. Now, after arriving at the station in a hansom cab Logan MacLain had summoned, she watched as a detective scribbled a few words of her statement onto paper.

Looking up, Inspector Herrin brushed a few strands of salt-and-pepper hair off his brow. "You believe the man in custody intended to rob you?"

"I'd say so. His actions and threats certainly showed as much."

The detective tapped the nib of his fountain pen against the pad. "The establishment is a free lending library. Do you keep substantial sums on hand?"

She shook her head. "I do not require payment for the use of the collection, but many of my patrons offer a small donation from time to time. Those funds are promptly deposited into the proper account."

"So, you have books. But little money. Is anything of value stored in the place?" The questions in his eyes spoke louder than his words.

"Nothing I'd think would have much worth to a thief. There is one thing you should know." She swallowed against a nervous lump in her throat. "The man insisted I had something he wanted. A jewel, of all things."

Inspector Herrin's attention lit on the garnet pin at her collar. "He attempted to steal your brooch?"

"I don't believe so." She touched a fingertip to the elegant piece that had once belonged to her grandmother. "He made no attempt to take it. He was after a far more valuable gem . . . a diamond."

The creases in the detective's forehead deepened. "I see." He cleared his throat. "You are quite sure his intent was not . . . an assault on your person?"

She rubbed her temples with her fingers, as if the gentle touch might soothe the dull throbs in her head. "I cannot be sure of his intentions. But I know what he said. He demanded that I tell him where a diamond had been hidden, a jewel I most certainly do not possess."

Inspector Herrin looked down at his notes. "At this point, he has refused to answer any questions. Not so much as his name. Mrs. Stewart, do you have any idea—"

From the corridor beyond the detective's office, a man's horrified shouts penetrated the closed door. "Good God!"

Heavy footsteps and epithets followed. Inspector Herrin leapt to his feet. "Mrs. Stewart—stay here."

Rushing from the room, he slammed the door shut behind him.

Her pulse raced.

What was happening?

Had her attacker escaped?

Amelia ran to the door and cracked it open. Cautiously stepping into the corridor, she spotted uniformed patrolmen crowded around an open cell.

Inspector Herrin barked an order. "I need a physician! Now!" He looked pale. Drawn. Was that blood on his hands?

An older man, more world-weary in his expression, trailed the detective out of the cell. "It's too late for that."

Inspector Herrin turned. "Bloody hell," he uttered beneath his breath. He'd spied her viewing the unfolding chaos. He scowled. "For God's sake, get the woman away from here. This is not a fit sight for a lady's eyes."

She looked past him. Her pulse hammered in her ears. Where was Mr. MacLain? He had accompanied her to the station house. Surely he had not been injured. Or worse.

Despite the detective's order, she edged closer to the cell. A towering patrolman stepped in front of her, blocking the scene.

From behind, a firm hand closed over her upper arm. She startled at the unexpected touch.

"Come with me, lass."

Mr. MacLain's husky rasp sent relief coursing through her. She whipped around to face him. Lines of tension etched his mouth and brow.

"All hell has broken loose," he said, settling a hand on her elbow. "This is no place for a lady."

Escorting her back to the detective's office, MacLain ushered her inside and closed the door. He led her to a chair, his tone grim. "The man who attacked you—did he have another weapon? Did he have a knife?"

"I don't know." She searched her mind. "I saw only the revolver."

Rubbing the back of his neck as though it ached, he stared at the floor.

Apprehension surged through her. "Tell me . . . tell me what's happened."

"The bastard who attacked ye is dead."

"Dead?" she replied, her words dulled by shock.

He walked to the window and looked out into the darkness. "Aye. And by his own hand."

Chapter Five

D EBATING HOW MUCH to tell her of what he'd witnessed, Logan turned away from Amelia. For the span of several breaths, he stared into the night, focusing on the sliver of moon against the stark blackness of the sky. In his life, he had seen violence. He had seen death.

By hellfire, he'd never encountered a more vile sight than what he had seen in that holding cell. The bastard who'd come after Amelia Stewart had died a violent death. Brutal. Bloody. Vicious.

God almighty.

He had watched as a detective retrieved a folding knife lying on the floor, inches from the man's right hand. How had her assailant smuggled a blade into the jail? Surely the guards had searched him. They would not have made such a careless error.

Had the cur actually taken his own life?

Or had he been silenced?

Turning back to her, Logan caught Amelia's hands in his. Her rounded face had gone pale, her mouth thinned to a taut seam. Was that fear in her sapphire eyes?

Damn the jackals who'd set this scheme against her into motion. If anyone tried to hurt her, they would pay a steep price. He'd see to that.

He drew his thumb over the back of her hand. Her skin was soft, smooth as satin. So very different from his. At his touch, her fingers trembled against him. If she'd been taken aback by his bold move, she did not show it. A current of awareness flowed between them.

Had she sensed the connection?

Her gaze softly questioning, the tension in her mouth eased. "You say he died by his own hand. Why would he do such a thing?"

"I don't have the answer, lass. But I know this much: I'll be damned if I am leaving ye to spend this night alone."

Her eyes widened. With a slight lift of her chin, she slipped her hands from his grasp. "I have no need for a bodyguard. I am a librarian. Not a damsel in distress."

"And I'm not blasted Prince Charming, out to slay some fairy tale monster. But as long as ye're still in danger, I'll take no chances with yer safety."

Lacing her fingers as if to steady them, she pulled in a low breath. "The man who attacked me is lying dead in that cell."

"The threat has not passed. Ye will stay with me, in my home."

The set of her jaw betrayed her response before she spoke the words. "Out of the question, Mr. MacLain."

"I will protect ye. But ye must listen to reason. Ye have to—"

She hiked a feathered brow. "Listen to reason?"

Bollocks. Hard-won experience had taught him never to utter those words to a woman. From the look in Amelia's eyes, he should have heeded the lesson.

A minor setback, at worst. He'd advance a rational argument to convince her.

"If ye look at this logically—"

Heat blazed in her sapphire eyes. "Rest assured, I am viewing your proposal through a lens of reason and logic. And I must tell you, the word that springs to mind when I consider the notion that I might sleep under your roof is *never.*"

"Surely ye know ye can trust me by now."

"Frankly, that remains to be seen," she said with a little huff.

"You've yet to explain why Paul would call upon you to protect me. And against schemers and murderers, no less. Perhaps some insight into the nature of your mysterious debt might inspire a bit more trust."

"That time will come," he said, doubting his own words. If Amelia knew the full truth of what had happened all those years ago—of the circumstances that had compelled her brother to pull a trigger to save Logan's life—she might never forgive him.

"Will it now?" Her tone told him she'd read the truth in his expression. "In any case, I've no intention of spending the night with a—"

"A man like me?"

"With *any* man."

"Ye're concerned for yer reputation?"

"You are not the only one the gossipy biddies like to talk about. Preserving my good name is rather a lost cause." A low breath escaped her slightly pursed lips. "I am most grateful for your assistance. But I have no intention of warming your bed."

For reasons he couldn't entirely work out, her insinuation stung. "Ye think that's what this is about, do ye?"

She gave a little shrug. "It is very late. At this point, I possess neither the strength nor the mental energy to puzzle out your true motives. I wish only to return home."

"Whatever the bastard was searching for is still out there. Ye don't know who's lurking about, who's waiting for ye."

The stubborn tilt of her chin ratcheted higher. "I had not expected you to be so melodramatic. Perhaps I should check my armoire for a monster or two before I lie down to sleep."

"A woman alone is easy prey. Surely ye know that."

"I will not be alone," she countered. "Have you forgotten about Heathy?"

Had the lass not been in harm's way, the notion of the four-legged mop of fur acting as her protector would have given him a chuckle. But at the moment, he was in no mood for amusement.

"I'll be damned if I'm leaving yer defense to that wee beast."

Her eyes glimmered with emotion. Was that a hint of fear? She was a strong woman, but she had to see she was still vulnerable.

Still in danger.

"Heathy is not a watchdog. But as you've seen, he's quite capable of deterring an attacker."

"We both know that mop on legs is no match for an armed man."

As he spoke, Detective Inspector Herrin returned to the office. His expression grim, he closed the door behind him. He turned to Amelia. "At this time, I have no further questions. I will summon a constable to escort you home."

"That won't be necessary," Logan said. "I will see to her safety."

The detective frowned. "Mrs. Stewart, I would not be doing my duty if I did not entrust the task of seeing you home to one of our men. They are of the highest character."

"That will not be necessary," Amelia said. "I do appreciate your concern, but I have confidence in Mr. MacLain's ability to see me safely to my doorstep." Was it his imagination, or had her tone been rather cheeky, as if she felt both men were worrying far too much over a threat she felt had been extinguished?

"Very well." Inspector Herrin pinched the bridge of his nose. "In that case, I will send a patrolman to escort you to the station house in the event that I have further questions."

"Thank you," she said. "Inspector, do you believe the man who attempted to rob me acted of his own accord?"

"At this point, there is no evidence that anyone else was involved. If he had an accomplice, you can be confident we will apprehend the lout." Weariness fell over the detective's features as he returned to his desk.

"Thank you, Inspector," she said, offering a warm smile, as if she'd found an ally.

She flashed Logan a sneaking glance. So, she thought she'd won this battle, did she?

"There's something else." The detective sank into his chair. He reached for the decanter on his desk. "Something you need to know."

Amelia's smile faded. "And what might that be, Inspector?"

"It has been a very long night," he said, pouring a hearty draught of brandy into a glass. "You're entirely certain you've had no prior acquaintance with the man who attacked you?"

"As I've told you, I had never laid eyes on him before this evening."

The detective nodded his understanding. "There is one thing that I find rather peculiar."

"What are ye getting at?" Logan pressed for an answer.

Herrin studied Amelia for a long moment. "Paul Anderson was your brother, was he not?"

A tiny vee formed between her brows. "You know very well he was. But what could he have had to do with any of this?"

The detective pinned her with his gaze. "That's what I was hoping you could tell us, Mrs. Stewart. You see, the man who died tonight carried your brother's calling card."

AMELIA STAYED BY Logan MacLain's side as they left the station house. She'd seen no need for an escort by a member of the police, yet another stranger whose presence she would have to endure on this horrid night. But she harbored no illusion that the streets of London were safe for an unarmed woman, much less after dark. Though the man who'd come after her was no longer a threat, she knew full well that more ordinary dangers lurked about at this hour of the night.

Casting MacLain a sidelong glance, she felt herself relax, if only a bit. Something about his very presence offered a sense of security, something she had not expected to feel. It may have been the confidence in his manner and the ever-so-serious set of his features, the sense that he was a man with a purpose he intended to fulfil. It might have been the image she carried in her mind of the capable way in which he'd dealt with the man who might well have killed both her and Heathy. Or, perhaps—just perhaps—deep within her, she wanted to believe his claim that Paul had trusted MacLain to be there for her when she needed him the most.

Amelia drew in a calming breath, then another. Regardless of whatever it was that made his nearness reassuring, she knew better than to give in to his urging to spend the night under his roof. Even if his motives were pure and chivalrous, unlikely as that might be, she certainly could not leave Heathy to his own devices all night long.

Weary to the bone, she longed for the comfort of her own bed. She'd be safe in her own flat. After all, the intruder could no longer hurt her. Even so, her thoughts raced. Inspector Herrin's revelation had shaken her to the core. Why in heaven had the brute possessed a card engraved with her brother's name? Surely Paul would not have associated with the ruffian who'd invaded her library.

Hazy gaslight cut through the darkness of the alley, bringing into focus an ebony-enameled coach. MacLain had sent a messenger to summon a carriage to transport her home. The rather stodgy conveyance was not at all what she'd expected. A pair of horses that looked to be well past their prime waited patiently to pull the coach. She glanced up at the driver's bench. A lean man with a thick mop of wheat-brown hair tipped his flat-brimmed cap while the silver-haired woman at his side smiled down at them. The woman held the reins in slender, gloved hands.

"I was starting to wonder if ye were ever going to show yer face, MacLain," the woman called from her perch. "Tim and I have been chilled to the bone."

"These things take time," MacLain replied. "I'd think ye'd remember that, given how many times ye fished yer husband out of jail."

"Those were the days. Ah, how I miss that man." The woman's voice bore a touch of sadness.

"I know ye do, Mrs. Langford. As do I."

Turning to Amelia, MacLain introduced her to the woman at the reins and the young man who'd accompanied her, the barkeep's assistant, Tim. Following the exchange of pleasantries, he opened the door and assisted Amelia into the carriage. He then turned his attention back to Mrs. Langford. "Now I'll ask ye to join Mrs. Stewart in the coach."

"'Tis a beautiful night. A grand time for a drive," she replied. "There's no need for me to be cooped up inside."

"I must insist," he said, his tone firm.

She shot him a scowl belied by the twinkle in her eyes. "I seldom find an opportunity to take the coach out at night. You're too blasted protective of me."

"Mrs. Langford, I would be obliged to ye if ye'd convince the lady I am not a scoundrel."

"Why in heaven would I want to do that?"

"Because it is the truth." He grinned. "Even if I am inclined to get my way."

The appealing touch of humor in his tone made Amelia smile despite the weary pounding in her head. She heard Mrs. Langford scurry down from the bench, impressively nimble despite the flowing wool of her skirt.

The older woman flashed a warm smile as she entered the coach. "Ye've no worries, MacLain. I'll get the lass on yer side."

"Ah, ye're in for a treat," he said to Amelia, wry amusement flavoring his words.

Mrs. Langford settled onto the bench across from Amelia, so near their knees almost touched. As she smoothed her skirts into place, she made no attempt to hide the fact that she was sizing Amelia up.

"So, lass, I understand ye're in a bit of a fix."

"I am confident the situation has been resolved," Amelia

replied, followed by a silent prayer that the words contained more fact than wishful thinking.

As the carriage rumbled down the street with MacLain at the reins, Mrs. Langford's mouth pulled into a soft smile. "Logan is of a different mind on the matter. Believe me, if he sees a threat, it's because one is there."

"I must disagree. The man who tried to harm me is dead," Amelia explained. The words seemed so very matter-of-fact, yet her pulse hammered with a fresh burst of fear.

"I know he is headstrong. Always has been, since he was a wee lad." Mrs. Langford lowered her voice as if she confided a grand secret. "But ye will not find a man more true to his word. Logan will watch over ye. He will not let ye down. Ye can count on that."

Welcoming the warmth in Mrs. Langford's smile, Amelia bit back the reply that had sprung to mind. In truth, she had no reason to count on Mr. MacLain. Nor to fear he would let her down. Hours earlier, Logan MacLain had been a stranger to her. The events of this evening had not changed the fact that she knew almost nothing about the man other than breathlessly spoken gossip. But there was no need to dismiss the older woman's confident assurances.

"He does appear rather determined to play the protector," Amelia said gently.

"When the courier brought the message to come for the two of ye, I breathed a sigh of relief. The barkeep had already spread the word about the nasty bloke who attacked ye. And in yer own home, no less." Mrs. Langford lightly touched Amelia's hand, her expression revealing a genuine concern. "But I shouldn't have worried over Logan. He's a scrapper. Always has been."

"I do hope it was not inconvenient for you and Tim to be summoned for an errand so late into the night."

"'Tis no trouble. Logan and his family have been good to me. I am happy to return the favor whenever I have the chance."

"I appreciate your help."

Amelia peered out the window, searching for a way to change the subject. The more they spoke of Mr. MacLain, the more inclined she was to like the man. Which was most unwise. It was far better not to trust him, far better to not give her trust to *any* man. No matter how appealing his raw courage might be.

"I quite enjoyed the outing, dear. That is, until Logan banished me from the driver's bench." Mrs. Langford shrugged. "He worries there might be danger afoot, what with criminals lurking about, chasing after ye."

A reply hovered on Amelia's tongue, but she held it back. There was no point trying to convince the older woman that Mr. MacLain's assessment of the situation was not entirely logical. Not that it mattered. Not really. In a few minutes, she'd be home in her own flat, with a cup of chamomile tea, and this dismal night would be near its end.

Minutes of engaging conversation passed between them before the carriage slowed to a stop, mere steps from Amelia's home. Mrs. Langford glanced out the window, then back to her. "Ye're the one who opened the lending library?"

The question conjured bittersweet memories. Her brother's smile as he'd first escorted her into the rather plain brick building that now housed her collection. The sense of accomplishment upon seeing the carpenters install the shelves to house the collection. Her delight when the first shipment of books arrived. Many hours of planning and work had gone into setting up the library. Paul had not fully understood her fierce desire to open an establishment women could view as a haven. But he'd supported her endeavors with his whole heart.

Amelia swallowed against a lump in her throat. "My brother also played a part."

Seeming to detect the emotion that had swept over her, Mrs. Langford placed a gentle hand over hers, a simple, reassuring touch. "Sometime soon, I may pay ye a visit," she said. "That is, if ye'll have me."

The uncertainty in the older woman's voice touched Amelia.

Did she fear she would not be welcomed by the ladies who frequented the library?

"I do hope you will join us," Amelia said. "I expect you'll enjoy the conversation as well as the collection."

Mrs. Langford flashed a grin. "I would relish time away from the tavern."

"We must take tea one afternoon," Amelia offered.

Mrs. Langford's eyes lit with enthusiasm. "With this chill in the air, I would enjoy a cup of Earl Grey."

"Would you now?" MacLain said as he appeared at the door. Extending a hand, he escorted Amelia from the carriage.

As she fished her key from her reticule, Mrs. Langford called out to her. "Good night, Mrs. Stewart. I've enjoyed our conversation, brief as it was."

"As have I," Amelia replied. Mrs. Langford waved from the window as Tim cracked the reins and the coach wheels rumbled over the pavement.

How very odd.

"Ye look puzzled," MacLain observed with a deliberately bland air.

She stared after the carriage as it clattered off into the fog. "I cannot help but wonder why the carriage is departing."

A hint of humor danced over his features. Drat the man. He had no right to look so devilishly appealing when he'd left her utterly confounded.

"How else did ye expect Mrs. Langford to return to the pub?" If only he didn't sound so very logical.

She turned to him. "I assumed you would see to that."

Slowly, he shook his head. "I've entrusted that task to Tim."

"Why?" she asked, though she suspected she already knew the answer.

A half-smile played on his full mouth as the coach turned a corner some distance down the road, evidently heading toward MacLain's tavern.

Now she was alone with him.

What in blazes was Mr. MacLain up to?

She swallowed against a lump of apprehension. "Dare I ask why you are still here?"

"As ye're not willing to spend this night at my residence, ye've left me no choice." His half-smile transformed into a sly grin. "Tonight, I will be *yer* guest."

Chapter Six

L OGAN FOLDED HIS arms with a casualness he did not feel, rocked back on his heels, and watched the set of Amelia's features shift like quicksilver. A brewing storm flickered in her gaze. Blast it, the lass's face expressed her feelings louder than words. She'd likely be damned poor at poker, telegraphing her thoughts with every flash of emotion in those gorgeous blue eyes of hers. As she took in his words, her teeth grazed her lower lip, the sight as tempting as any he'd seen in a very long time.

Too damned long a time, in fact.

He wanted to kiss her. No, not *want*. The word was far too tame, not even close to describing the sudden hunger to taste her sweetness.

In his youth, he had spent months that seemed an eternity as one of the crew on a ship that sailed across the Atlantic. He'd found beauty in the white-capped waves of summer storms, even as the wind would howl around them, fierce as a banshee's cry.

Like those turbulent ocean waters, Amelia was beautiful.

Fascinating.

From the slight tilt of her chin to the way her half-parted lips countered the cool ire in her eyes, Amelia could draw him in with the crook of a finger. Something about her he couldn't attempt to define—something so genuine, it seemed to render her incapable of guile—rekindled a yearning he had thought long extinguished.

If a man was not careful, he'd be swept into the deep. Over

his head in dangerous waters.

He would not let a fool's desire get the better of him. He'd come to make good on his pledge. There could be nothing more to it than that. Seducing Amelia was out of the question. A woman like her deserved a man who'd come home to a fire in a hearth every of night of his life.

No, she was not meant for a man like him.

He wanted no part of love, no part of the charades that inevitably went along with it. Once, when he was younger and far more foolish, he had thought to make a life with a woman he'd adored, offering that lass his heart and his passion and his name.

But that was not enough. Not for his beautiful bride-to-be. Not for her family and their blasted highbrow aspirations. Maeve had revealed that brutal truth not long before they were to speak their vows. Another man had offered for her hand in marriage, a man who could give her both the riches and the title she craved.

Now, when he hungered for a woman, he sought pleasure. For himself. For the woman in his bed.

But love was a myth, no more real than the dragons in a childhood fairy tale.

Love was for fools.

So, he would settle his debt.

He would protect Amelia. Whatever the risk. Even if it meant putting his own neck on the line.

Reining in his rebellious thoughts, he tore his gaze from her mouth. What in blazes had come over him? It wasn't as if he was a wet-behind-the-ears lad.

He met the storm in her eyes. "In case ye wonder if yer ears are deceiving ye, they're not."

"Well then, that settles it," she said, her tone cooler than her gaze. "When you claimed my brother had sent you, I wondered at your motives. But now, it's clear. It would appear you've gone mad."

Mad. He considered her words. "Seeing as I'm on a fool's errand to play the protector to a woman who does not want to be protected, I am inclined to agree with ye."

"In that case, I trust you will be on your way." She turned her back to him and marched up the steps. "I am more than capable of letting myself in my own residence, locking the door behind me, and pulling the bedcovers up to my chin to settle in for the night."

He joined her on the small porch as she fished her key out of her reticule. Throwing him a hint of a scowl over her shoulder, she looked as if she wanted to sigh but thought better of it. "I intend to spend the night in my flat. *Alone.*"

He shook his head. "Mad or not, I won't be leaving ye on yer own tonight."

She whipped around as if he'd pinched her. "I will *not* remain under the same roof with you tonight, Mr. MacLain. Not here." Her full mouth pinched together before she added, "Not on the blasted moon."

"The bastard named Jack was the first to come after ye. But I'd wager my last coin he won't be the last."

"I suspect you will lose that bet." She cocked her chin, then once again showed him her back as she fiddled with the lock.

"I will not leave ye defenseless."

"Please, go. I do not wish to disturb my neighbors."

As she whispered the words, a sudden movement caught his attention.

He turned.

Across the cobblestone road, a shadow against the apothecary's shop shifted, low against the brick.

Probably a stray dog. Nothing more.

He turned back to Amelia. Suddenly, he caught the motion again, out of the corner of his eye.

The silhouette crept closer. Not so low to the ground now.
Not an animal.

Gaslight flashed against metal clutched in the man's hand.
Bloody hell.

"Mr. MacLain," Amelia continued, "I assure you, I do not

need—"

He took a step closer to her, putting his body between Amelia and the man lurking in the shadows. In his mind's eye, he worked out a strategy.

But first, she had to be safe behind a sturdy door.

He kept his voice low. "Go inside. Now."

"You are not—"

A *crack* thundered through the night.

Bollocks!

Instinctively, he threw himself over Amelia as the bullet slammed into the wall above them. Fragments of brick tumbled over their shoulders. Pressing her against the side of the porch, he heard her gasp, felt her voluminous skirts fan out beneath her.

"Good heavens!" she cried out. "You'll be hit!"

The notes of anguish and fear in her voice stunned him. Her concern had not been for herself. But for him.

That was a bloody first.

"I'll hold him off." He unholstered the revolver he'd worn beneath his coat. "Go inside. Lock the door behind ye."

Another shot rang out.

The slug splintered a wooden sign. Its remnants dangled over the window, an arm's length from their heads.

Bugger it. Was the bastard in the shadows that damned poor a marksman? Or did he only intend to send a message?

Amelia's key scraped against the lock. Her body tensed against him, and he felt the uneven cadence of her breaths. Finally, the hinges squawked a protest, the door creaked open, and she darted inside.

"Bolt the door," he told her, training his attention on the gunman.

"But you—" Concern colored her low tones.

"I know what I'm doing," he ground out. Bloody hell, he hoped he was right. "Do not open this door until ye hear the sound of my voice."

She gave a reluctant nod. The hinges squeaked again, and he

heard the lock fall into place.

Crouching low, he scanned the street. The gas lamp cast hazy shadows against the buildings on either side of the road.

No sign of the shooter.

Out of the darkness, a cat darted over the cobbles.

Gaslight from the lamp at the corner beamed dimly through the fog. In the darkness beyond Logan's line of sight, boot heels thudded against the pavement.

Heading to the alley.

Running away.

Blasted coward.

Logan followed the frantic beat of the assailant's footfalls. The bastard seemed to blend into the darkness, but the pounding against the pavement guided Logan through the thick mist.

He moved toward the alley, weapon at the ready. "Come out, ye bloody coward."

He couldn't see the gunman.

Couldn't take a shot.

Within the shadows, metal clattered against stone. He spotted a refuse can tipped on its side. Had the gunman toppled it in his rush to flee?

Senses on alert, Logan continued his pursuit. In the distance, horses whinnied. Carriage wheels rumbled over the street. Reaching the end of the alley, he spotted an elegant coach racing into the night.

Bugger it.

The gunman had escaped.

AMELIA MILLED ABOUT the library, straightening shelves that were already in perfectly reasonable order, completing minor tasks as if doing so might soothe her nerves. Growing weary of the mindless activity, she moved to the window, ducked behind the curtain, and peered into the gaslit night.

No sign of Mr. MacLain.

Uttering a quiet prayer for his safe return, she crossed the room and began tidying another shelf. Somehow, nothing about this night made sense. While she remained locked behind a sturdy door, Logan MacLain was out there, putting himself at risk. She'd watched through the window as he began to pursue the gun-wielding coward who'd hidden in the shadows. A dull ache pulsed deep within her. At that very moment, he could be lying wounded in some dank alley.

And all because he was determined to protect her.

Why had Logan MacLain—of all the men in London—set his mind to playing the part of her champion? What was the debt he owed her brother?

Curled on his little pillow near her desk, Heathy watched her every move. Despite his curiosity, he showed no inclination to join her. To the contrary, the pup happily nibbled a bone, content to observe her as she undertook one chore after another.

The clock on the wall chimed.

Midnight.

Surely this new day could not possibly be as disturbing as the last. In mere hours, her life had transformed from one of pleasant, rather predictable routine to what seemed a bad dream.

Suddenly, Heathy's head snapped up. The bone in his mouth fell to the rug. Letting out a little growl, he padded off to the door.

Amelia's pulse raced. What had he heard?

No need to be afraid.

A shiver crept along her spine. Drawing in a calming breath, she retrieved the pistol she kept in her desk. With any luck, she would not be forced to pull the trigger.

A heavy rap sounded upon the door. "Let me in."

MacLain's voice. *Thank heavens!*

Relief rushed through her. But still, she needed to be sure. She needed to know wild hope had not deceived her senses. "Tell me again, Mr. MacLain."

"Open this bloody thing." His tone was low and raw. Unmistakably *him*.

She released the bolt and threw open the door.

He hiked a sable brow as he met her gaze. "Would I be speaking the truth if I said ye're glad to see me?"

"Indeed, I am." There was no need to be coy. This night, they had been through far too much to play games.

He closed the door behind him and locked it.

Glancing over him from head to toe, she forced a casual tone. "It would appear you are still in one piece."

A half-smile tugged at his mouth. "Did ye fret over me, lass?"

It wouldn't do to confess how she'd worried. Lord knew the man was arrogant as it was. "Not for one moment," she fibbed, not quite convincingly.

Eyes narrowing with obvious doubt, he cocked his head. "I don't believe ye. But ye know that, don't ye?"

"Perhaps I did worry, Mr. MacLain," she admitted. "If only a wee bit."

"I figured that might be the case." He plowed long fingers through his hair. "I'd appreciate it if ye'd stop calling me *Mr. MacLain*. Logan will do just fine."

"It would not be proper . . . to use your given name."

He'd rested his elbow against a bookshelf and leaned his head against his hand. His features betrayed his weariness, but the glimmer in his dark eyes was not dulled.

"What on God's green earth would make ye think what's *proper* matters to me?"

"It matters to *me*." Even if the bastions of society viewed her as somehow *less* because of what she'd been through, that had only shored up her determination to hold to her own standards.

"Aye." He studied her for a long moment, as if she were a puzzle he couldn't entirely piece together. "I will respect yer wishes."

"Thank you."

He glanced at the weapon she still held. "Ye know how to

shoot, do ye?"

She set the gun on her desk. "My father taught me when I was a girl. We'd have target practice at our house in the country."

MacLain rubbed his neck as if to ease an ache. "Keep the pistol within easy reach. Don't let down yer guard. The gunman escaped." His voice was low, his words matter-of-fact. But she sensed his frustration. His restrained anger.

"I suppose there was nothing to be done about it. The element of surprise worked to his advantage."

"I spotted a carriage at the end of the alley. I believe it was there, waiting for him." A muscle clenched in his jaw. "By hellfire, I let him get away."

As MacLain spoke, Heathy strolled up to him. Seeming to forget about snarling and growling, he wagged his tail enthusiastically while sniffing MacLain's trouser leg.

"A fine guard dog, indeed," MacLain said. "The wee beast might well thrash an intruder to death with his blasted tail."

"Heathy is quite the traitor, isn't he? And to think, you're not even the one who feeds him."

"I will have ye know dogs are fine judges of character."

"Well, this one's judgment leaves something to be desired."

"Bloody shame the ball of fur cannot talk. Ye could train him to address me as *Mister* as well. I'm sure he'd want to be a proper little beast."

"I suppose my attempt at propriety is rather a lost cause," she admitted. "The very fact that you're here, well past midnight, is entirely improper."

"So it is." His eyes darkened as they met hers. "But as long as there's a jackal out there looking to put fear in yer heart, ye're stuck with me. I will not be leaving ye tonight."

Chapter Seven

Y**E'RE STUCK WITH** *me. I will not be leaving ye tonight.*

Amelia didn't want to admit it, not even to herself, but Logan MacLain's arrogant words were the most reassuring she'd heard in a very long time.

Still, she could not permit him to stay here. To stay with *her.* Her cozy flat above the library was warm and quite comfortable. But there was only one bedchamber.

Only one bed.

And she certainly was not about to share *that* with him tonight.

"If ye think ye can talk me into leaving, ye'd be better off getting a good night's sleep." His tempting mouth quirked at one corner. "Ye've no worry that I will have my way with ye, or whatever the hell it is ye think scoundrels do."

"Have your way?" She kept her voice deliberately bland.

Devilish amusement gleamed in his eyes. "Sorry to disappoint ye, but there will be none of that tonight. I am weary to the bone, and as I understand it, properly ravishing a woman takes effort."

Warmth flamed in her cheeks. *I rather fancy the prospect of being ravished by a rogue.* The words she'd spoken so blithely while Beatrice carried on about Logan MacLain held a definite irony now. She'd certainly known how to tempt fate, hadn't she?

"I've far greater concerns than fear of being ravished, by a rogue or otherwise." She hiked her chin and steadied her voice.

"Tell me, Mr. MacLain. Why are you determined to play the hero?"

"I'm not anyone's hero. But I'll be damned if I will stand by while cowards terrorize a woman." He cast Heathy a glance. "Even if the lass happens to possess a fierce guard dog disguised as a mop."

"If Heathy had not planted his teeth in that ruffian's leg, things might have turned out differently," she pointed out.

"True," he agreed with a nod. "I regret ye had to go through that. If I'd known the bastard intended to come after ye, I would not have left ye on yer own. Even then."

The all-too-recent memory of the intruder's thick-fingered hands on her body unleashed a shudder of revulsion. She straightened a pile of books on her desk, as if the simple task might help her shake off the sickening sensation.

"I am no worse for wear," she said.

"Ye're a poor liar, lass."

He touched her face, brushing the pad of his thumb over her cheek. Gentle. Comforting. Surprising her with his tenderness.

"I suppose I am." Fending off another shiver, she rubbed her arms briskly. "Still, the man did no lasting harm."

"I don't know why the coward attacked ye. But I do know this much—he's not the only one who has ye in his sights. I will not leave ye on yer own to face the threat."

Determination blazed in his eyes. She was not going to win this battle. Truth be told, she was not entirely sure she wanted to. Having him near offered comfort and reassurance she had not felt in quite a long time.

"Very well," she relented. "But only tonight."

He rubbed his jaw, skimming his fingertips over a growth of new beard. "That's a start."

She squared her shoulders. "Only *this* night, Mr. MacLain."

"We'll see about that." His mouth hitched at one corner, not quite a smile. "I take pride in my powers of persuasion."

The hint of challenge in his gravel-edged voice intrigued her, even as a single word echoed in her thoughts.

Persuasion.

Spoken in the man's gravel-edged tones, the word conjured images of seduction. Of surrender. My, Logan MacLain was an arrogant one, wasn't he? And she . . . well, she was not about to give in to any man's *persuasion.* Much less a known rogue.

No, she knew better. The man who had left her a widow had taught her well.

Meeting MacLain's perceptive eyes, she infused a layer of ice into her voice. "I would not count on those powers."

"They haven't let me down yet."

"*Yet* would seem to be the key word in your statement." Steeling herself, she pulled in a soft breath. "Given the events of this evening, I must accept the validity of your argument and allow you to stay close. But only for this one night. If I were alone here, I would be far too on edge to even drift off to sleep."

"The validity of my argument, eh?" His eyes narrowed as he studied her. "Ye do intrigue me, Amelia. Ye've the face of a woodland fairy, but yer words bring to mind a discussion with my solicitor."

An emotion she couldn't quite name stirred deep within her. He'd used her given name. Perhaps she should be taken aback by the familiarity. But somehow, spoken in his husky brogue, it felt so very intimate. So very right.

Ye do intrigue me.

Logan MacLain knew how to set her off balance, no matter her determination to remain unaffected by the man. No one had ever dubbed her intriguing. And only one other person in her life had ever compared her to a fairy, woodland or otherwise. The very thought of it brought a twinge of emotion in the vicinity of her heart.

But she would not give Mr. MacLain the satisfaction of knowing he'd unsettled her. Hiking her chin, she spoke in a bland tone.

"In any case, it's far better that I am not alone tonight."

The way he looked at her unfurled heat through her body as

the faintest hint of a smile played upon his full mouth.

"Even if that means spending the night with a wicked rogue?"

"Indeed," she said, hoping to sound resigned. "I intend to see about getting some rest."

"My weary bones would welcome sleep," he agreed.

Doubt reared its head. "There is one thing . . . one thing I must know if you expect to earn my trust."

The flickers of amusement left his gaze. "Tell me what ye need of me, lass."

"You say my brother sent for you. I need to understand why . . . why he chose you."

"Paul knew he could count on me."

"Because of the debt you owe?"

"That is one factor."

"Why else, then, Mr. MacLain? Out of all the men in London, why you?"

"Yer brother knew he could trust me. He never doubted I'd have his back. And now, he is counting on me to protect the person he most treasured." A muscle in his carved jaw flexed. "I will not betray his trust. Nor yers."

The intensity in his gaze left her nearly breathless. She glanced away, steadying herself against a sudden wave of emotion.

"I would like to see the letters you received," she said.

"They're secure in my safe. I'll take ye there in the morning. Ye can confirm they are in yer brother's hand."

She veiled her gaze with her lashes. "Thank you."

"Now, we've settled one matter—I will not be leaving ye tonight. But I have another question." His attention raked over the abundance of shelves. "Where in blazes do ye sleep in this place?"

"My flat is upstairs," she said, collecting her thoughts. "Unfortunately, there's only one bedchamber."

A slow grin spread over his features. "Well, if ye're thinking we will be sharing it, think again. I already told ye I'm too bloody tired to be ravishing a woman, much less one I am sworn to protect."

"Well, that's quite a relief," she teased in return. "I would hate to have to sic Heathy on you."

He cast the dog a sidelong glance. "Ah, the furry warrior. Now I can rest easy."

She couldn't help but smile. "I'll have you know he is truly fierce when he wants to be."

"As I said, ye're a poor liar." He caught her hand in his. Gently, he drew her closer. "Believe me when I say this—ye're beautiful, lass, and if ye were any other woman, I would barter my soul to warm yer bed. But I came here to keep ye safe. Even from a rogue like me."

AT THE TOUCH of his hand to hers, Logan knew he'd made a mistake. Blast it, he never should've touched her.

Never should've looked into those ocean-blue eyes that could draw a man far out of his depth.

Far over his head.

Her skin was warm and smooth as fine silk. No doubt the rest of her would feel as good against his body.

Bugger the twist of fate that had set her off limits.

By thunder, he was tired. But the weariness had not stopped his male body from responding to this, the simplest of touches. Hadn't kept him from going rock hard at the innocent brush of her fingertips against his.

Her almond-shaped eyes had darkened to the color of the sky after a summer storm, hinting of an elemental desire. Had she felt it too, this low-simmering heat he could rapidly kindle to a blaze?

Deep within, an instinctive hunger stirred. What in blazes had come over him? He knew better than to be drawn to her. The man who had once been his friend had trusted him to protect his sister. Amelia was out of his reach.

Damned shame his rebellious body didn't understand that truth.

A heavy silence fell over them. Behind them, the rhythmic swing of the clock's pendulum marked the moments as Amelia seemed to study him. Was she trying to puzzle out his true intent?

A touch of a smile lifted the corners of her mouth. "I'm not so certain you are a true rogue, Mr. MacLain. Of course, I've heard the tales. But I know better than to believe every snippet of innuendo that comes along."

"Ye're a clever lass." He drew the pad of his thumb over the back of her hand. In response, her eyes widened, ever so slightly. "Sooner or later, ye'll figure out the truth."

"Perhaps," she said, gently easing from his hold.

"I will stay down here in the library for the night," he said, setting his mind on an overstuffed chair near the front window. Not the most welcoming of accommodations, but it would do.

"There is a settee in the back of the library." Her gaze skimmed over him from head to toe. "It's not quite long enough. But it should offer some degree of comfort."

He shrugged. "Believe me, I have bedded down on worse."

"Very well." After retrieving her pistol, she crossed the room and mounted the staircase. "Goodnight, Mr. MacLain." Halfway up the steps, she turned back to him. "Heathy will stay down here. In the event of an intruder, you can count on him to sound the alarm."

Was that amusement in her tone?

"I've no need to use that wee beast as a sentry."

She smiled impishly. "Goodnight, Mr. MacLain."

And with that, she continued her ascent.

Casting aside the good sense he'd been blessed with at birth, Logan allowed his gaze to trail Amelia's movements until she closed the door at the top behind her. The metallic squawk of protest distracted him, if only for an instant. Good God, did every hinge in this place require oil? He would see to it in the morning.

He spotted the small sofa Amelia had suggested. One glance, and he ruled it out. Too blasted short. Settling instead on a heavily cushioned wing chair, he stretched out his legs and rested his boot-clad feet on a well-used ottoman.

Keeping his revolver at the ready on the table beside him, he closed his eyes. Before long, he began to fall into slumber.

Suddenly, something touched his hand.

Something wet.

And warm.

He jerked awake.

Bollocks. Staring down at the culprit, he laughed. Amelia's pet wagged his tail, oblivious to the fact that it was high time for man and beast alike to be asleep. The ball of fur on legs was no more a guard dog than he was a bloody duke.

He forced a scowl. In response, the pup wagged his tail even more vigorously.

Pulling himself to his feet, Logan spotted the dog's bone. Somehow, the pup had managed to wedge it partly between a shelf and the floor.

Scooping up the bone, he set it before the animal. "Heathy, ye little mutt, it would seem ye've won this skirmish."

Sprawling back upon the chair, Logan stretched out his legs. Wearily, he stared at the ceiling, waiting for sleep to return. Thank God he was exhausted. If not, thoughts of the woman lying in the bed upstairs might well have kept him awake through the night.

Chapter Eight

*A*ND NOW, THE *rogue has opened that den of sin.*

As Amelia strode through the massive oak doors of the Rogue's Lair, her friend's scorn-filled assessment of McLain's tavern played in her thoughts. Somehow, this *den of sin* was not at all what Bea had described.

Amelia had expected . . . well, she wasn't quite sure what she'd expected. But she certainly had not anticipated the sight of gleaming hardwood floors, the crackle of cozy flames dancing in a massive stone fireplace, and the welcoming smile that lit the eyes of a plump, silver-haired woman who busily polished the high wooden tables. The pub was rather quaint. Perhaps even charming.

Morning light streamed through large windows with intricate designs in stained glass. Of course, the atmosphere in the Rogue's Lair would likely prove quite different after dark as the usual patrons poured into the place, seeking a cold draught and a friendly ear to which they might confide their troubles.

The barkeep, a gray-haired man MacLain addressed as Murray, acknowledged their presence with a nod and went about his preparations for the day's customers. As MacLain offered Amelia a quick introduction to the barmaid cleaning the tables, an elegantly dressed woman garbed in peacock blue from head to toe strolled through the door.

Flashing a scowl, she headed straight for MacLain. Her thick dark hair had been swept back from her lovely face with lavish silver and mother-of-pearl combs. The scattering of silver threaded through her hair hinted that she was a bit older than the man she regarded with a sullen pout.

"So it's true, then." She sauntered up to the counter. "I heard you played the hero last night. How very surprising."

MacLain regarded her as though the sight of her had triggered an ache in his neck. "Why are ye here?"

"I wanted to hear the truth . . . straight from your mouth."

"Ye've wasted yer time, Elspeth. There's no grand secret to reveal."

"Any other evening, you would've had a grand time separating a bloke from his coin over a few rounds of cards. But last night, you rushed off to the rescue." She lifted a pale brow. "Logan MacLain, am I to believe you've become a protector of widows in peril?"

He shot her a dagger-filled stare. "Go home."

Elspeth's icy gaze swept over Amelia. Tiny lines crinkled deep around her eyes. "I must say, your gallant charade makes more sense now." Her mouth tipped up into a rueful smile. "Somehow, I'd thought a *librarian* would be older. And far more plain."

Librarian. The contempt in the woman's cool voice pricked at Amelia like a thorn beneath her heel. Pulling in a steadying breath, Amelia bit back the utterly unladylike response that sprang to her lips. She squared her shoulders. If Elspeth— whatever her undoubtedly improper relationship to MacLain might be—thought to intimidate her, she was sorely mistaken.

"At the moment, you have me at a disadvantage, Miss . . ."

"My name is Elspeth Gilroy." She toyed with a jade brooch at her throat. "Mrs. Elspeth Gilroy. You may have heard of my dearly departed husband. He had a rather unimaginative penchant for naming businesses after himself."

Mrs. Gilroy. One of MacLain's dalliances, no doubt. Did she fear Amelia harbored a notion to take her place? *How utterly absurd.*

Amelia forced a placid expression. "Since you are so very curious about the events of last night, I will tell you that Mr. MacLain was quite courageous. Chivalrous, in fact."

"Chivalrous? I don't believe I've ever heard that word used to describe you." Elspeth's gaze drifted over MacLain's long, lean form. "Well, that was then. Now, shall we see to a bit of . . . recreation?"

A muscle in MacLain's jaw flexed. He slowly shook his head. "Those days are in the past."

"Is that so?" A look of clear challenge simmered in Elspeth's gray eyes. "I could change your mind."

"Go home to yer fine mansion." MacLain's low voice rumbled hard as flint.

Elspeth gave a little huff. "Very well. I had not expected you to be so tedious." As she walked to the door, she turned back to Amelia. "If you believe you can change him, I would suggest you think again. Some men cannot be reformed."

"Reformed?" Amelia scoffed. "I do not know what drivel you've heard, but it's utter rubbish."

Elspeth shrugged. "For your sake, I hope it is."

With that, she stormed out into the street. The slam of the door reverberated against the stone wall, as if punctuating the woman's exit.

"Mrs. Gilroy does have a flair for the dramatic, doesn't she?" Amelia turned to MacLain. "Are you going to tell me what that was all about?"

MacLain slowly shook his head. "Not if ye threatened me with a dozen years of torment sleeping in that lumpy chair of yers."

"Lumpy chair?" She shot him a frown. "I will have you know that piece has been in my family for generations."

He cocked a brow. "That instrument of misery is a family heirloom?"

"My great-grandmother brought it from Wales," Amelia replied crisply.

"Blasted shame she didn't give it to the bloody Tower. They might've used it for torturing the condemned."

"Now there's a story worth hearing, if only after a whisky or two." I'll look forward to hearing the tale," the barkeep spoke up. "For now, tell me, Mrs. Stewart, are ye well? Mrs. Langford mentioned the ordeal ye endured last night."

Welcoming the change of subject, Amelia met the barkeep's kind eyes. "The situation was alarming, to say the least. But I suffered no lasting harm."

"Thank God Logan was there to watch over ye," Murray said.

"The lass had no cause for worry. She possesses a guard dog, fiercest little beast I have ever encountered," MacLain added with a grin. "Murray, if ye need me, we'll be in my office."

He escorted Amelia up a spiral staircase and led her to a room near the end of the corridor. Closing the door behind them, he motioned her to a Chesterfield chair that faced a large writing desk. Struggling to distract herself from a fresh wave of apprehension, she perched upon the edge of the elegant leather wing chair and focused on the intricate carvings on the legs of the desk. If only her nerves would settle down. She needed to see the letters for herself. Had Paul actually composed the messages? She could not rest until she knew the truth, no matter how painful.

She drummed her fingertips against the cushion of the chair. "You're confident both of the letters came from Paul?"

"Both letters arrived by private courier." MacLain crossed over the blue and ivory wool carpet to the wall behind the desk. Jostling one of the wooden panels behind the desk, he slid it open, revealing a stout iron safe. "I recognized his script. I am counting on ye to confirm my assessment."

With smooth, sure movements, he manipulated the dial, and the lock released. He opened the weighted door to reveal a small book stored within.

When he handed her the leather-bound volume, Amelia's breath caught. Her hands trembled as shock washed over her. Everything about the book, from its maroon leather binding to the lettering on its spine, was all too familiar.

"The book has significance to ye," MacLain said, observing her reaction.

"Yes." Dragging in a low breath, she opened the cover and gulped against a sudden lump in her throat. With the tip of her pointer finger, she traced the inscription penned in indigo ink on the title page.

To my dear Pixie . . .

Years ago, when she was still a girl in braids, her brother had dubbed her a pixie, flitting about and driving her governess to distraction. If she closed her eyes, she could still hear Paul's voice, claiming in a childish taunt that somehow, she'd lost her fairy wings. Given her penchant for mischief, her mother and father had found the pet name rather fitting, while her beloved grandfather took a liking to the name. In his heart, Amelia was his little pixie, an imp no one could ever tame.

A rush of memories cascaded over her without warning. She blinked hard against a swell of emotion. Not even the most skilled forger would have known to use the affectionate nickname.

"Good heavens," she whispered, turning to MacLain. "My brother gave me this book of poems many Christmases ago. How did you come to possess it?"

The set of his jaw hardened. "The first letter had been placed within the pages of this book."

Oh, dear. Of all the books in her private library, why would anyone choose this collection of poetry to send to Logan MacLain?

Seeming to sense her pain, he gently touched her shoulder. "Had ye loaned it to anyone?"

"Never." Bitter tears brimmed in her eyes, but she blinked hard, determined to hold them back. "I thought I had misplaced it. I've been heartsick."

"Whoever took it wanted to be sure to connect ye with yer brother."

"Indeed," she agreed. "May I see the letter?"

He removed a folded leaf of stationery from the safe. "This is Paul's handwriting, is it not?"

Fresh grief swelled within her. This imprecisely penned letter might well have been the last Paul had ever written. The very idea roiled her insides and tormented her with quiet misery. Her gaze swept over the page. Her pulse raced as she read and reread the ominous warnings scrawled in Paul's characteristically brash script.

Her heart thudded, feeling as if it might actually crash against her ribs. "My brother wrote this message. I have no doubt."

With a nod, MacLain placed another note in her hand. "This came with yer brother's watch." Was that an undercurrent of pain in his voice?

At first glance, she saw her brother's bold strokes, the long, angular lines so typical of his script. Quickly scanning the brief missive, she paused, then read it again more slowly, careful to take in every nuance of Paul's warning.

Fear mingled with the sadness deep in her heart. "I am confident Paul wrote this as well."

"These messages make it clear that ye're in danger."

"I don't…I simply do not understand." Pressing her fingertips to her temples, she searched for words. "I am not positive I even want to."

Shivers traced an icy path along her spine. Hands trembling, she stared down at her brother's brash scrawl. Once again, she took in the words that seemed a desperate confession.

I have kept too many secrets. Like a fool, I believed I could shield Amelia. But I can no longer protect her. If you are reading this, I have met my fate. My dear sister does not deserve to suffer the consequences of my deeds. She is innocent. But the jackals want what is theirs. They will show no mercy. I cannot defend Amelia, but I have faith you will protect her. MacLain, I know that you will do whatever it takes to keep her safe. I am putting my full trust in you.

Bowing her head, she lost the battle against the tears pricking the backs of her eyes.

"Oh, Paul." She swiped away a rebellious drop, then another. "Dear God, what have you done?"

AT THE SIGHT of a lone teardrop trickling down Amelia's cheek, an instinct Logan had thought long buried returned to life. For years, he had walled off his own heart, but now, as he reached for Amelia, he wanted only to comfort her. Gently touching her arm, he reassured her. He was there to ease her fears. There to help her uncover the secrets behind her brother's death. There to protect her.

"Paul wrote of jackals," she said in a near whisper. "Of more than one."

"The man who attacked ye was not the only one to have ye in his sights." He placed his hand over hers, an undemanding caress. "Yer brother knew this was coming, Amelia. I know the man he was. Paul would've protected ye himself if there'd been any way, but he knew they would get to him first. So he sent for me."

Rising to her feet, Amelia laced her hands together, as if to still them. Restlessly, she went to the window, drawing back one panel of the drapes, bringing sunlight into the room. Turning to him, she met his eyes, then veiled her gaze with deep brown lashes. "Even as a girl, I held no fear of the dark. But now, it seems I must be wary of what lurks behind every shadow."

"If ye'll trust me, I will keep ye safe." He drew her closer. The subtle aroma of lavender on her skin filled his senses. "Ye have my word."

"Your word as a gentleman?" The faintest of smiles touched her lips.

"As a gentleman. As a rogue. Does it really matter?"

Her stormy eyes met his gaze. "There's something you need to know . . . if you've set your mind to helping me, that is."

"Ye know I have, lass."

"I won't be content hiding like a frightened child behind four walls. I will not rest until I find the scoundrel who killed Paul."

"Ye think I will try to stop ye?"

Slowly, she shook her head. "I would prefer that you assist me."

"I meant what I said." He lightly brushed away a tear on her cheek. "I will be at yer side."

She shook her head. "This is not your fight."

He tipped her chin up with his finger and gazed into beautiful eyes that glistened with unshed tears. "The blazes it isn't. I won't let ye face this alone."

Her teeth grazed her lower lip. "Tell me—how did you know where to find me?"

"I'd known of Paul's connection to yer library, but I had no cause to seek ye out. Not until now."

Turning back to the window, she peered out at the street below. "You have mentioned a debt you owe to my brother. I'm asking you to tell me what happened."

Like a blow he had not seen coming, ugly memories flashed through his thoughts.

Moonlight glinting off a dagger's blade.

Blood—his blood, soaking his linen shirt.

The flash of a gunshot.

God only knew how he'd struggled to lock the images deep within the recesses of his mind. The memories would be a part of him until he took his last breath.

He'd been a young man on that fog-shrouded night at a tavern by the sea. Too blasted arrogant. A bloody fool, getting himself in over his head. Determined to make his own fortune, he'd convinced himself he could handle the risks.

Damned shame the cost had been so steep.

He and Paul Anderson had forged a strong friendship. In

truth, they'd been brothers in spirit. With his keen intellect and fierce ambition, Paul was a man who strove to live by his wits. He'd wanted no part of violence. But what happened that dreary night had cleaved their bond in two. Now, his sister deserved to hear the truth from his lips. That much, he could give her.

"Yer brother was forced to take a life." Odd, how even now, speaking the words felt like a blade to the gut. "He killed a man to save my neck."

Amelia kept her back to him, but he could see the way her shoulders tensed. "He was a gentle man." A hush of pain clouded her voice.

Gentle. So many years before, Logan's mum had used that very word to describe him. He had been a boy in those days, whiling away lonely hours shooting targets he'd set on flat stones and daydreaming of a time when he would be old enough to leave the simple life of the countryside and seek his fortune.

Burying the quick jolt of pain deep within himself, he shoved the fragments of memory aside. He had to focus on Amelia, on offering the lass what little comfort he could.

"Paul faced an ugly choice. He did what he had to do."

"When . . . when did this happen?"

"Years ago, while we were at university."

She pressed one hand to the window pane, her slender fingers splayed against the glass. "You're telling me that all these years, Paul carried this horrible secret."

"He wanted to protect ye from the truth." Logan rubbed at an ache in the back of his neck. "He blamed me. And he was right. If I hadn't been looking for shortcuts, he would not have had to pull the trigger."

She spun on her heel. Facing him, her chin thrust up, resolute. "In my heart, I know this much—if my brother killed a man, he had no choice. You cannot shoulder the blame."

Ye're wrong, lass. If Amelia knew what he had done to set the wheels in motion that night, she might well think differently on the matter.

He studied her for a long moment. Her unadorned beauty drew him in. The trust in her eyes seemed a clear contrast to the cynicism he saw every time he looked in the mirror.

Amelia demanded nothing from him. Unlike Elspeth, who sought sensual delight without any thought of trust or caring or faith in him as a man. The widow harbored no desire for sentimental emotions. She had taken all the pleasure he would give. Just as he'd taken from her.

Sudden need coursed through his veins. He wanted to trace the curve of her face, as if he could commit her vibrant beauty to memory.

He wanted to shield her, to protect not only her body, but the spirit in her eyes.

And, blast it, he wanted to kiss her.

Despite his noble intentions, if one could call them that, he hungered for the feel of her rounded curves against the length of his body and the taste of her lips.

But this was not the time.

And it sure as bloody hell was not the place.

"I trust that someday you will tell me more of the story." Her softly spoken words mercifully pulled him from his thoughts.

"Someday, Amelia, I will tell ye. But for now, I will not set aside the vow I made that night. Yer brother trusted me to watch over ye."

"You must promise me that you will exercise caution."

"Do not worry yerself over me. I know how to fight, and I know how to win. Ye've seen that with yer own eyes, have ye not, lass?"

"I must admit, you have been most impressive, Mr. MacLain." Her voice, low and smooth as velvet, touched him like a caress. "But I intend to play a role in my own defense."

Ah, the lass had spirit. Despite the slight quiver of her chin, her tone held courage. She would not surrender to fear.

"Fair enough," he replied. "I do have one expectation of my own."

"And what might that be?"

"Ye find it improper to address me by my given name. But if the tavern blokes hear ye calling me *mister*, they'll wonder if my da has come back from the grave. MacLain will do. That's what everyone calls me."

"A reasonable request," she agreed.

As she gave a little nod, a rogue tendril slipped from her primly pinned hair. Gently, he tucked the rebellious curl behind her ear. The small intimacy shot a bolt of awareness through him, and the most subtle of smiles touched her lips. Sunlight streamed through the window, highlighting traces of red gleaming in her silky gold tresses. Her eyes darkened with feeling, with concern over him, no less. No other woman had ever looked at him with such genuine emotion.

Had ever looked at him like *that*.

Bloody hell, she was beautiful.

More beautiful than a man like him could find words to describe.

The expression in Amelia's smile and her eyes tempted him. Even the tiny little vee of a frown between her expressive brows drew him in.

From the first, he'd intended to defend her. Had been determined to protect her. But now…now he wanted to hear his name on her lips.

By hellfire, he wanted *her*. A powerful hunger coursed through his body. Desire. Need. And something more. Something far more fierce. Far more dangerous.

With ruthless discipline, he took control of his will. Of his heart. A woman like Amelia deserved more than a man like him could ever offer. She deserved more than passion. More than pleasure. Amelia deserved the one thing he could not give. Love was not in the cards.

Not with her.

Not with any woman.

All those years ago, he had given her brother his word. And

he would honor that vow. No matter the cost.

He would protect her.

Even from himself.

✿

Chapter Nine

G IVING IN TO the nervous tension brewing within her, Amelia paced before the large stone fireplace in MacLain's office. When she'd been a girl in braids, Amelia had endured more than one scolding from a lemon-tart governess who'd had tried with little success to direct Amelia to channel her energy—nervous, or otherwise—into more subtle, more ladylike actions. But as Logan MacLain laid out his strategies for ensuring her safety, the even footsteps over his plush carpet seemed precisely the thing to ensure her fragile sense of composure. That is, until he spoke the words that stopped her in her tracks.

"It goes without saying that ye will need to take up residence in my home." He spoke the words as if he'd stated an unarguable fact.

My, the man was arrogant. Well accustomed to getting his way, she supposed. A more prim and proper woman than herself might have feigned indignant shock. After all, it wasn't every day that a known rogue proposed a respectable widow take up residence with him.

Fortunately for both of them, she hadn't given a fig about being prim, let alone proper, for quite some time.

"What you are suggesting is utterly scandalous," she said matter-of-factly. "But you already knew that, didn't you?"

"I did," he agreed. "We both know I don't give a damn about scandal. What I am proposing is the most practical option for keeping you safe."

"Goodness, the gossips will have a high time with such an arrangement, won't they?"

"Ye're not afraid of tongues wagging, Amelia." His eyes flashed with challenge. "Ye've more backbone than that."

"You do have a point. Given the circumstances, perhaps there is no better alternative."

"So ye agree . . . ye will stay with me?" He frowned. "Just like that."

Was it her imagination, or did he seem a bit let down by her ready agreement?

"I suppose it is the wisest decision. I do hope I have not deprived you of an opportunity to exercise those powers of persuasion you take such pride in."

"Ye could say that you have." A half-smile tilted his mouth. "I was looking forward to the challenge."

She went to the table beside the wing chair and poured a cup of oolong tea from a pot Mrs. Langford had placed there. "I consider myself a logical woman. I've far more pressing concerns than a blot on my so-called good name."

"That's not it. Not all of it, at least." He slowly shook his head. "Yer decision to stay with me is not a simple matter of logic."

"You think not?"

"It is a matter of trust." His husky, gravel-edged voice seemed a caress. "I will not let ye down. I will justify that trust."

Trust. The word echoed in her thoughts. Good heavens, he was right. Deep within, she did trust this man who had been a stranger twenty-four hours earlier. Logan MacLain was bold. He was brash. And she suspected he'd earned his reputation as a rogue.

But her every instinct vouched for him as a man of courage. Perhaps, even, of honor. He would abide by his promise to her brother. And he would help her find justice for Paul.

"There is one thing." Sudden doubt twisted in the pit of her stomach. "I will not leave Heathy behind."

"That goes without saying. Though I may regret it when the wee beast sinks his little teeth into my leg." He flashed a grin. "We certainly would not leave behind such a fierce guard dog."

Drat the man, Amelia thought as his smile reached his eyes. Logan MacLain had no right to be so blasted appealing.

No. She corrected herself. *Appealing* didn't even come close to the full truth.

A sudden clatter of wheels against the pavement beyond the tavern drew her attention back to the window. Peeling the curtain back again, she spotted his carriage rattling down the street with Mrs. Langford at the reins.

"Where in blazes is she off to now?" he muttered over her shoulder, amusement flavoring his tone. "Murray must have wanted some peace and sent her on an errand."

Hearing the smile in his voice, she turned to him. "How did Mrs. Langford come to be your driver?"

"Now that is a question I've asked myself more than once. Most nights, I'd prefer to be at the reins of my phaeton. Truth be told, Mrs. Langford is the only reason I keep that blasted box of a coach."

"So, am I to understand that you maintain a carriage you do not need, so that a woman—a woman old enough to be your mother, no less—may drive it through the town as she pleases?"

"Aye, that about sums it up."

"Is she kin to you?"

His expression shifted, as though a fond memory had drifted into his thoughts. "She is now."

"I sense a tale behind your words."

The curve of his mouth eased, not quite a smile. "While I was a lad, Mrs. Langford's husband drove for my father. He was a conventional man, as was my da. Neither allowed a woman to take the reins."

"But you are not nearly so conventional."

"Ye do see things clearly, don't ye?" His mouth tipped up at the corners. "Now, Mrs. Langford has her chance."

Very unexpected, Mr. MacLain.

The hint of sentimentality in his words intrigued her, even as the crisp notes of his shaving soap—bergamot, perhaps—awakened her senses. Her pulse picked up its cadence, and she battled an utterly improper desire to graze her fingertips along the hard edge of his jaw, to explore the texture of his skin with her touch.

Her gaze danced lower, trailing over his long, lean body. He was temptation come to life in a slightly rumpled linen shirt and ebony trousers that hugged long, muscular legs. And with a pinch of sin and a dash of wickedness thrown in for good measure.

She had faith in his ability to protect her from the scoundrel who'd made her a target. He would protect her from *that* menace.

Pity she was not nearly as confident of her own capacity to resist the rogue's charm in Logan MacLain's smile.

And now, she would be sleeping under his roof.

Perhaps I have gone a wee bit mad after all.

She'd do well to remember that he had likely tempted many a willing woman with that gravel-edged brogue of his and the flash of desire in his midnight-dark eyes.

Women like Elspeth. The wealthy widow had eyed MacLain with a hunger that exceeded her scorn for Amelia. Well, Mrs. Gilroy had nothing to worry about on her account. MacLain was a rake of the first order.

Amelia knew better than to fall into the bed of a man like him.

Didn't she?

Giving her head a little shake as if that might clear it, she fixed her attention on the gem-colored panes in the transom over the door. She had to focus on something—anything, really—other than the man who stood temptingly near.

With effort, she regained some control over her renegade thoughts. "Your office . . . the establishment, actually . . . is rather different than I'd imagined,"

"Not what you expected, eh?"

"Not at all." Her gaze lit upon the intricately carved sideboard behind his desk. A silver platter, crystal glasses, and what appeared to be a decanter of fine whisky added an elegant touch. "I had expected a den of inequity to appear more . . . sinful."

"Ye make a valid point, lass." Humor flavored his words. "Are ye're thinking I should commission some nudes? Portraits of beautiful women just as the good Lord made them might draw even more patrons. The gents would flock to this place."

The glimmer in his eyes told her he wasn't serious.

Not entirely, at least.

"I am suggesting nothing of the sort."

"Paintings of bonny lasses behind the bar would be a more pleasant sight than Murray weaving about after he's sampled a pint too many."

"I prefer it just as it is," she said truthfully.

"Ye're quite sure of that, are ye? I don't want the townspeople to be saying my place is not a fine setting for a bit of debauchery."

Heat rose in her cheeks. His devilish grin left no doubt he'd spotted her blush. Well, she was not about to let him think he had left her at a loss for words.

"From what I've heard, this tavern is regarded as a haven for wickedness."

He eyed her for the span of a heartbeat, perhaps two, his expression bold as they came. "A haven for wickedness. I do like the sound of it."

The challenge in his half-smile kindled a touch of spirit in her. The feeling was refreshing, more so than she wanted to admit.

"Perhaps you might rename this establishment," she suggested cheekily. "Den of Wickedness has a unique flavor."

"I'll give the matter some thought. But at the moment, I have a question for ye."

"And what might that be?"

"The patrons who frequent yer library are a genteel sort. So why in blazes would respectable ladies discuss drunken debauchery?" He cleared his throat, as if for effect. "Am I to believe ye possess books on that particular subject in yer collection?"

Oh, dear. She certainly had not expected *that.*

"It isn't as if we gather around the desk, talking about . . ." She glanced up, making a show of studying the stained-glass window above his desk.

His eyes darkened with a blend of amusement and an emotion she could not quite describe. "I believe the word ye're looking for is *sin.*"

She hiked her chin. "I assure you, we do not discuss such matters."

"Such matters, eh, Amelia Stewart?" A sly smile played on his full mouth. "Have ye considered that a lady might benefit from a bit of sin now and then?" Posed in that husky burr of his, his question seemed a delicious challenge.

Perhaps if you are the one with whom I've chosen to sin.

MacLain had drawn her in, his words a prelude to seduction.

Nonsense. She'd allowed her fanciful thoughts to run wild. Given the subtle quirk of his mouth, he'd been teasing her. Well, if he thought to get the better of her, Amelia was not about to give him the satisfaction. It was only fitting that she respond in kind.

"I am inclined to agree." She met his gaze and took another sip from the delicate teacup. "Pity a worthy match for such an endeavor is indeed a rare find."

At that moment, his expression brought to mind a spy gathering intelligence on his quarry. She'd intended her statement to be shocking. Evidently, he'd detected the underlying truth.

"A worthy match, eh?" he pressed. "Tell me, Amelia, what is it that ye seek in a lover?"

A lover.

She set the cup down on his desk with a little *clink* against the saucer. Her mouth had gone dry, but she composed a response. "A certain boldness would be desirable. As well as a bit of daring."

His sable brows hiked. "Only a bit, eh?"

"Certainly not to the point of recklessness."

"I figured as much, given ye're a sensible lass. So, a woman desires a man who's bold and daring—but not too daring." He gave a somber nod, countered by the glint of humor in his eyes. "I should commit this to memory. Ye never know when I might find myself pursuing a clever lass like yerself."

"A touch of wickedness also holds an appeal." She summoned a tone of authority. "But only in the proper measure, of course."

"Aye, in the proper measure." Again, those dark eyes flashed. "Of course."

Absently, he scrubbed his hand over the dark stubble of beard on his jaw, stirring a fresh rush of heat to flood Amelia's cheeks.

Would his touch be tender?

Would he command a response from her with the slight roughness of his skin against hers?

She was playing a dangerous game, wasn't she?

Logan MacLain was a man skilled in all manner of delicious wickedness. A true rogue.

She glanced down to her toes, making a valiant effort to banish the wanton notions. Didn't she know better than to engage in a flirtation, much less with this man? Heaven only knew nothing good would come of it.

She could not let down her guard.

Hadn't she already learned a bitter lesson about men who could coax a woman out of her corset with little more than persuasive words and a flash of desire in their eyes? Before they had wed, her husband had eased away her doubts with his seductive promises. If only she'd realized she was not the only woman Edward wanted. Innocently—perhaps foolishly—she'd believed spoken vows could change him.

She'd been so very wrong.

The truth of it still seemed a dagger to the chest. But the years had brought a bitter wisdom. Trusting a man to pleasure her body was one thing.

But entrusting a man with her heart was quite another matter.

A light rap upon the door provided a welcome distraction from her thoughts. She didn't know who'd come up to MacLain's office, but she offered silent gratitude for the interruption.

He moved to the door. After verifying the identity of the visitor with a gruff question, he cracked open the door and plucked an envelope from the unseen man's outstretched hand.

"Mr. Caldwell instructed me to say it's for yer eyes only," the messenger said in a youthful voice.

"Good enough," MacLain replied.

"Any message ye'd like me to relay?"

MacLain shook his head. "Ye can be on yer way now."

With that, he closed the door, tore open the seal of the envelope, and glanced over the missive. He bit off an epithet between his teeth.

His expression grim, he turned to her. "Did yer brother have any interest in the occult?"

A shiver traced over Amelia's nape. Images from a deck of unusual cards flashed through her thoughts. "I was aware of a passing curiosity. There was a woman . . . Paul met her quite some time ago. She told fortunes."

"Ye recall her name?"

In her mind's eye, Amelia pictured a striking beauty with a cascade of auburn hair. "Helen Tanner, if memory serves. He was rather taken with her, but after Papa discovered she fancied herself to be a fortune teller, he forbade Paul from seeing her."

"But he didn't listen."

"No, I don't believe he did," she said. "At the time, Paul did not confide in me. I was little more than a girl fresh from the schoolroom, but even then, I could see he was drawn to her. After a time, she ended their relationship and sailed to America. I never heard her name again, not until a year or so ago."

"What happened then?"

"Paul mentioned casually, perhaps too casually, that she had arrived in London."

"And ye've no idea why she returned to London?"

"At the time, I thought she wished to rekindle her relationship with Paul. But now, I'm not so certain something else did not motivate her return."

MacLain gave a solemn nod. "We need to find her. She may be in danger."

"I believe she left England after my brother's death."

"There's reason to believe she's back." MacLain placed the missive on the table. "I took the liberty of asking my business partner to make some inquiries. The man who attacked ye last night had been asking around about a woman—a fortune teller. She calls herself Madame Helena."

✦

Chapter Ten

READY FOR TROUBLE as he escorted Amelia from her home, Logan counted himself ready to face most any threat that might arise. Before leaving the Rogue's Lair, he'd strapped a *sgian dubh* to his calf and holstered a gun beneath his jacket. He'd inspected the derringer she carried in her reticule, judging with his own eyes that it was a viable weapon in the event something rendered him unable to defend her. Determined to ensure her safety, he'd mentally mapped out the spots along the way to and from her residence where an assailant might hide in wait. He thought he was well prepared to watch over Amelia.

Bloody hell, he'd been wrong.

He could not have predicted that Amelia would thrust a leather travel case containing her wee beast—a decidedly unhappy wee beast at that—into his hand. Nor that she would flash a deliberately sweet smile as she made her request that he, of all people, transport the dog to his coach.

When he started to scowl, signaling that he'd prefer a night in the Tower to the task, her delicate brows knit into the beginning of a frown.

"Heathy *is* exceedingly unhappy. Perhaps I should reconsider . . . leaving, that is."

"The dog will be well enough once he can take leave of this little box."

She nodded, her weary expression making it clear that the

wee beast was not the only one who felt no joy at leaving her home.

"You're quite right," she said. "I suppose we should hurry along."

"My housekeeper will see to it that the dog has an abundance of bones to gnaw on and whatever else it is that he fancies."

"He'll like that," she said half-heartedly. "I'll gather my things."

With that, she turned on her heel, leaving him standing on the front steps, bearing cargo that *yipped* in an infuriatingly steady rhythm. Bloody hell, was the dog actually counting the beats between his plaintive barks? If the good townsfolk were to witness the sight of *The Outlaw MacLain* hauling a mop with teeth, they'd bloody well enjoy a hearty chuckle at his expense.

"Well, well, Logan MacLain. If this isn't a rich sight."

Blast the infernal luck. Hearing the laughter in the man's familiar voice, Logan tossed a glance over his shoulder, spotting Finn Caldwell as he cut a quick path across the street.

Holding the carrier steady as the squirming dog within let loose a mournful howl, Logan met his cousin's questioning gaze.

"Murray said ye'd be here," Finn said. His eyes narrowing, he stared at the bag. "Good God, man, that *is* a hound, isn't it?"

"Unless the lass's clothes have come to life, I'd say it bloody is."

Finn chuckled. "And a fearsome little beast he is."

"I'll have you know he *is* quite fierce," Amelia said as she emerged from the library, carrying a bulging traveling bag in her hand. "There, there, Heathy. You've no need to fret."

As if in hearty disagreement, the dog barked more vigorously. Blasted shame the pup didn't realize he was not likely to stir a fright in any creature larger than a field mouse. His niece's wee tabby kitten wouldn't even bat an eye over the dog.

"Naughty boy," Amelia scolded lightly. "Hush."

Finn hiked a brow. "I presume she is speaking to the hound."

"Ye're still an arse, Caldwell," Logan muttered.

"Ah, tell me something I didn't already know." As Finn laughed, his attention lingered on Amelia. She'd hiked her skirts to the ankle while making her way down the stairs.

"I take it you are a friend of Mr. MacLain," she said as she stepped onto the pavement.

"Cousins. I have far better taste in friends," he said. "Finn Caldwell, at yer service. It is my pleasure to make yer acquaintance."

A raw epithet sprang to Logan's lips, but he thought better of it. "If ye're attempting to win over the lady, she will not be impressed by whatever it is ye're calling wit."

"Mr. Caldwell, if you would be inclined to assist me, I have another satchel." Her expression bland as porridge, Amelia motioned to the entry. "It's just beyond the door."

"Never let it be said Finn Caldwell is not a gentleman."

Amelia's mouth curved in the faintest of acknowledgement. "Oh, and if you would, please grab Heathy's bag as well."

"Heathy?" Finn repeated.

"My dog."

Finn's forehead furrowed. "The hound possesses his own satchel?"

"Of course." Amelia flashed a smile.

"Consider it done, lass."

She stepped aside, and Finn bounded up the stairs. Logan shot him a glare. God above, his cousin was bloody shameless.

"I take it he fancies himself to be charming," Amelia said in a conspiratorial whisper.

"If that's what ye want to call it."

Amusement played on her rosy mouth. "I have little use for a charming man. I much prefer an honest one."

"In that case, ye're in bloody luck. I'm not inclined to spout silky drivel."

As she placed her traveling case on the floor of the coach, Finn descended the steps, an over-stuffed carpet bag in one hand and a blue satchel embroidered with a large black "H" in the other. A metal bowl and a well-gnawed bone protruded from the case. By Zeus, she'd actually monogrammed the dog's bag. Amelia Stewart was nothing if not surprising.

In place of his typical smug smile, Finn flashed a scowl. Logan let loose the rumble of laughter he'd held back. At least he wasn't the only man whose fearsome reputation was at risk of crumbling to dust.

"Do ye intend to tell me why ye're here?" he asked Finn as his cousin set the bags inside the carriage.

"I understand ye're taking her to yer place. Someone needs to watch yer back." Finn motioned to his carriage. "I'll follow ye there."

"Ye know of a threat?"

"None that I have confirmed." Finn's expression revealed more than his words.

Amelia's top teeth grazed her plump bottom lip. The worry in her eyes was like a fist digging into Logan's gut. "Has something else happened?"

Finn shook his head. "But we can't let down our guard."

"We'll keep ye safe," Logan assured her. "Ye can count on that."

FROM HER COMFORTABLE seat within MacLain's carriage, Amelia took in the scene as they made their way to his West End townhouse. Through the back window, she spotted Finn Caldwell at the reins of his sleek conveyance as he trailed their coach at a discreet distance.

Peering up at her from his spot by her feet, Heathy yipped for attention. Amelia slid a finger through the mesh at the end of his case and petted his head. "Oh, hush. You'll be out of there soon enough."

Turning back to the window, she drank in the fine craftsmanship of the elegant brick and mortar buildings lining the streets as the carriage made its way over the cobblestone pavement.

The carriage slowed as they approached a stately red-brick townhouse with gleaming black shutters. An ebony gaslight on a pole near the front windows lent the premises an understated charm.

MacLain climbed down from the driver's bench and escorted her from the coach to the entry of the house.

"Welcome to my home." His tone was casual, but the expression in his eyes betrayed the intensity of his mood.

Amelia gulped a breath and gripped Heathy's carrier more tightly. To her dismay, the dog fidgeted and barked, announcing their presence.

As soon as MacLain opened the polished wood door, Mrs. Langford hurried to greet them. Looking past them, her smile lit her eyes. Amelia glanced over her shoulder as Mr. Caldwell strolled through the entry.

"Ah, if this isn't a pleasant surprise," Mrs. Langford said. She flushed like a young lass and touched her fingertips to her cheek.

Caldwell's smile carved an appealing dimple in his cheek. "The pleasure is mine, Mrs. Langford."

Amelia caught the sour glance Logan shot his cousin. As if to announce his dismay at the attention everyone was receiving except him, Heathy let out a bark, then another.

A vee etched between Mrs. Langford's brows. She leaned closer to get a better look inside the satchel. "Goodness, is that what I think it is?"

As if in reply, Heathy barked, a bit less plaintively this time.

"A wee hound." Mrs. Langford looked to MacLain. "Why, he's so very much like the one yer mum had when ye were a lad."

MacLain met her gaze. "Ye still remember old Silas?"

"Who could ever forget the valiant little creature? No vermin dared trespass in yer mum's home, not with Silas in residence."

"That was a long time ago," he said.

"I remember ye playing with the pup," Mrs. Langford said

with a touch of wistfulness. "Back in those days, ye did not even come to my chin. Yer mum was none too pleased by the dirt the two of ye would drag into the house."

MacLain rubbed his jaw, the look of a pleasant memory softening the set of his features. Something in his expression—something Amelia couldn't quite define—fascinated her. What an imp he must have been as a boy, a handsome lad with mischief dancing in his dark brown eyes.

Caldwell chuckled under his breath. "Getting soft-hearted, are ye?"

MacLain's jaw hardened. He'd displayed a side of himself Amelia suspected he did not usually reveal. "The dog earned his keep, I will give him that."

"Just as Heathy does," Amelia spoke up proudly.

His brow furrowed. "The dog's a wee terror, he is."

Caldwell leaned toward Heathy's case. He drew back quickly when a growl met his action. "That he is." He chuckled. "Why, I'm shaking in my boots."

"Heathy can be a wee bit cantankerous, but I'm confident he will warm up to you," Amelia said. "In time."

A primly attired wisp of a woman whose dark hair was generously sprinkled with silver entered the front hall. "Cantankerous, you say?" Wry humor played on her thin mouth. "In that case, the dog will be right at home among this lot of scoundrels."

"A warm greeting, as usual, Mrs. Garrett." MacLain's mouth hitched up at one corner, not quite a grin. "No one could accuse ye of dripping honey to gain favor with yer employer."

"Would you have it any other way?" she replied.

"I do value honesty. But I place even more worth on yer lamb stew," MacLain said. "A finer cook ye could not find in all of England."

"It's a good thing you were blessed with that smile. I've no doubt it has helped you charm your way out of many a fix." The woman's eyes warmed as she turned to Amelia. "As my employer is taking his fine time offering an introduction, I will see to that task myself. I am Mrs. Garrett. You must be Mrs. Stewart."

MacLain slanted the older woman a glance. "Impatient as ever, I see."

Mrs. Garrett flashed him a little scowl that appeared to be for effect. "I keep house, and from time to time, I prepare meals for MacLain—on those rare occasions when he's actually in the residence."

Amelia offered a smile. "Pleased to make your acquaintance."

"As ye can see, Mrs. Garrett's cheerful disposition endears her to all she meets," Caldwell said with a cheeky grin.

Mrs. Garrett's mouth tightened, as if she held words perched on the tip of her tongue that she'd thought better than to voice. Waving him away, she turned to Amelia. "If there is anything you need while you're under this roof, please do not hesitate to let me know. I will be seeing to your accommodations."

"Thank you," Amelia said as Heathy yipped again.

Mrs. Garrett bent down and spoke gently to the dog. Her smile seemed as genuine as Heathy's enthusiasm while he wagged his tail.

"The little fellow is a good judge of character." She turned to Finn, her eyes narrowing. "'Tis no wonder he growled at you."

"Ah, ye've a cold heart," Caldwell protested as MacLain chuckled under his breath.

"You'd do well to remember that. Your sly ways do not work on me," the housekeeper said. "As long as I am here, you will treat the ladies in this house with the proper regard." She sent Amelia a wink that told her she had an ally under MacLain's roof.

"Mrs. Garrett, I trust you will find suitable accommodations for Mrs. Stewart's pet," MacLain said.

"If it's no trouble, I would prefer that Heathy stay in my room," Amelia said.

"It's no trouble," Mrs. Garrett replied. "I'll see to the darling pup's comfort."

MacLain's brows hiked. Standing behind the housekeeper, he

mouthed the words *darling pup* to his cousin.

"As I recall, ye did not regard yer own grandson so kindly when he paid ye a visit," MacLain pointed out.

Mrs. Garrett's thin shoulders rose and fell. "I don't expect this pup will be nearly as insolent as my kin. His mum—my harridan of a daughter—is raising the lad to be a hellion, she is." She let out a little sigh. "At least I do not have to worry about the influence the two of ye will have on a dog."

"True enough," MacLain agreed. "Finn and I will see to Mrs. Stewart's bags. And then, we have matters to discuss."

"If Mr. Caldwell is involved, it is safe to assume the matters are not fit for a lady's ears," Mrs. Langford spoke up. "I'll be happy to help Amelia to settle in."

"This time, I am only the messenger." Caldwell raked a hand through his wavy wheat-brown hair. "Fit for a lady or not, Mrs. Stewart needs to hear what I've learned."

Chapter Eleven

AMELIA PACED THE floor of MacLain's study. Staring down at the intricate design woven into the rug beneath her feet, she struggled to hold her tongue as the allegations Finn Caldwell uttered clawed deeper and deeper at her chest. Each calmly spoken word seemed a sharp dagger to the heart.

Mr. Caldwell was mistaken. Surely the information he'd gleaned from his so-called sources was wrong. It simply had to be.

The very idea that her brother had become entangled with criminals was ludicrous. Paul had been many things in his life.

But he was no thief.

Finn Caldwell's accusations could not possibly have merit.

But as she studied him, seeing the solemn truth in his eyes, the pain in her heart grew more intense with each beat. Mr. Caldwell had no reason to deceive her.

Unlike her brother.

For months before Paul's death, she'd suspected he was hiding something. He'd become unusually reticent, especially when she inquired about his trips to the Continent. Deep down, she'd known he was harboring secrets.

Had he been trying to protect her?

Or had he feared she would be ashamed of him if she knew the truth?

"I know this is not pleasant for ye," Caldwell went on. "But we need ye to tell us about yer brother's dealings."

"Paul was an authority on the art of the Renaissance. He traveled the Continent in search of works of interest to his clients."

Caldwell nodded. "What do ye know of his clients?"

"He acquired works for museums and public galleries, for the most part. Though from time to time, private collectors employed his services."

Standing by a well-stocked bookcase, MacLain leaned an elbow against a shelf. "What do ye know about these collectors?"

"Paul shared very little with me. His clients demanded a high level of confidentiality."

MacLain nodded. "What do ye recall of his travels in the months before his death?"

"He spent several weeks in Paris. He returned shortly before he died."

"What business did he have there?" MacLain pressed.

"I don't know. As I've said, my brother did not often discuss his ventures with me."

"I don't wish to upset ye, but the facts are plain. Yer brother was involved with some very bad people." The furrows in Mr. Caldwell's forehead betrayed his tension. "We need to know why."

"Paul was not a saint. Not by any measure." She dragged in a deep breath. "But he was *not* a criminal."

"We can't ignore the truth. There's good reason to believe he'd been working with schemers and cheats," MacLain said, gritting out the words as if they pained him. "He got himself in over his head."

A swell of brutal emotion crashed into her. "My brother was neither a thief nor a swindler."

"We are not here to sully Paul's name." A tiny muscle in MacLain's jaw ticked. "But we need to know what in blazes he did that made ye a target."

"I was able to track down information on the fortune teller, the woman who calls herself Madame Helena." Caldwell said.

"I'm told she also has ties to your brother. Why would he involve himself with a charlatan?"

"Charlatan?" she repeated dully. An image of Helen laying out her arcane cards in a distinct pattern on a silk-covered table flickered through her thoughts. At the time, Helen's fascination with interpreting the images had seemed an amusement, a bit of harmless fun.

"Helen Tanner deceived gullible men," Caldwell said. "Was yer brother one of them?"

"My brother was no fool. Paul's interest in Helen had little to do with her fortune telling cards." Amelia stared down at her hands, searching for the right words. "She was his mistress."

"Could she have lured him into a scheme?" MacLain asked.

"Paul was not naïve." She let out a low breath. "But it *is* possible she deceived him."

Caldwell stood and went to the window. "Did he ever refer to a man who calls himself Mr. Hawk?"

Amelia searched her mind. "The name is not familiar. Is he a collector?"

"The man is an art thief," Caldwell said. "My sources believe yer brother aided Hawk in his schemes."

Amelia met his hard gaze. "I've told you—Paul was not a criminal."

"I'm not here to pass judgment. But my sources—"

Amelia squared her shoulders, shoring up her resolve. This was all quite beyond belief. "Your sources? I presume they have names."

Caldwell regarded her for a long moment. "I am not at liberty to reveal their identities. But ye can trust they are reliable. Word on the street has it that Hawk believed yer brother and Miss Tanner betrayed him."

Amelia gulped against a searing lump in the back of her throat. The very thought that Paul had consorted with criminals was nearly beyond comprehension. Yet, deep inside, she could not deny how his behavior had changed in the time before his death. He'd seemed to keep his distance from her, becoming colder. Evasive. So much had seemed out of character. At the time, she'd suspected he'd developed an overfondness for the gaming tables. But this . . . this was far worse that she'd ever imagined.

"You believe this man called Mr. Hawk . . . killed Paul?"

Caldwell's tone was raw. "Yes."

Yer brother and Miss Tanner betrayed him. The revelation struck like a slap to the face. Dear God! If Mr. Hawk had murdered Paul over some act of disloyalty, would Helen be next?

Glancing to MacLain, she read his grim expression. Her pulse raced. "Helen is in danger. We have to warn her."

"Don't worry, lass. We'll find her," Caldwell said with a brisk confidence.

MacLain pinned her with his dark gaze. "Ye'll stay here, where ye will be safe."

Amelia shook her head. "Even if you locate her, she won't believe you," she said. "Helen needs to hear the truth from someone she knows. She trusted Paul. And she will trust me."

"I won't allow it," MacLain said in a tone that brooked no dissent.

Amelia cocked her chin. "You *will* need me. Helen will not confide in you."

MacLain's eyes narrowed. "But ye think she will talk to ye? Bloody unlikely."

"I believe she will tell me the truth, if only for Paul's sake."

MacLain regarded her for a long, silent moment. "I will not expose ye to danger."

Amelia forced a little shrug. "We may work together to find Miss Tanner. Or I will make inquiries on my own. The choice is yours."

He flashed a scowl. "Ye are a confounding, headstrong woman."

"I consider that high praise." She met his fierce look with a little scowl of her own. "You know I am not bluffing," she added for good measure.

"Much as it pains me to admit it, she's right," Caldwell spoke up. "We'll have a better chance convincing Helen Tanner to tell us what she knows if she can confide in someone she already knows."

MacLain slowly shook his head. "That is too damned risky."

The note of concern in his voice warmed Amelia's heart. The most talented of thespians could not have feigned the emotion.

She allowed a faint smile. "If anyone dares to threaten me, I am entirely confident you will teach them the error of their ways."

"That goes without saying." MacLain plowed a hand through his hair. As Amelia's gaze trailed the path of his fingers, a longing to touch him kindled deep within her.

"We will protect her," Caldwell said, his tone resolute. "Ye know we can."

Amelia planted her hands on her hips. She would find justice for her brother, one way or another. And now, she had acquired allies in the battle. "So tell me, gentlemen, what is our plan?"

Chapter Twelve

Alone in his private office at the Rogue's Lair, Logan savored the quiet. He draped his jacket over the back of a chair, went to the sideboard beneath the window, and poured two fingers of good whisky from a decanter that had been in his family for generations.

Weary to the bone, he eased back against the leather of a well-padded chair, stretched out his legs, and willed himself to relax. Taking a drink, he studied the play of gaslight and shadows against the ceiling. Tension held him alert. God only knew he'd never planned to play the protector.

Not for Amelia Stewart. Not for anyone. But he would defend her. He would keep her safe.

No matter the cost.

At first, he'd been determined to honor the vow he'd made so long ago. But now, his need to keep Amelia safe had more to do with the woman herself than a promise he'd uttered in his youth.

Since the moment he'd strode through the door of her library, much to the shock of her prim patrons, his world had shifted on its axis. Before he'd first laid eyes on Amelia, his drive to restore this once-decrepit tavern to its former glory had consumed his energies.

He would bring the Rogue's Lair back from the brink of ruin, just as he'd once pulled himself up from the shattered depths of loss and betrayal. He'd spent years in America fleecing British fops gone west, night after night plying his mathematically precise skill at cards in rough saloons that brimmed with guns and rotgut whisky. When he'd tired of the smoky rooms and drunken fools, he upped the stakes, risking his ill-gotten gains on wildcat wells that had the good grace to gush oil, and with it, a fortune. Weary of an existence where he never knew when he'd end up on the wrong end of a gun, he'd returned to England.

Since landing in London, he'd poured money, time, and energy into the old pub his kin had believed a fool's purchase. Despite their doubts, the sense of history in this tavern had spoken to him. This place would be his home, its restoration his greatest accomplishment.

Until suddenly—unexpectedly—he'd been drawn into another quest, this one far riskier. And far more crucial.

It was as if a temporary madness had overtaken him. He had not felt himself capable of caring about a woman in a very long time. God only knew he didn't want to. Not since he'd watched the lass he'd been engaged to wed enter a rich man's carriage and leave him behind.

Forever.

In those moments of pain and the miserable years that followed, he'd believed his heart too hardened to ever hold feelings for another woman.

Until he'd seen the quiet storm in Amelia's sapphire blue eyes.

Closing his eyes, he pictured her in his mind. When she cocked her chin defiantly, a challenge had flashed over her delicate features. By Zeus's thunder, she was beautiful, even if she didn't seem to know it. Amelia had not been bent on seduction. But she'd drawn him in nonetheless. Her intentions hadn't mattered to his body, not in the bloody least.

Even though he craved her beauty, he could rein in that hunger.

Blasted shame the need in his soul was another matter.

He relished her determination, the courage and spirit that had led her to insist she would seek out Helen Tanner on her own. She'd forced his hand in the hunt for the fortune teller.

By hellfire, he had been a fool to give in. He was sworn to protect her. But he did not doubt she would rush headlong into trouble, caution be damned, if he'd tried to exclude her from the search. She was desperate to talk to Helen Tanner—not only to warn her of the danger, but to glean whatever information the charlatan might have that would answer the questions that tore at her. At least this way, she'd have the protection he could offer.

For some reason he didn't understand, Amelia had faith in him. Faith that he could lead her to Helen. Faith that he would defend her, no matter the odds. By thunder, he would justify her trust.

At the moment, Amelia was at his home, safe behind stout, bolted doors not even Goliath could break. In his mind's eye, he pictured her pacing a trail over the carpet as she waited to put their hastily cobbled-together scheme into play.

Finn had gone into the night to make the rounds of his contacts, searching for some clue to Helen Tanner's hideaway. Bloody good thing his cousin knew how to blend in with the high society types who flocked to midnight séances as readily as he could slide into the city's underbelly. Someone knew where the fortune teller had gone. It was a matter of time before Finn convinced some bloke to reveal her secret.

A muffled noise just beyond the front door tore him from his thoughts.

A bark, of all the blasted things.

He would've described the sound as grumpy if it had come from a human being.

Bollocks.

"MacLain, are you in there?" Amelia called.

He threw open the door. The perceptive gaze of the woman who'd consumed his thoughts met his eyes.

"I take it this is not a pleasant surprise," she said before he could get a word out of his mouth.

"Ye are a clever lass, aren't ye?" Forcing a bland tone, he motioned her and the dog into the room.

"I realize I'd agreed to occupy myself at your home tonight. But unfortunately, fate had other notions."

"Fate, is it?" He pinned her with what was meant to be a steely gaze, but she merely hiked her chin as if to counter his expression.

"Mrs. Langford offered to take out the carriage. She's downstairs, chatting with Mr. Murray."

"Somehow, that does not surprise me."

"She does seem to be rather fond of him," Amelia said. "Sadly, I do not sense the feeling is mutual."

"Now, that is an understatement," Logan said. "I see ye brought yer guard dog."

"Of course. After all, there is no way of knowing what sort of brute we might encounter." Her coral lips curved into a smile. "Heathy did enjoy the outing. I do believe he finds the night air quite refreshing."

The dog stared up at him, as if uncertain whether to give a little growl or to plead for a treat. The poor wee beast wore a blue bow on his ridiculously ornate silver collar.

As if on cue, her pet began to sniff about. Good God. Was the dog looking for a place to relieve himself in his office?

"Heathy, naughty." She curled the end of the dog's pale blue leash around her hand and brought him closer to her skirts. "I am quite confident he would deter an attacker."

"If the villain is concerned about a dog piddling on his trousers, he might think twice."

"I'll have you know Heathy is well trained. He does *not* have accidents."

As the last syllable passed her lips, the dog sank his pointy teeth into the edge of the carpet, a costly rug Logan had acquired on his last voyage as lieutenant on a merchant ship.

"I take it he has not been as well-schooled on the matter of property destruction."

"Oh goodness, Heathy," she scolded gently.

Seemingly chastised, the dog released a mouthful of carpet and regarded Amelia with mischief-filled eyes. Was the spoiled little beast actually grinning?

Forcing his attention back to the matter at hand, Logan shot Amelia a look he'd intended to be commanding. "Do ye care to explain what compelled ye to venture out tonight?"

"Something came up." Her tone made it clear the scowl he'd perfected while an officer on a rowdy ship's crew had not fazed her in the least.

"Something?"

"Something related to our plan . . . a matter of great urgency."

"So ye persuaded Mrs. Langford to disregard my instructions?"

Amelia's mouth thinned. "She understood the need to reach you. I do hope you will not be upset with her. She was only trying to be of help."

He scrubbed a hand against his jaw. Amelia's concern for his driver touched something deep within him. It seemed a lifetime since he'd encountered someone outside the small circle of souls he trusted who gave a damn about anyone other than themselves.

"Ye've nothing to worry about where Mrs. Langford is concerned." He rubbed the back of his neck, easing out a knot of tension. "But what was in yer head, lass, risking both yer necks?"

Challenge glimmered in her eyes. "Do you want me to tell you why I'm here? Or would you prefer to glare at me a bit longer?"

I'd bloody prefer to kiss that teasing little smile off yer perfect mouth.

By hellfire, the woman was maddening. Somehow, that made her all the more enticing. He wanted to hold her. Wanted to touch her until she was too weak in the knees to think of anything but the taste of his mouth and the feel of his fingertips upon her skin.

Blast it, his own body threatened to betray him. Dragging his attention to a generations-old dagger mounted on the wall, a solemn symbol of pride in the Clan MacLain, he shifted his stance and tamped down the sudden hunger, if only enough for rational thought to prevail.

Logan glanced down at the floor, spotting Amelia's dog as he set his sights on a pair of boots stowed under his desk. If Heathy—poor mutt with that atrocious name—had his way, the leather would soon lay in shreds.

Silently thanking the dog for the much-needed distraction, Logan snatched up his boots. Was he going daft, or had the pup actually looked disappointed as he set them out of his reach?

A bland smile touched Amelia's lips. "Heathy has no fondness for shoes."

"I've no inclination to test yer theory."

"If you don't mind . . ." She strolled over to the sideboard and looped the dog's leash around a stout wooden leg. "This will ensure that Heathy stays out of mischief."

The dog sank upon his haunches, his expression fairly shouting that he would not be so easily deterred. He turned his head, seemingly intrigued by the play of light against the cut crystal bottle. Finally, the wee beast had something else to take his interest. With any luck, he'd be quiet and still while Logan got to the bottom of Amelia's unexpected arrival.

Folding his arms, Logan leaned against his desk. "Tell me, Amelia Stewart, what compelled ye to put yerself in danger—at this hour of night, no less?"

Her expression was placid, though her eyes sparkled with the look of a truth she was eager to reveal. "Mr. Caldwell no longer needs to search for Helen."

"What in blazes are ye saying?"

"I know where she is." Amelia paused, glancing toward the clock on the wall. "To be precise, I know where she will be at midnight."

Her words plowed into him. This had the markings of a trap.

Damned if he'd let her rush headlong into it.

"How do ye know this?"

"Helen sent a message by courier tonight. This time, it was addressed to me." Amelia retrieved an envelope from the reticule dangling from her wrist. "She has information . . . about Paul."

"Bloody hell."

"I quite agree." Amelia handed him the note. "I suspect the messenger might've been the same lad who delivered the letters from Paul."

God above, that was it. Helen Tanner had sent the parcels. She'd ensured the letters from Paul had made it into Logan's hands.

And now the fortune teller was aware that Amelia was staying at his residence.

How the hell had she come upon that knowledge?

Quickly, he scanned the message. "If that woman thinks we will agree to her terms, she's mad."

"I do not believe that is the case. But there's really no alternative, is there? She needs to know that she's in danger. And I need whatever information she is willing to offer."

"Ye've no idea what ye'll find there. God only knows who could be lying in wait. I'll be damned if I will let ye rush in on your own."

"I cannot imagine you would. After all, there is that mysterious debt you owe my brother."

"This has nothing to do with a debt," he said, the words as honest as any he'd ever spoken. "Ye should know by now that I would not leave ye to harm."

Her eyes seemed to darken as she studied him. "I do believe you mean that, Mr. MacLain."

"Logan," he corrected.

"Very well . . . Logan. Since you will be putting yourself in harm's way yet again, I suppose we might as well proceed to given names."

"It's about blasted time."

He'd expected her to counter his statement, but she smiled, a wistful look in her eyes. "I do believe I am beginning to enjoy having a bodyguard."

"Are ye now?"

"Oh, yes. If only the gossips could see me now, accompanied by a strapping Scotsman on a perilous quest. And at such a scandalous hour, no less." A hint of a smile played on her soft features. "The only thing more intriguing than scandal is sin. Wouldn't you agree?"

He cocked a brow. "I'd wager ye'd appreciate a taste of sin."

Intrigue glimmered in her eyes. "Wickedness does possess a certain allure. But in my experience, it is rather overrated."

He took her hand in his, drawing her closer. "I could convince ye a bit of wickedness is a delight to be savored."

"You seem rather confident."

His gaze was drawn to her like a moth to the flicker of a flame. "I've no doubt."

"In due time, perhaps, you will leave me thoroughly . . . convinced." Her words seemed a dare, a challenge he knew better than to accept.

Damned shame his good sense had flown out the window.

Before logic could overrule the hunger deep within him, he caught her in his arms. Holding her close, he could feel every rise and fall of her chest, sense every beat of her heart.

"Would that please ye, Amelia?"

Her mouth curved, a perfect temptation. "Yes." The single word was uttered in a husky voice, a siren's song he did not have the strength to resist.

A true madness filled him. Drinking in the heat in her sapphire eyes, he drew the pad of his finger over the curve of her face. "In my world, there is never a better time than the present."

As if under his spell, Amelia nestled against his long, lean body. His natural heat penetrated the layers of clothing which separated them. Gently, he framed her face in his hands. So warm. So strong. He regarded her with a sense of fascination. Ripples of awareness coursed through her, and she stilled. There'd be no harm in a simple kiss, would there?

It wasn't as if she were an innocent. She could savor a mere taste of passion in his caress.

Nothing would come of it.

Yes, she could tell herself that.

His eyes thoughtful, he watched her, taking his cues from her. Holding back. Logan had sensed her hesitation. He had given her time to change course.

Not so very wicked, are you now, Mr. MacLain?

His hands slid lower, and she smiled to herself. He caressed the small of her back before his fingers settled at the flare of her hips. She let out a low, calming breath and allowed her fingertips to glide over the silk of his silver-gray waistcoat, taking in the flex of the powerful muscles in his shoulders.

Subtle notes of bergamot on his skin stirred her senses. The heady aroma conjured a longing deep within.

With a smile that would tempt an angel to sin, Logan met her gaze, offering a moment for her to slip away from his embrace. Allowing her one last chance to guard her heart.

Pity her craving for his caress was far more powerful than her desire to protect her heart. Unwilling to deny herself this delicious pleasure, she coiled her arms around his neck. With a whisper, she invited the intimacy of his touch.

He dipped his head low to taste her lips. Slowly, at first. Teasing her. Tempting her beyond all reason.

Until she lost herself in delicious sensation.

Passion surged, nearly a tangible thing. Losing herself in a whirlpool of feeling, she closed her eyes. His long fingers splayed against her corseted ribs, and he held his muscles taut, his strength restrained.

Logan wanted more. In her heart, she knew that undeniable truth. Yet he took nothing she did not offer.

She sighed against his full, utterly delectable mouth.

Suddenly, a crash of glass against the floor tore Amelia from her bliss.

Logan's head jerked up. In unison, they turned to the source of the noise.

A crystal goblet lay shattered beside the carpet. Near the mess, Heathy sat not quite peacefully, guilt clear upon his canine features.

Her suspicions confirmed, Amelia rushed to the sideboard and scooped the dog into her arms. Frowning, Logan surveyed the scene.

Oh, you've done it now, Heathy. You'll be banished to your travel case. No more running about for the likes of you.

Logan's forehead furrowed. He leaned down and reached for one of Heathy's paws. Tiny lines crinkled around his eyes as he examined each paw in turn.

How very fascinating. Was kindness another weapon in his rogue's arsenal?

How very unfair of Logan MacLain to take her by surprise and further erode her defenses.

"The wee beast avoided injury." Taking a step back, Logan looked down upon the scattered shards. "I cannot say the same for the glass."

"Heathy must've fiddled with his leash and jarred the sideboard. I'm quite sorry—"

"Do not worry yer head, lass." He tapped a finger to the decanter, a faint grin pulling at his lips. "Now if the pup had ruined my whisky, that would be another matter entirely."

Amelia glanced down at the unusually quiet dog in her arms. Pity Heathy had not been so well-behaved moments earlier. She would still be savoring Mr. MacLain's kiss.

"I'll find something to clean it," she said.

He shook his head. "Do not trouble yerself. I'll have Murray send up one of the barmaids to take care of the mess."

"Thank you." She swallowed against a sudden, nervous lump in her throat. "In that case, I suppose Heathy and I should be on our way. Miss Tanner is expecting me at midnight."

"If ye are intent on this meeting, ye know I will be at yer side."

"If you insist," she said. It went without saying that his presence would give an attacker pause.

"As for the dog, Mrs. Langford can take him with her when she returns home."

Amelia nodded her agreement, even as a vein in her temple throbbed. "I'm afraid I should not have agreed to have you accompany me. You see, Miss Tanner instructed me to come alone."

"I don't give a damn what the woman told ye." Logan's tone made it clear he would not be swayed. "Ye'll not be walking into a trap. Not while I am watching over ye."

Chapter Thirteen

W ITH LOGAN BY her side, Amelia made her way along fog-draped streets to a rough-hewn workman's tavern. A gas lamp on the corner cast hazy light over the pub's massive door. Instinctively, Amelia lifted a hand to cover her face as a fetid stench wafted from the gutter beside the stone and brick building. Good heavens, the place was dismal, far worse than she'd imagined. What measure of desperation had driven Helen Tanner, a woman who had displayed a taste for elegance and expensive surroundings, to take refuge in this putrid place?

As they neared the entrance, a slovenly man stumbled out of the place, muttering foul words with each uneven step. He cast his bleary gaze at Amelia, leering at her until he glanced at her imposing escort. Mumbling a vulgarity under his breath, he turned on his heel and drunkenly staggered away.

Steps beyond the building, a rustling in the shadows unleashed a shiver down Amelia's nape. Was a creature scavenging in the darkness? Or was something more threatening waiting to strike?

She dragged in a low breath, as if that could steady her nerves. Goodness, she was letting her imagination run away with her, wasn't she? Seeming to sense her twinge of fear, Logan reached for her, placing his fingers on her arm in a light but steady touch. Odd, really, how his presence reassured her. Days earlier, she could not have imagined taking comfort in his nearness, in the strength of his determination to watch over her.

"I suspect someone connected with the rotter who came after ye is waiting to finish what he started." His voice was low and rough-edged as he gestured to the crudely painted image of a jester on the tavern door. "Any woman Paul might have fancied would never take up residence in this hellhole."

"She's here." Amelia looked up to the windows on the upper floors. "I'm quite sure of it. Helen would not deceive me."

He cocked a brow. "Ah, that's right, a fortune teller who cheats gullible fools. Honest as the day is long, she is."

"Actually, this tavern may be a clever choice for a hideaway. No one would think to look for her here."

"With good reason."

"I must admit, I am thankful I do not have to face what lies within this place all on my own."

He caught her hand within his long, warm fingers. "So, Amelia, ye did not wish to wander alone into a lion's den."

"Lion's den? A wee bit dramatic, wouldn't you say?"

"I know what I'm talking about, lass. Stay with me."

"You think I don't know how to deter an overly amorous gent?"

"Not when ye do not have yer growling little beast to defend ye."

"An excellent point. Just think, if I'd brought Heathy along, you could be at home, asleep in your bed."

"There is not a chance in Hades I would see ye venture into the night on yer own, wee guard dog or not." His jaw hardened. "Don't let yerself get separated from me. By this time of night, even the blokes still on their feet are deep in their cups."

Taking in his somber expression, she bit back a retort to his commanding tone. They were heading into a world he knew well. She'd be wise to take him at his word.

He opened the door and led Amelia through the entrance. Gas lamps on the wall cast sparse light over the patrons. Staying close, Logan's possessive stance sent an unspoken signal that she was under his protection. A man who stank of liquor and sweat grinned at her from a table, his ugly expression betraying the gist of his thoughts. Another towering drunk ambled toward her. This one boldly reached out, daring to try to touch her.

Logan clamped a hand over the man's forearm. "I'd think twice if I were ye."

Though taller than Logan by half a head, the drunk's eyes betrayed a flicker of fear. With a nod, he waited for Logan to release him, then beat a hasty retreat.

Steadying her resolve, Amelia scanned the crowd. She spotted a gaunt-faced scarecrow of a man sitting by himself in the corner. His eyes gleamed with interest as he motioned to her with a slight crook of his finger. When she met his gaze, he nodded, confirming his action had been intended for her.

Logan had seen the gesture as well. He nudged her protectively behind him before escorting her to the table.

"She's waiting for you." The straw-haired man inclined his head toward the spiral staircase. He shot Logan a glare beneath hooded lids. "But only the woman."

"I'll take no orders from ye," Logan shot back, voice hard as flint.

The man's shoulders lifted and fell in a shrug. "I am only the messenger," he said, his attention drifting to the ale in his glass. "Look for the crest."

Curving a hand over her wrist, Logan led Amelia to the stairs. "Stay alert," he warned as they began their ascent. Despite his comforting presence, Amelia's mind raced. Was Helen Tanner the key to uncovering the truth behind Paul's death? Or was this another attempt to prey on Amelia's still-raw grief?

As they reached the landing, Amelia saw that each room bore a sign on its door that depicted an animal—a crudely painted lion, a bear that looked decidedly unhappy, a rooster depicted with overly ornate feathers. She spotted a vivid emblem on a door at the end of the corridor, a coat of arms in shades of blue and gold. The painter's work displayed a precise talent, unlike the other rather crudely rendered images.

Keeping his dagger at the ready, Logan scanned the hallway as they proceeded to the room. Amelia lifted her hand to knock on the ebony-enameled door, but before she made contact, it swung open.

Helen stood in the doorway. Behind her, an oil lamp on the table of the small, shabby room cast scarcely enough light to illuminate her features, her familiar green eyes now shadowed against her ashen, hollow-cheeked complexion. Wrapped in a plain cloak in gray wool, she'd covered her hair with its unadorned hood, but she could not hide all of her abundant curls. Helen's hair had been a glorious copper-red. Now, the tendrils were dull as ashes in a hearth. Had she deliberately disguised the vibrant hue?

Amelia bit back her little gasp of surprise. It scarcely seemed possible that this wraith of a woman was the vivacious beauty who'd once laughed and smiled as she told Amelia's fortune. What had she suffered since Paul had been killed?

"You were to come alone." Helen's whisper-quiet tones confirmed her identity. "You'll get us both killed, you little fool."

Amelia met her cold stare. "You will have to trust him. Or I will have to be on my way."

"I know better than to trust anyone. Even you." Helen's mouth thinned to a hard slash, but she stepped aside, allowing them to enter. She closed the door and bolted it behind them. "But I want the bastards to pay for what they did."

"Ye know who murdered her brother, do ye?" Logan questioned.

"I do not know who killed Paul." The despair in Helen's voice seemed a warning. "But I know who wanted him dead."

"Then tell us," Amelia pressed. "Please, I must know the truth."

Helen laced her fingers into a knot. "What did Paul tell you about his last trip to Paris?"

"As I understood it, he went to acquire a painting for one of his clients."

Slowly, Helen shook her head. She tipped back the hood, allowing a better look at her overly thin features.

"He lied to you." She twisted her hands, as if the words she spoke were a misery. "I only wish he had lied to me as well."

Logan pinned her with his gaze. "Tell us what ye know, Miss Tanner."

"Your brother did not go to France in search of an artist's work. He was there to perform a very specific task for . . . shall we say, an unusual client. After he returned, he was not the same."

Amelia dug her fingers into her palm, battling the apprehension welling within her. "What happened to him?"

"A man was murdered." Helen dropped her gaze to her linked fingers. "In cold blood."

Pulling in a low breath, Amelia fought for calm. "Surely Paul was not involved."

"He played a role." Helen's voice cracked "He didn't think there would be violence. The plan was sophisticated. No one would even know a crime had been committed. But something went wrong."

"Please, Helen, tell us what happened," Amelia implored.

"One of Paul's clients was a criminal—the man calls himself Mr. Hawk. He deals in art forgeries and . . . worse. Much worse. This time, he'd schemed to pass off a painting as a newly discovered Rembrandt. He paid your brother to provide authentication of the piece."

"But how could Paul have allowed himself to be deceived in such a way?" Amelia asked, grasping onto a faint hope that he'd been an unwitting participant in the plot. "He had a thorough knowledge of Rembrandt's works. How could he have believed it was genuine?"

"He didn't." Helen's voice was little more than a rasp. "Paul knew it was not real . . . he knew what he was doing."

"Why?" The world tilted beneath Amelia's feet. "Why would

Paul involve himself in such a reprehensible scheme?"

Helen stared down at her hands, seeming to search for the answers. "He owed Mr. Hawk quite a large sum. Hawk had some sort of connection with the gents at one of the clubs Paul frequented. Paul had always had a taste for playing cards. But it turned into something he didn't want to control. Especially when it seemed he couldn't lose."

"But his luck turned." Logan's tone was grim.

"Ah, that is an understatement." A rueful expression thinned her mouth. "At the time, I wondered if the games had been rigged. To my eyes, it seemed he was being manipulated by a masterful cheat. I suspect I only knew the half of it. Through an associate, Hawk advanced Paul funds to cover his losses. Enough to avoid ruin."

A terrible understanding washed over Amelia. "But then the debt came due."

"Paul knew he'd lose everything. He would be destroyed. When Hawk's representative offered an arrangement that would settle his debt, Paul believed he had no choice. He traveled to Paris and offered an appraisal that was an utter lie." Helen sighed. "If only that had been the end of it."

Logan studied her, questions in his eyes. "You believe Hawk had Paul killed?"

"I don't *believe* Hawk ordered Paul's death. I *know*."

"You have proof?" Logan demanded.

"There is evidence." Helen moved to the window, brushed back the drapes, and peered down to the street below. "After he returned from France, Paul learned of a murder in Paris. The collector he'd deceived had been murdered. The killers stole a fortune in jewels from a safe in the unfortunate man's home."

Amelia's blood chilled. "Dear God."

"Paul suspected Mr. Hawk's involvement." Helen's slender shoulders trembled. "But he was afraid to go to the authorities. If he'd confessed what he'd done, he would have been sent to prison. Or worse. The guilt tormented him. There was no escaping it. He needed the truth. So he confronted Hawk's representative." Miserable regret colored through her tone. "Oh, God, I should have stopped him."

Logan allowed Helen a moment to collect herself before pressing for more. "What happened then?"

"Mr. Hawk's representative claimed Hawk had no part in the murder, but he offered Paul an incentive," Helen said. "In exchange for his silence."

"An incentive?" A raw bitterness rose to the back of Amelia's throat. "Of what sort?"

"Paul would not tell me what they had discussed. He thought I would be safer that way. But he spoke as if the man had offered him a rare treasure."

Treasure. The word echoed in Amelia's thoughts. The man who'd attacked her in the library had demanded answers she had not possessed.

Where is the bloody treasure?

Where is the blasted diamond?

Had Paul accepted a precious gem as payment from a killer? *Dear God.* Suddenly, the floor seemed to sway beneath her feet. She pulled in a breath to steady herself.

"Please tell me Paul did not accept the bribe," she said, though the look of sadness on Helen's face was all the answer she needed.

Helen stared down at her hands. "If only I could."

A muscle in Logan's jaw clenched and unclenched with tension. "He took the bait."

Helen brushed a tear from her cheek. "He planned to use it as evidence against Mr. Hawk."

Logan pinned her with his gaze. "Tell me where I can find the man who works for Hawk."

"I can't." She turned away from the window. "I don't even know his name."

"Do ye possess Paul's correspondence?"

Helen gave her head a miserable shake. "Only the letters he'd trusted me to deliver to your hands."

"Surely he gave some hint as to where Mr. Hawk's associate could be found," Amelia persisted gently.

"I don't know. Now, the cold-blooded bastard who sent his thugs after Paul wants me dead." Helen's words seemed to catch in her throat. "And I suspect they will come after you as well."

"So that's it, then," Logan said. "Hawk—whoever the bloody hell he really is—wants the bribe he'd given to Paul."

"Paul assured me he'd hidden it away somewhere safe, in a place where Hawk's thugs would never think to look," Helen twisted her hands in a miserable knot. "But now I fear he lied to me."

Amelia met Helen's stricken gaze. "Please, tell us where he hid it."

"I can't." Helen laughed, the sound low, nearly crazed. "You see, Amelia—he entrusted the treasure to you."

AMELIA REACHED FOR the back of a nearby chair, bracing herself as the shadowed walls of the cave-like room seemed to close in on her. She dragged in a breath to ease her racing pulse. "You're mistaken. My brother gave me nothing for safekeeping."

"I know what he told me." A small sob cracked Helen's voice. "I saw the fear in his eyes. He knew Mr. Hawk would try to silence him. But he thought he had more time."

Logan's eyes narrowed. "When did Paul give ye the letters ye sent to me?"

"He left the letters with me on the night he died. He knew Amelia would likely be in danger . . . he knew he would need your help." Helen went to the window and eased back the curtain again, just enough to peer into the darkness. "Paul told me to hide them away. Until they were needed."

Amelia joined her at the window. "Where did you take refuge?"

"This was not the first time I'd had to stay out of a dangerous man's reach. I know how to disguise myself, how to hide in plain sight. That skill has aided my survival as much as my knowledge of the tarot."

"How did you know to deliver the letters?" Amelia asked gently. "Why now?"

"I heard talk on the street that a man was looking for me." The curtain shimmied from Helen's hold. She turned to Amelia. "And for you."

"Thank you for alerting Mr. MacLain." Amelia clasped Helen's hand in hers. "You may have saved my life."

"Your brother meant the world to me. He regretted everything he'd done. It tore at his heart to think he'd put you in danger. I could not live with myself if something happened to you." Helen's eyes glistened with tears. "These days and nights since he's been gone have been hell on earth. Soon, I will be away from this place."

"Paul loved you, Helen. Tell us how we can help you."

"Don't worry about me. In the morning, I will be on a steamer sailing far away from here. Far from the bastard who wants me dead. And you—you must do what Paul would've wanted you to do. You must leave this city. You must go away, far out of Mr. Hawk's reach. If you don't, even a man like MacLain won't be able to save you."

As THEY MADE their way from the tavern to his carriage, Logan drew Amelia nearer, even as he held his senses on high alert. Detecting no sign of a threat on the hazy street, he led her to the carriage where Finn Caldwell awaited their return, lounging against the conveyance as if he didn't have a bloody care in the world.

"I don't understand." Amelia's voice was raw with fresh grief. "Not any of this. Why would Paul do such a thing?"

"Yer brother was a good man. But if the woman is telling the truth, desperation can drive a man to cast aside his principles."

"If only he'd told me what he was going through."

"He feared ye'd think less of him."

An all-too-familiar tension clawed at his insides. God only knew he'd had a bitter taste of shame. He'd spent his youth looking for a quick path to riches. Until his arrogance in a cesspool of a pub nearly led him to an early grave.

Paul had saved his neck that night.

Bloody shame he had not been able to return the favor.

He'd never told his father what happened that night when Paul had taken the shot that saved his life. In Da's eyes, Logan had been a wastrel. God only knew he hadn't needed one more reason to be ashamed of his son.

Months after that bitter night, Logan had confided the truth to his older brother. Ewan had listened to the tale without judgment. He'd understood Logan's hunger for a life beyond Da's notion of a respectable existence.

Logan shoved the bitter memory to the back of his mind. Bugger it, he'd no cause to dwell on regrets best left buried. He had to focus on protecting the woman who walked at his side.

Her expression had turned pensive. "I would have stood by him," she said. "I would not have looked upon my brother with scorn. But he wanted . . . I suppose he needed to shield me."

"Paul would've done anything to protect ye, no matter the cost."

"I don't believe Helen was lying. But perhaps she's got it wrong. At least some of it," Amelia said. "The notion that Paul gave me a treasure to hide is pure folly. Surely he would not have wanted to put me in danger."

As they neared the coach, Finn opened the door and let down the metal steps. With a tip of his hat to Amelia, he climbed onto the driver's bench.

Logan assisted her into the carriage. How on earth was she able to navigate the narrow treads while her cumbersome skirts swayed about her legs? As she settled herself on the upholstered bench, Logan confirmed their destination with Finn, then joined her inside the compartment.

Resting his elbows on his knees, he leaned closer. "Amelia, did yer brother give ye anything before he was killed?"

"Nothing of great value. There was one thing, a gift I truly cherished." Amelia's eyes went wide, and her body tensed, as if every nerve in her body had fired at once. "Good heavens! The doll!"

Chapter Fourteen

A S THE CARRIAGE rumbled away from the decrepit pub Helen used as her hideaway, her words echoed through Amelia's thoughts.

You see, Amelia—he entrusted the treasure to you.

Why would Helen have uttered such a blatant untruth? It did not feel as if she was lying. Her tone had not held even a trace of deception. It seemed Helen believed what she'd said.

How very peculiar.

A dreadful suspicion gnawed at Amelia. Had she been wrong to trust Paul? She'd known he had his secrets, but she had never imagined he would deceive her. Had he used her faith in him to his own advantage?

Pressing her head back against the carriage's upholstered seat, she closed her eyes and pictured the delicate Fashion Lady he'd brought back to her from Paris. How she cherished the heartfelt gift. Had the elegant doll meant nothing more to Paul than a means to an end, a means of concealing a stolen gem?

Now, as the watch in her reticule ticked well past the midnight hour, she would retrieve it before anyone connected with Hawk realized its significance. Time was of the essence. Logan understood that just as she did. A stranger would destroy the doll without a moment's thought.

And then they would come for her.

Just as the intruder had that dismal night when Heathy's

sharp teeth and Logan's courage had protected her.

Logan broke the silence. "Ye truly think yer brother stashed a gem in a blasted doll?"

Opening her eyes, she met his gaze. "It is a logical theory. The man who attacked me spoke of a diamond. Paul gave me the doll after he'd returned from Paris . . . after the murdered collector's jewels were stolen."

"To my mind, it'd be too damned much trouble. If I wanted to conceal a stone worth a bloody fortune, I wouldn't waste time fiddling about with a blasted doll."

"I disagree," she countered. "No one would think to look there."

"I knew yer brother well, lass. If he'd needed to stash a stolen gem, I'd wager my last shilling that he would not have chosen a method that would require carefully concealed alterations. He would not have had the skill, nor the time. But if I'm wrong—if the stone is there—we *will* find it."

OH, DEAR.

A moment—perhaps two—after Amelia lit the sconce on the wall and light beamed through the library, she heard herself gasp. *Good heavens.* Her heart sank. They were too late. Someone had invaded the place she viewed as a haven. Someone intent not merely on searching the library, but on destruction and havoc. Reaching the rumpled carpet near the circulation desk, she scanned the chaos.

Chairs upended and drawers in her cabinets hanging ajar.

Books strewn about the floor like so much refuse.

A vase, or what was left of it, lay in pieces on the floor beside her desk. The single rose it had held was surrounded by a small puddle of water and shards of crystal. Anger and grief welled in her chest. Years earlier, her favorite aunt had given her the vase as a cherished gift. Now, it lay hopelessly shattered.

"Bloody bastards," Logan said, his voice hard as he inspected the space for intruders. "They will pay for this, Amelia. That, I promise ye."

Bracing herself with a hand pressed against her desk, she surveyed the damage. The stuffing of a plump wing chair had been torn out through a slash in the upholstery and now lay loose upon the seat. Ruined. Utterly ruined.

Her attention settled on the now-vacant space on the shelf where she'd kept the doll. Her pulse raced. Had the intruder made off with it? Could they have known that Paul obtained the doll while he was in Paris? Or had they indiscriminately snatched up anything that might have been used to hide a jewel?

She glanced toward Logan. He stood rather still, his expression grim as he looked down at something on the floor.

Her gaze trailed his. A surge of grief blended with raw anger. *Oh, my beautiful doll.*

Ruined.

The intruder had not stolen the Fashion Lady. No, this was far worse. The despicable lout had torn her cherished keepsake to pieces.

She went to Logan's side and began to gather up what was left of the doll. The head with its lovely painted face was still intact. That was some comfort. But its elegant silk gown had been torn away, cast aside like a scrap of rubbish. Stuffing oozed out of its leather body through a crude rip down the middle. Goodness, even its tiny limbs had been sliced open and pitched to the floor.

Crouching beside her, Logan retrieved several mutilated pieces. "Blast it, Amelia. I know how much this meant to ye."

She examined the Fashion Lady's unmarred face. "They tore it to pieces and took what they were looking for."

"Or they came up empty-handed." Logan lifted up the doll's damaged body. "There's one fresh slash by a blade, but no sign the doll had been cut before tonight. Paul could not have hidden anything inside it unless he'd opened it up."

She examined the doll beneath the gas lamp. "You're right.

The stitching appears to be untouched. Unless Paul repaired the damaged seam."

Logan touched the small of her back, the warmth of his hand offering unspoken comfort. "Not bloody likely. Yer brother couldn't even mend a rip in his trousers."

A smile tugged at Amelia's mouth. "Mend a rip? Why, I doubt he could've threaded a needle."

"Ye miss him." Logan's words sounded low and husky. "I can hear it in yer voice."

"More than you can imagine. He always knew how to make me laugh." She stared down at the delicate doll cradled in her palm. "He cared for me. And now his last gift has been torn to bits."

Tears stung the backs of her eyes. She blinked them away, willing herself to stay strong. Still, a rebellious drop streamed down her cheek, then another.

Gently, Logan brushed them away. He drew the pad of his thumb over her bottom lip. "We will find the bastard who did this, Amelia. I'll make it right."

She gulped against a fresh wave of raw emotion. The past hours had been filled with stunning revelation, with secrets and deceit. Now, she wanted more than anything to believe him.

Lifting her eyes to meet his deep brown gaze, she felt a sudden racing of her pulse. A sudden boldness awakened within her.

Perhaps it was the way he looked at her, his gaze taking her in as if he found her rather fascinating.

Perhaps it was the rush of sensation that had nothing to do with fear.

If she were wise, she would retreat to her warm chamber in his spacious home, curl up with a piping hot cup of tea, and make it through this night without stirring a proper scandal.

Pity she didn't give a fig about rumors and gossip and what few tatters were left of her good name.

Her eyes lingered over the contours of his cheek, trailing the line of his shadowed jaw. How she longed to draw her fingertips over the path.

If she dared to explore the texture of his skin, would he think her wanton?

Or would he find her touch far too chaste?

Giving in to instinct would be dangerous. She couldn't afford to be vulnerable. Not even to him. She certainly knew better than to surrender to the temptation gleaming in a rogue's eyes.

Drawing a calming breath, she folded her fingers against her palm and resisted this newly intense craving for contact. For a long, silent moment, she drank in his carved, masculine features, imagining the caress of his full, seductive mouth.

Heaven knew a woman could find herself lost in his kiss. A woman foolish enough to succumb to temptation, that is.

His mouth curved at the corners, an instinctive awareness darkening his eyes. Had he sensed her renegade thoughts?

For a heartbeat, she thought he'd draw her closer.

Thought he might be so brazen as to kiss her, right there and then, in the midst of the chaos.

But he did take her in his arms.

He held her then. The muscles in his arms were taut with restrained strength. Powerful. Yet so very gentle.

His eyes met her gaze, seeming to search for the answer to an unspoken question. He drew his thumb over the curve of her face. His touch was smooth. Gentle. Nearly reverent.

But he did not kiss her.

Ah, she had to keep her wits about her. She had to keep a level head. Meeting his gaze, she carefully schooled her features. She did not dare to betray her emotions, much less the twinge of disappointment she'd felt when he held back.

A respectable woman would not be disappointed.

A respectable woman would be relieved.

But with each beat of her heart, she wondered more and more if being a *respectable* woman was highly overrated.

Suddenly, the bells at the door jangled, tearing her thoughts back to reality. Logan's hold fell away, and she turned to see Finn

Caldwell navigating the cluttered floor, stepping around books and furniture in his path. "Looks like the fortune teller was telling the truth. The bastards are after something all right."

Logan met his words with a scowl. "Blasted cowards, terrorizing a woman. Believe me, they will regret what they have done. I will see to that."

THE MOON HUNG low in the sky as Logan escorted Amelia to his home. With Finn at the reins and Amelia comfortable within the coach, Logan sat on the driver's bench, scanning for threats, weapon at the ready. A keen alertness surged through him. Despite a weariness that went bone-deep, his senses were tuned for any sign of danger in the night. Fortunately, their route proved uneventful while the horses clopped a steady path to his townhouse.

Upon their arrival, they were met by a visibly relieved Mrs. Langford at the door. After seeing for herself that they'd returned unscathed from their covert meeting, she poured Amelia a cup of hot chamomile tea and saw her to her bedchamber. Making no secret of his need for sleep, Finn took to another room for a few hours' rest, while Logan retired to his study.

Retreating to his quiet sanctuary, Logan stripped off his waistcoat, rolled up his shirtsleeves, and poured himself a drink. He leaned against his desk, stretching out his legs as he downed the whisky and stared up at the shadows on the ceiling. A peculiar energy set his mind racing. How in blazes could he protect Amelia against a ruthless cur who operated like an unseen puppet master, pulling the strings of men who did his bidding without revealing his true identity?

Paul's letters had warned of a clear danger to his sister. But Logan had not expected that Paul would have gotten himself mixed up with brutal thieves and cheats. The web of treachery he'd become trapped within now threatened Amelia.

By hellfire, he'd get to the truth.

He would find the elusive Mr. Hawk. The bastard would pay for what he'd done to Paul. And to Amelia.

The pain on her fairy-delicate features when she'd found her doll torn to pieces had been like a bareknuckle blow to the gut. The curs who'd invaded her library had not merely searched for some blasted hidden treasure. They had inflicted deliberate destruction and chaos. They had wanted to cause fear.

But why? What could the bastard think to gain from terrorizing Amelia?

If Mr. Hawk and the cowards working for him thought Amelia was vulnerable, they'd soon discover she was under his protection. They would learn an ugly lesson, indeed.

Logan took another drink. By hellfire, he would stand by her. He would not—could not—let her down.

When he'd held her in his arms, her irises had darkened to the hue of sapphires fit for a queen's crown. He'd seen the flicker of heat, an elemental fire she could not entirely hide. But there had been more. Something far more rare had glimmered in the depths of her gaze. Without a trace of guile or a hint of an ulterior motive, she had looked at him as a man who would stand at her side, come hell or high water.

In those beautiful blue eyes, he'd seen trust.

In the years since the lass he'd planned to wed had cast aside his love in favor of land and a title, he had realized an ugly truth. Maeve's pretty words of devotion had suited her purposes. In the end, she'd left his heart battered. Now, he knew better. If a man was smart, he wouldn't give a damn if a woman—or anyone else for that matter—looked upon him as anything other than a rogue.

But now, Amelia had put her faith in him.

The realization stirred a conviction deep within him. He wanted her to believe in him, to know that he would be there for her. And he would do whatever it took to justify her trust, no matter the cost.

A light tap upon the door tore him from his thoughts. Amelia stood in the entry. "I see you are still awake. I do hope I'm not disturbing you."

"Of course not," he said. "I thought you'd gone to sleep."

She shook her head, her unpinned tresses cascading over her shoulders. Tugging on the sash of her deep blue dressing gown, she seemed suddenly self-conscious. "My mind is rather stubborn tonight, I'm afraid. I simply cannot clear my thoughts and drift off."

"Ye can rest now, Amelia," he said. "Ye're safe here."

"It is not a matter of fear." She padded over the carpet until she stood not quite within arm's length. "I have searched my mind, again and again, for some hint Paul might've given me, something I may have missed. How could he have kept such a devastating secret? It must have been sheer torment."

Logan set the tumbler on the desk. "He wanted to protect you."

"He should've trusted me." Pain gave her voice a smoky tone. "He should have told me he was in a fix. We would have found a way to make it through . . . before he got himself in too deep."

"I don't think he knew yer true strength, Amelia. Ye're a woman of honesty, of courage."

Emotion glistened in her eyes. "I would like to believe that's true."

He stepped closer, a single footfall, near enough to touch her. Near enough to pull her closer. Near enough to enfold Amelia in his arms and kiss her until any thought of what had happened in the library had been banished to the back of her mind.

"I see yer gentleness . . . yer vulnerability." He reached for her, taking his time as he drew tiny circles against her palm. "Yer skin is soft. Smooth as silk. Some might look at that flawlessness and think ye fragile." He pressed a kiss to the back of her hand before he lifted his gaze to hers. "But I know better. Ye're a strong woman, Amelia."

The most subtle of smiles curved her mouth. "You do believe that, don't you?"

"Aye. Ye've a backbone of steel, lass," he said, releasing her. "Do not ever forget it."

"I do hope you're right."

Her deep blue eyes flashed with what seemed a subtle challenge. In a heartbeat, Amelia veiled her gaze with her lashes, as if she'd revealed more than she had intended.

But he had seen a truth she could not deny. She enjoyed his touch, the fleeting, not-quite-innocent contact, just as she'd savored the moment they'd given into temptation at the tavern.

Wickedness does possess a certain allure. But in my experience, it is rather overrated.

When Amelia had spoken the words, he'd sensed a hint of a dare in her tone. But then, his impulsive kiss had turned into more.

Her lips had tasted of desire. Of passion. And yet, there had been an innocence about her sweet response that confounded him. She was a widow. No doubt she'd learned the ways of men and women. But she had reacted to their caress as if the experience of seduction was very new.

God above, how he wanted to teach her true pleasure. Skin to skin. Heat kindling with each touch. With each kiss.

Amelia would respond to him. She would mirror his passion. Deep within, he knew that much to be true.

But he knew better than to risk the alliance they were building. She trusted him to protect her. To defend her. To tell her the truth. For now, that would have to be enough.

Or so he'd thought until she reached for him.

Dancing her fingertips along the line of his jaw, hunger flickered in her gaze. "I want you to do something for me." Her voice had gone low. Sultry.

Curiosity warred with the instinct to taste her lips. "And what might that be?"

The tips of her fingers danced idly over him. Gently touching his hair. Skimming the skin above his collar where his overly long strands grazed his neck. Trailing the angle of his jaw.

God above, was this some bittersweet torment she had devised for reasons only she could fathom?

"Promise me you will not take foolish risks," she said. "I could not bear it if you were harmed."

"I've outgrown foolish risks," he said, even as he contemplated taking one. If he kissed her again—truly kissed her—would she welcome the caress?

Or would he shatter the fragile connection they had forged?

She studied him. Her mouth curved slightly at the corners, as though she'd read his thoughts. "But only foolish risks, I take it."

Holding himself still, he nodded. For the span of several breaths, he watched her. Allowing her time to make her wants clear. Time to retreat if she needed to pull back from this moment. Time to retire to her own room.

Her own bed.

A soft sigh escaped her. She edged closer, closing the space between them.

Again, she nibbled her lower lip. "Some risks are worth taking, are they not?" Her voice was silky, softly confident.

He curved his arms around her, bringing her closer. "Indeed."

She did not ease away. If anything, she intensified the contact. "At times, I wonder if I still have the courage to take a risk."

He drank in her beauty. "If ye didn't, ye wouldn't be here . . . here with me."

"As I recall, you were rather confident that I would appreciate . . . oh, how did you phrase it?" She flashed a sly grin. "Oh, that's it—a taste of sin."

Blast it, she was intent on driving him to madness. But he held his voice steady. Casual, even. "I do recall that conversation. And I stand by my words."

"Is that so, Logan MacLain?"

Much more of this, and he would call her bluff. Ah, his name would be on her lips. But uttered with need. With passion. Rather than the challenge that now flavored her tone.

"Could you have any doubt, Amelia?" He spoke her name as a caress.

Her eyes widened, ever so slightly, as color rose to her cheeks. A lush smile tempted him beyond all rational thought.

"Very well, then," she said softly. "Shall we put your theory to the test?"

♞

Chapter Fifteen

B ENEATH HER DRESSING gown, Amelia wore a prim cotton nightdress with sleeves down to her wrists, but at that moment, she felt as vulnerable as if she were unclothed. And yet a sense of boldness coursed through her.

She had come to him. Logan had not tried to lure her into his bed. But he wanted her. Just as she wanted him. The truth crashed over her like a storm-tossed wave. This moment was what she'd long hungered for.

Even if the very thought of loving another rogue pinched her breath away. Feeling every beat of her heart in her ears, she gazed up at him. Was she a fool to pursue this moment? Hadn't she learned a bitter lesson about surrender all those years ago?

But still, she craved his nearness, taking comfort in his strength and his courage. Above all, she had yearned for his kiss and the tender need in his touch.

She looped her arms around his neck, canting her head up, savoring his warmth. His eyes met hers, his gaze intent, seeming to study her. Was he giving her time to change her mind? Couldn't he see how she desired his kiss? How she wanted *him* with a fervor unlike any hunger she had ever known?

Passion flickered in his dark eyes. His desire stripped away any trace of hesitation.

He splayed his hand against her back, the feel of his long, strong fingers gentle against her, even as he held her tight. A faint smile tugged at his delicious, tempting mouth.

"May I kiss ye?" The question was uttered in a voice edged with gravel.

Amelia drank in this moment. The fire in his gaze. The warmth in his touch. The heady, masculine aroma of shaving soap. Heavens, she didn't want it to end.

Her teeth grazed her lower lip. "Yes."

When he lowered his head to claim her lips, she closed her eyes. Drinking in the delicious caress, she savored the taste of him. The feel of him. The possessiveness of his kiss.

In an act that seemed driven by pure instinct, he held her closer, so near the heat of his body seeped through the silk of her dressing gown and the sensible fabric of her nightdress. So near he could not deny the proof of his masculine need, hard and demanding, stirring her own desire to a place where she could no longer reason away her own longings.

As he deepened the kiss, a gruff groan against her mouth betrayed his hunger. Amelia wove her fingers through the silky hair curling at his nape, holding him as fiercely as he held her.

Wanting him.

Needing him.

An unexpected little gasp from the doorway shattered Amelia's bliss. "Oh, my." The words hushed, but quite purposeful, may as well have been an explosion.

Logan's hands fell away as if she had suddenly turned molten hot. Muttering an epithet beneath his breath, he turned to the door.

Amelia followed his gaze. She felt her own eyes go wide. Sudden mortification crashed over her. Mrs. Langford stood inches from the portal with what seemed a rather cheeky smile on her face.

"Goodness, I did not mean to interrupt ye—" The older woman touched a hand to her cheek, as if to emphasize her blush. "Carry on, dears."

Logan shot her a glare. "Doesn't anyone sleep in this bloody house?"

Mrs. Langford's little grin betrayed her amusement. "I was wondering the same thing. I heard ye moving about and thought ye might be in the mood for a bit of warm milk. I'll be on my way now."

"Sleep well," Logan said, not bothering to hide his annoyance.

"The two of ye as well." Was it Amelia's imagination, or had the silver-haired woman thrown Logan a wink?

"Not bloody likely." Logan waited for Mrs. Langford to make her way down the corridor before turning to Amelia, his expression one of a man who'd been doused with water from a glacial spring. "Ye'd best be off to bed now, Amelia. With some luck, we might manage a few hours' rest."

Amelia reached for him, touching his cheek gently. "If you are concerned for my good name, I'm not."

"Mrs. Langford would never utter an ill word against ye. She's quite fond of ye." His expression softened into a smile. "But the woman's timing definitely leaves something to be desired."

"Perhaps it was better timing than we might've thought."

He regarded her silently. The heat in his gaze penetrated her defenses, but he only swept his lips against her cheek, the most gentle of butterfly kisses. "Ye may be right, lass. But at the moment, I am not inclined to agree."

FORCING HIMSELF TO rest, Logan made his way to his bedchamber and slid beneath the covers. He fell into a fitful sleep and rose shortly after sunrise. By the time Amelia strolled into his study after the clock struck nine, he was pouring through a stack of documents Finn had delivered that morning.

She'd pinned up her long reddish-gold curls, framing her face with soft tendrils, while her dark gray walking suit intensified the stormy blue color of her eyes. Even with slight shadows of weariness, her softly rounded face and rosy mouth were beautiful. Too blasted tempting.

Tearing his gaze from her plump mouth, he cleared his throat. "Ye slept well?"

"I drifted off." She glanced down at the carpet, seeming preoccupied by her thoughts. "Considering my horrid dreams, I almost wished I hadn't slept at all."

"I seldom dream. When I do, it always seems to be the same memories, again and again."

Lifting her gaze, her brow furrowed. "I take it your dreams are not fond recollections."

He set the papers aside on his desk. "To some, sleep is a refuge. But I prefer the waking hours, when I can control my fate."

She studied him. "Can you now?"

"'Tis the plan, Amelia." He rose and came to her side. "It's high time we broke our fast. Mrs. Garrett is eager for ye to have a taste of her cooking."

"I'm afraid I have little appetite this morning."

"Ye would not want to wound Mrs. Garrett's feelings now, would ye?"

"Very well," she said without enthusiasm. "But I will be on my way to the library immediately after we dine. I cannot rest until I've put it back in order."

"I'll accompany ye."

"I don't think that will be necessary. Surely the hooligans would not return during the morning hours." Weaving her fingers in a nervous knot, she pulled her mouth into a prim seam. The woman who'd passionately tasted his kiss the night before seemed to have departed the residence.

"Ye cannot count on the rotter to use caution. The bastards that ransacked the place were reckless."

"You do have a point," she said, resignation marking her tone. "Your assistance would be helpful. Now that it's daylight, perhaps we should do a thorough search. In my heart, I don't want to believe that Helen was lying. But still, the notion that Paul stashed a treasure in some secret cache is rather far-fetched."

"Far-fetched or not, someone believes it's there. We need to find the truth."

"Indeed." Her gaze fell on the fingers she'd laced loosely together. "To know that my brother was not honest with me . . . the very thought of it cuts to the bone."

"He wanted to keep ye out of this ugly scheme." Gently, he placed his hand over hers. "I won't allow the cutthroats to draw ye in deeper. Ye can count on this, Amelia—I will put a stop to the threat. One way or another."

Chapter Sixteen

A s Amelia entered the library with Logan at her side, his steady presence offered a sense of security. Somehow, she knew she could count on this man. Days earlier, they'd been strangers. But now, she felt an instinctive bond.

Trust.

And perhaps, something more.

Surveying the chamber, she pulled in a breath. Even Logan's nearness could not ease the tumult in the pit of her stomach while she made her way through the chaos.

How dare the curs invade her sanctuary!

The light of day brought the damage into harsh view. So much of the vandalism seemed utterly pointless, more the product of rage than of a purposeful search for a hidden valuable. Moving toward a chair that had been tipped on its side, its stuffing strewn about the floor, Amelia blinked back angry tears. Near her desk, she spied a flowerpot shattered on the floor. Dirt and uprooted plants lay among the bits of broken pottery. Utterly senseless. There'd been no true reason for the destruction.

No reason beyond a desire to instill fear.

She squared her shoulders, feeling a surge of determination course through her. If the intruder thought she would scurry away like a frightened mouse, they'd soon discover their error. The heathen who'd ransacked this place would not leave her cowering in a fit of despair. No, she would restore order from the chaos.

Just as she would find justice for her brother

Logan righted a toppled set of shelves. Turning to her, the set of his jaw betrayed the anger that simmered below the surface. He crouched down, gathering remnants of stained glass that had once formed a lovely lampshade. "Damn the bastard."

"Perhaps they found what they were searching for." An oddly hopeful notion ran through her thoughts. "If they did, they may be finished with me."

Rising to his full height, Logan bit off an epithet. "Finished or not, they will pay for what they've put you through."

The conviction in his voice was a comfort. Her gaze wandered over his long, lean body. How would it feel to go through life with a man like him by her side, strong and courageous and resolute?

Forcing her attention back to the mess that surrounded them, she sighed. If she were wise, she would do well to keep Elspeth's cold glare in her thoughts. The jealous scorn in her eyes had been as vicious as a slap to the face. She'd wanted the pleasure of his touch. Most likely, Elspeth did not crave a place in his heart.

If only I could say the same.

If only she could look upon a night in his arms—a night in his bed—as a passionate escape. And nothing more.

She wanted more. Needed more.

She'd do well to protect her heart.

To protect herself.

Busying herself with a pile of papers that had been tossed to the floor, she set them on her desk and banished her musings far to the back of her mind. Moving a stack of books back onto a shelf, and then another, she set about putting the displaced volumes strewn over the floor back in place while Logan explored the back rooms of the library. The rather mindless task offered some comfort. Until an obnoxious pounding of the brass knocker against the front door tore her from the momentary peace.

"Mrs. Stewart, I know you are in there," a man's voice bellowed. "I need to speak to you."

She spun on her heel. The timing could not have been worse. "Drat the luck."

Logan met her eyes. "Ye know who's calling?"

"Yes." She resisted the urge to sigh. "Unfortunately."

"I'll send the bloke on his way."

She placed a hand on Logan's shoulder. "That would not be wise. You see, Mr. Driscoll is the owner of this building."

His dark brows quirked. "At what point did ye gather I'd follow the wisest course?"

Despite the storm of nerves churning within her, she could not help but smile. "In any case, I suppose I should let him in."

"As ye wish." Logan opened the door, meeting the landlord's cold gaze.

Amelia stepped forward to greet the burly man garbed in an inexpertly tailored tweed overcoat. "What brings you here today, Mr. Driscoll?"

The man stared up at Logan. "So, I see the rumors are true. You've taken to keeping company with—"

"With what?" Logan's tone could have cut diamonds.

Nervously, the landlord shoved his hands in his pockets. "I must say, I had not expected to find the likes of you here, MacLain." Looking past Logan, he scanned the room. His bushy brows settled into a harsh line. "What in God's name has happened?"

Amelia hid a bit of pillow stuffing in her skirt pocket. "A bit of a mishap. Nothing more."

"I'm acquainted with your hound's penchant for mischief, but this is beyond that little beast's capacity for destruction." Mr. Driscoll scowled. "I understand you've had trouble recently—the kind of trouble that is not good for my investment."

"As you may have heard, I was the victim of an attempted robbery." Amelia held her voice steady.

"Who in blazes would want to make off with a trove of

books?" Mr. Driscoll reached down to pluck a lace doily off the floor. "And cheap fripperies."

Amelia tucked another piece of pillow into her pocket. "Now that is a question for the local constable."

Mr. Driscoll's mouth settled into a stark line. "As I understand it, a ruffian paid you a visit, then promptly ended his own life?"

"I assure you, that brute's presence was not a *visit*."

"Call it what you will. I will not tolerate criminals on these premises." The landlord puffed his chest, as if doing so might shore up his own courage. "It is my duty to notify you that an investor has an interest in this building."

Logan folded his arms and leaned against a desk, deceptively at ease. "Yer investor will have to find another place."

"We'll see about that." Mr. Driscoll shot him a scowl. "I'd be a fool to refuse this offer. Cecil Mansfield is a most generous fellow, I might add."

"Mansfield." The name echoed in her ears.

"So, you've heard of him. The man is looking to expand his galleries."

Logan regarded him coolly. "The lady is not leaving."

"For now, MacLain." The landlord's Adam's apple bobbed in his throat. His attention darted back to Amelia. "And to see with my own eyes that you've taken to cavorting with the likes of him . . . it seems you've made my decision for me."

"My lease is paid in full through the end of the year. Surely you have not forgotten that fact."

The landlord's expression hardened. "Might I remind you, this is my property, Mrs. Stewart. I will protect what is mine."

With the ease of a powerful cat, Logan closed the distance between Driscoll and himself, crushing the man's lapels between his fingers. "If word that ye've harassed this woman gets to my ears, ye will answer to me. Understand?"

Mr. Driscoll replied with a nervous nod.

"It's time for ye to go." Logan gave him a shake before he dropped his hands. "Before I give ye a reason to regret coming here today."

A current of elemental awareness raced through Amelia's core. For a heartbeat, perhaps two, she couldn't tear her eyes away from Logan. His confident actions and flint-edged tones spoke of raw power.

Most impressive, Mr. MacLain.

Forcing her attention back to the landlord, Amelia watched Mr. Driscoll's surly march to the door. Stumbling, he kicked a small braided rug out of his way. He muttered a foul word beneath his breath as he stared down at the cause of his misstep. A floorboard had tipped up ever so slightly, not quite even with the other planks.

"I see the ruffians you associate with have damaged my property," he ground out. "Your brother is not here to negotiate another lease. I will see you gone from my property."

"Ye're trying my patience," Logan warned. "Get out."

"I'll be on my way. For now." Driscoll's thin mouth curved into a sneer. "Believe me, Mrs. Stewart, you've more to worry about than the likes of me."

FOLLOWING CLOSE AT the landlord's heels as the man made his retreat, Logan steeled himself against the urge to teach the bloated toad a well-deserved lesson. Driscoll knew the recent hell of grief Amelia had endured. Yet the foul-tempered bloke had treated her with undisguised contempt. Only the reality that she would witness the ugly scene had kept Logan's instincts in check. If the man dared to turn back to the library, Logan would take the opportunity to provide that instruction, there and then.

Satisfied that Driscoll was indeed on his way, he turned back to Amelia. "Don't let him intimidate ye. The coward backed down in the face of a man who knows how to use his fists."

She busied herself placing another stack of books in place upon a shelf. "Paul once considered Mr. Driscoll an ally, if not a friend. But of course, that was in the past. At one point, they were partners in an enterprise."

"An enterprise, eh?"

"They shared an interest in an art gallery. I was not privy to many of the details, but there was talk of an investor, a silent partner."

"Hawk?"

A tiny crease between her brows deepened. "I don't know who invested in the venture. It was all rather hush-hush."

Logan held back the thoughts that came to mind. An investor could have many reasons to wish his involvement kept a close secret, especially if the funds were tarnished by crime. What kind of dishonest schemes had Paul gotten himself into?

"Ye'll get no more trouble from the likes of Driscoll," Logan reassured her. "Or he will answer to me."

Faint lines of tension feathered around Amelia's mouth. "I cannot imagine Paul wished you to take on every unscrupulous man in town on my account."

"He knew I'd watch over ye." Telling himself he wanted only to touch the rebellious curl that had escaped Amelia's rather-severe bun he reached out, tracing the curve of her cheek with his thumb. "Not that Driscoll would be a challenge to send running for cover. Even yer ball of fur with teeth could chase off that bag of hot wind."

A slight smile tugged at the corners of her mouth. "I do believe you're right."

"Do ye now?"

Her smile lit the room. "Absolutely."

The tempting curve of her lips stirred a longing deep within his chest. A hunger, physical in nature.

Yet more.

Infinitely more.

He wanted to make Amelia smile every day. He wanted to be the one who brought her joy. And God above, he wanted to taste those sweet, lush lips.

Unable to stop himself, he spoke the truth. "I'm of a mind to kiss ye, Amelia."

"Are you now?" The husky notes of her voice were a subtle seduction.

He smiled. "Ye do realize we are actually alone. No nosy old woman to walk in at precisely the wrong moment."

She flashed a cheeky little grin. "No dog to wreak havoc."

"Not so much as an ill-timed bark."

"Quite so," she said. Her brow furrowed. "Unfortunately, Mr. Driscoll may return."

"If he does—and especially if he walks in while I have ye in my arms—he will regret it."

A soft, teasing challenge filled her eyes. "It would seem you are rather intent on kissing me, Mr. MacLain."

He cupped his palm against her cheek. Her skin was velvet soft against his. "Would ye like that, Amelia?"

Her gaze locked with his, vibrant and tempting. "I do believe I would."

Without another conscious thought, he took her in his arms. Smoothing her curls from her face, he studied her. Her eyes were the color of a stormy sea, tiny flecks of gray darkening the dusky blue of her irises. Bloody hell, she was beautiful.

This near, he could feel the gentle rise and fall of her every breath. Her mouth curved into the most tempting of smiles.

Amelia wanted this. She desired his touch. She invited his kiss.

She wanted *him*.

Dipping his head, he tasted her sweet lips. Ah, it seemed Amelia had been made for him. The subtle fragrance of lavender filled his senses as her slender arms curved around his back. Bringing him closer. Gentle. Yet possessive.

He could not get enough of her.

He deepened the caress. Her response unleashed a wave of need coursing through his body. With a breathless, simmering heat, she kissed him. Giving and taking. Leading him to the brink of control. God above, she was more enticing than any woman he had ever known.

Sliding his hands along the length of her back, he ran his fingertips over her gently rounded bottom. Holding her close, he nested his erection against her softness. What he wouldn't give to dispatch with the row of buttons on the back of her dress, peel the layers of clothing from her delectable body, one by one, and teach her the true depth of his hunger for her.

But by hellfire, this was not the time. And it was not the place. She deserved more than a quick tumble in her own flat. In her own bed. Amelia deserved to be tempted. To be seduced. To be loved until she was mindless with pleasure. She deserved to be held in the arms of the man who adored her all through the night.

That time would come.

But for now, he had to maintain control. He had to do what was right. He had to keep the focus on protecting her.

Summoning the strength to let her go, he gently eased his mouth from hers. His muffled groan sounded like a roar to his own ears.

She met his gaze, her eyes wide and luminous. "Most impressive, Mr. MacLain," she whispered, gracing him with the most teasing of smiles. "Most impressive, indeed."

Chapter Seventeen

S UNLIGHT BROKE THROUGH a haze of clouds as Logan escorted Amelia through bustling streets to the Rogue's Lair. Close by her side, he remained alert for any sign of a threat while taking in the ordinary acts of people going about their business, plying their trades and hawking their wares. He'd take no chances with her safety. The bastard who'd invaded her library had lurked about under cover of night. But there was no reason to believe he would not make a more risky move.

A white-haired bird of a woman standing on the corner of a street not far from the tavern caught his eye. Her small peddler's cart was laden with bouquets of flowers. Smiling to himself, he decided to take a detour. Leading Amelia to the rickety cart which had seen better days, he selected a handful of violets tied with a slender blue ribbon. When he pressed a coin into the old woman's hand, she stared down at it, brows furrowing in confusion. Lifting her pale, gray gaze, she offered an adamant shake of her head.

"Sir, you've made a mistake," she said as she tried to return the coin.

He smiled. "It's not an error."

"But . . . you've paid too much."

"'Tis money well spent," he said and placed the bouquet in Amelia's hand.

The flower peddler's eyes twinkled with understanding.

"Bless you. And the pretty lady."

Moments after they'd left the flower peddler, still smiling by her cart, Amelia lowered her voice to a near whisper. "That was most generous."

"She's too proud for charity," he said.

Amelia lifted the modest bouquet to her nose. "Well done, Mr. MacLain."

Continuing to the tavern, Logan wondered at the unusual quiet as they stepped through the door. To his ears, the place was still as a tomb. Peculiar, even given the mid-morning hour. The thud of his boots against the gleaming wood floor was magnified by the near silence. Neither Murray nor Tilly, the barmaid, stood behind the counter.

Bloody odd.

The door to the backroom swung open with a squawk of the hinges. The barkeep carried a platter filled with clean glasses. Logan felt the tension in his muscles ease.

"Oh, it's ye." Murray set the tray on the counter, turning to stack tumblers on a shelf behind him. "When I heard the door open, I thought Caldwell had returned."

"He was here?"

"Not quite an hour ago." The tension in the barkeep's expression contradicted his bland tone. He seemed to be avoiding eye contact. "I take it ye have not heard the news."

Logan leaned an elbow on the bar. "What in blazes is going on?"

Murray frowned. "I don't know if this is fitting conversation . . . with the lady present."

Amelia squared her shoulders. "I urge you to speak freely. Please, tell us what you've learned."

Murray cleared his throat. Why was he stalling?

Logan's patience frayed. "Out with it, Murray."

"Finn brought news." The barkeep raked a hand through his hair. "There's been another death."

Amelia curved her hand around Logan's forearm, seeming to

steady herself. "Good heavens."

A chill slid over the back of Logan's neck. "What are ye saying, Murray?"

The barkeep set another glass on the shelf. His hand shaking, he nearly toppled the stack. "A woman died last night." He glanced at Amelia, then quickly looked away. "Finn said she was an acquaintance of yers."

"He must have told ye her name." Logan pressed.

Murray nodded grimly. "Helen. Helen Tanner."

Amelia's gasp sounded like an alarm in his ears. "Dear God." Leaning against his shoulder for comfort, her voice quivered. "Did he tell you . . . did he say how she died?"

Murray avoided her gaze. "The lady fell from a high window."

WITHOUT WARNING, AMELIA'S world went topsy-turvy. The floor seemed to shift beneath her as if she stood on sand washing out with the tide. Her knees trembled, and she clasped Logan's arm, holding tight.

Logan coiled an arm around her waist, bracing her against the stunning revelation. "Ye're sure of that, Murray?"

"Yes." A look of regret fell over the barkeep's features. "I should not have spoken of it in the lady's presence."

Amelia managed a brisk shake of her head. "No, I needed to hear the truth."

"It must come as a shock to ye." Compassion flowed in the barkeep's voice.

"Indeed, it does." She slowly made her way to a chair. "I only need to sit for a moment, to steady myself. I was not prepared for such horrible news."

"I take it ye knew the lady," Murray said.

"We were acquainted." Her chest tightened and her pulse

thundered in her ears. Struggling to retain her composure, she fanned herself with a trembling hand. An hour earlier, she'd been focused on her library and grieving the destruction of a doll, of all things.

And all the while, Helen had lain still on the pavement.

Alone.

Dying.

In the morning, I will be on a steamer that's sailing far away from here. Far from the bastard who wants me dead.

Had Helen believed her own words? Or had she merely sought to ease her own fears?

The jackals had killed her in the same way they'd murdered Paul.

How very cruel.

Turning to the bar, Logan poured brandy into a crystal glass. "Amelia, ye've gone pale. Ye'd benefit from a sip."

"Thank you." She downed a few sips, welcoming the calming warmth of the spirits. She glanced toward the door as Finn Caldwell marched in. He met her gaze, then threw Murray a scowl as he read the truth on her features.

"Ye were not to tell her," Caldwell said in a low, hard tone.

"I insisted that he tell me what he'd learned," Amelia spoke up. "I do not have the luxury of insulating myself from unpleasant truths these days, especially those connected to my brother's dealings."

"What've ye found out?" Standing behind Amelia, Logan lightly rested a hand on her shoulder. "Bear in mind, there is a lady present."

Amelia sighed. "All of this talk of a *lady's presence*. Do not attempt to shield me. At a time like this, I assure you that ignorance is not bliss."

Caldwell kneaded his neck as if it ached. His attention flickered to the glass in her hand. "Ye might find it beneficial to take another drink before ye hear what I've got to say."

"That will not be necessary," she said.

"Very well." He sounded resigned. "The detectives have already ruled Helen Tanner's death a suicide."

"Bloody fools." Logan bit off the words between his teeth.

Amelia could not contain her frustration. "How can they make such a determination so swiftly? There has been no investigation."

"And there won't be." Caldwell stared down at the rug for a long moment before meeting Amelia's gaze. "Not one of the detectives gives a damn about her death. In their eyes, she was a cheat who bilked gullible fools out of their money. It's not difficult to call it a suicide and carry on."

"How very convenient," Amelia said in disgust.

"There's more, isn't there?" Logan said. "I know ye better than to think ye didn't get someone to talk."

"Ye know me well, don't ye, MacLain?" Caldwell said without a smile. "One of the constables who found her was talkative. For a price. The gent now has enough blunt to sate his taste for cheap liquor for a month."

"Please tell us what you've learned," Amelia said.

With a look of clear reluctance in his eyes, he hesitated for the span of a few heartbeats.

Amelia held her voice steady. "I need to know, Mr. Caldwell."

With a half-hearted nod, he fished a fortune-telling card from his pocket. "A watchman at the hotel discovered her before dawn." He held out the card. "This was found near her body. She may have held it when she fell from the window."

The Lovers.

Amelia swallowed hard against her revulsion. "How macabre."

"There's more." Caldwell turned over the card and placed it on the bar. "I can't make out all the letters, but it appears someone scratched a word into the surface."

Amelia took the card to the window and held it up to the glass. Pulling in a breath, then another, she studied the markings.

Sunlight brought the crudely etched letters into relief.

Dear God. A bitter taste rose to the back of her throat.

"It's faint, but I can read it. It says…" She choked out the word. "Betrayed."

Chapter Eighteen

*B*ETRAYED.

A horrible sense of dread swept over Amelia.

Had Helen believed they'd led the killer to her?

"The lovers." Logan leaned closer, examining the fortune telling card. "By hellfire, what was the woman thinking?"

Amelia tapped a finger against the card. "There's no way to know if she intentionally selected that card, but I suspect the choice was deliberate."

Caldwell nodded his agreement. "Had she been betrayed by a lover?"

"Perhaps." Searching for other markings that would bring Helen's message into focus, Amelia lifted the card into the light again. "Or perhaps she meant a man and woman taking part in deception."

Had Helen assumed Amelia and Logan were lovers who'd betrayed her for their own interests? Or was the card intended as a warning? Was someone they trusted in league with Paul's killer?

Logan's brow furrowed. Had he read her suspicions?

"One thing's for certain," he said, taking the card from her hand. "She did not take her own life. The woman was hellbent on getting away from this place."

"Away from her killer," Amelia agreed.

"She damned near made it," Caldwell said. "Now, ye'd be well advised to take Amelia away from the city to somewhere the killer won't be able to find her."

"Out of the question." She'd hiked her chin, strengthening her tone in adamant refusal.

"The hell it is," Logan countered. "Finn's making sense. I know just the place."

Amelia planted her hands on her hips and looked him square in the eye. "I will not leave."

Logan plowed his long fingers through his hair. "I'll take ye to my family home. My kin will keep ye safe."

"I see no need to leave the city. I have confidence in your abilities." Seeing the conflict in his dark eyes, she considered her words carefully. "I know you are determined to protect me . . . to keep the vow you made to my brother. But I cannot hide forever. The devils who killed Paul want the blasted treasure. They've already found Helen. Even if I evade them for a time, when I return, they will be waiting."

"The lass has a point." Caldwell said, his tone gruff as though it pained him to voice the words.

Surprised, she turned to him. Heaven knew she hadn't expected either of the men to agree with her without having to vigorously press her case.

Logan shot him a scowl. "What in bloody hell are you saying, Finn?"

"I'm thinking there's another way—another layer of defense," Caldwell said, his expression cryptic. "Ye know what I'm thinking, don't ye, MacLain?"

"Blast it, ye cannot be seriously considering—"

Caldwell nodded. "Ye know what I would do if I were in yer shoes."

"Not a chance in Hades." Logan bit off the words between his teeth. "I'd rather endure a night in the Tower."

Caldwell cocked a brow. "They don't still use the rack, do they?"

Logan shrugged. "I've never had cause to find out." He let out a long, low breath. "If we do this, it will be for Amelia's sake."

Amelia studied him. If only the infernal man would offer some hint of the mysterious plan they were hatching. "Might I ask what dreaded act you're contemplating?"

"It's not so much *what*," Caldwell said dryly. "But *who*."

Amelia pondered the single word. *Who.* "Another dashing scoundrel to the rescue?"

"Not exactly," Caldwell replied.

Was it her imagination, or had he actually grinned at the thought?

"Very well. I'll do it." Logan pinched the bridge of his nose. "Ye'll convey the message?"

"Consider it done," Caldwell said.

Logan cast another scowl his way. "Ye're enjoying this too bloody much."

"Aye, that I am." Caldwell chuckled, then motioned to the barkeep to pour him a drink. "That I am."

"I've got a feeling I'm going to regret this," MacLain said without elaboration as Caldwell downed a gulp of Scotch.

"Most likely. We both may come to regret this," Caldwell said rather cheerfully, then took another drink. He nodded to Amelia. "This errand calls for liquid courage."

With that, he placed the tumbler on the bar, marched to the door and strolled onto the street. Suddenly, the space seemed all too quiet. Appearing rather awkward, Murray mumbled something about a recent delivery of whisky, then shuffled into the backroom.

Amelia met Logan's eyes. "Well, do you plan to tell me what this is all about?"

"If I had my way—and it might still come to that—I'd take ye to my family's home. Ye would be safe there. No one would dare attack the MacLains on their own land."

"Even if that is true, at some point, I will have to return to London."

He offered a weary nod. "The next best thing to getting you out of the jackals' reach is to bring security to ye."

What in heaven did the man mean? He had already stepped into the role of protector. Surely she did not need another. "I've no need of a bodyguard. Nor do I intend to scurry away in fear. I feel quite secure right here in the city."

"It's not enough. I need to know ye're being protected while I am tracking down Hawk. With only Mrs. Langford and Mrs. Garrett in the residence, ye'll be vulnerable."

"Are you are forgetting Heathy?" she countered a bit cheekily.

"How could I overlook the fierce wee beast? The dog's teeth might well put a hurting on a man's ankles or even his shin. But I need someone who can secure the premises when I am not here—someone with opposable thumbs and a reasonably good aim."

"If I am understanding this correctly, the person you are summoning to your home evokes thoughts of the Tower of London."

"Aye," he said with a nod.

"And you expect me to be in their company twenty-four hours of the day?"

The grim set of his mouth relaxed, not quite a smile. "I'd say ye have a clear understanding of the situation."

"And if I do not wish to spend my days with a rather odious bodyguard?"

"I suspect she will be more fond of you than she is of me."

Amelia hesitated. "She?"

He nodded.

"Does *she* have a name?"

Logan nodded again. "Doesn't everyone?"

"And what might that name be?"

"Mrs. Johnstone."

Amelia sighed. "That tells me very little."

"Elsie Johnstone is kin to me, on my mother's side, the raiding and pillaging side."

"Ah," Amelia mulled his words. "Am I to believe this mystery woman is also an outlaw?"

He shrugged. "When I was a lad, she did mention something about a train robbery or two. More recently, rumor has it she worked for Pinkerton in America."

"Rumor has it?" she pressed.

A smile played on his lips. "I'd rather ye make up yer mind for yerself. She'll have no cause to breathe fire like a dragon in skirts with ye. After all, ye've never hidden a frog in her bed."

"A frog? In her bed?"

Logan grinned. "Or a snake in her armoire."

"Good heavens."

"In my defense, the reptile was not particularly dangerous."

"Well, I suppose that is a relief." Amelia took in the twinkle in his eyes. It seemed unfair that he was so appealing. And without having to try. She pulled in a breath and collected her thoughts. "I take it these acts occurred when you were a boy."

He gave a solemn nod. "But my aunt has a very long, very vivid memory."

"In that case, what makes you think she will agree to come here?"

Logan looked at her as if she'd asked him how he knew the sky was blue. "She is kin to me. And kin stick together."

"I'd like to think so."

"Besides, her curiosity will get the better of her."

Amelia frowned. "Curiosity?"

"She'll be eager to see the woman who inspired me to play the knight in tarnished armor."

Chapter Nineteen

*T*HE KNIGHT IN *tarnished armor.*

Logan had uttered the words casually. Perhaps, even flippantly. In all truth, he bore no resemblance—in word or deed—to Sir Lancelot. By thunder, he'd never considered himself a chivalrous man. But he'd done a fair enough job of defending the beautiful lass who now pondered his words, a spark of interest in her beautiful eyes.

"Knight?" she questioned as her gaze roamed over him. Pursing her lips, she slowly shook her head. "It doesn't suit you. Not at all."

"You think not?" He met her response with arched brows, making no secret that she'd caught him off guard. "Shall I trade my revolver for a mace?"

"Please don't misunderstand," she went on, a touch of mischief dancing in her eyes. "You are courageous. And daring. You most definitely possess gallant qualities. But I imagine a knight would be rather stuffy and predictable, clunking about in armor that needed polishing all the time."

"Ye'll get no argument from me on that. I will not be polishing any armor or, as ye put it, clunking about in the blasted stuff."

A faint smile touched her plump mouth, the amusement in her eyes fading to a thoughtful expression. "When I was quite young, I wanted so badly to enjoy a bit of adventure. To be bold. But my father had other notions." She sighed. "You're not at all concerned with propriety, are you?"

"I've had little use for it. It serves no purpose."

"I suppose a man can live his life without paying heed to the rules of society." She glanced away, as if she considered a dark memory. "A scandal would not upend his existence."

He caught her hand, smoothing his thumb over her fingers. Her skin was smooth as satin, her hand small within his. But not weak. Not fragile.

"It depends on the existence he's chosen, lass. I've never had to give a damn about what others thought of me."

She lifted her gaze to his. "I used to care what others thought of me. Quite a bit, actually."

"But now?"

Her shoulders lifted and fell. "I've cultivated a circle of friends whose trust I value. As for the rest—well, they may speak ill of me as they please. They relish a good scandal."

Driven to ease the pain her even-toned voice could not hide, he drew her closer. "Ye're a good woman, Amelia. Kind-hearted and strong. The gossips are liars, the lot of them."

"No, not liars. Not always." Again, she looked away, as though pulled in by memories. "A wife who leaves her husband offers ample fuel for scandal."

A low current of anger rippled through his veins. He knew she was a widow. Had Amelia been mistreated by the man she'd married?

She turned back to him, squaring her shoulders in that way of hers that conveyed her inner strength. "I married for love, you see. As it turned out, my husband did not. Even after we'd spoken our vows, Edward had no intention of giving up his mistresses. Nor his drunken outbursts. I began to fear him . . . to fear what he was capable of. That's when Paul stepped in."

"He helped ye to get away from the lout?"

"Yes." Amelia's mouth thinned. "He brought me into his home while he sought legal counsel to help me escape my husband's control. One night, after leaving his club in a drunken rage over another man's wife, Edward was thrown from his horse. I was told he died instantly. Suddenly, I was a widow. But that changed little. After all, it was no secret that I had sought a divorce. My reasons were of no consequence to those who take their amusement by spreading their cruel barbs."

Gently, he tipped up her chin, meeting her gaze. Her eyes glistened. Was she holding back tears?

"To hell with the fools who'd have seen ye endure a living hell."

"To Hades with them, indeed." Spirit filled her quiet words. "I have my library. I have my friends and patrons. And I have Heathy."

"Ye've also got a man who's hell-bent to lock after ye, Amelia. I will be there for ye."

Her rosy lips curved up at the corners, her subtle smile pulling him in like a wave crashing to shore. He drank in the subtle curve of her mouth, the vibrant spirit in her eyes. Blast it, if Murray wasn't likely to wander in from the backroom at any moment, he would've kissed Amelia right then and there.

"I'd like to think so," she said, a teasing lilt coloring her words. "None of the biddies who live to spread their gossip can boast of a dashing scoundrel charging to the rescue, now can they?"

"Scoundrel, eh?" Slowly, he traced the curve of her face with the pad of his thumb. "The man ye're looking at is neither a gallant knight not a dark-hearted scoundrel, but an ordinary man who set out to make his own fortune."

"Logan MacLain, you are far from an ordinary man."

Her eyes sparkled like a Highland loch at the first light of day. Bloody hell, when she looked at him that way, with her interest set on him and him alone, she was damned near irresistible.

He could hear Murray in the back room, going about his work. The din of metal hitting the floor clanged through the door. The barkeep had dropped a tray or a pot or something— bugger it if Logan cared what it was.

At the moment, all he gave a damn about was the woman who stood before him. And how bloody much he wanted to kiss her.

What was it about Amelia that made the prospect of a mere kiss seem a seduction?

His arms eased around her, bringing her close. She was warm and soft and tempting, despite the layers of clothing covering her gentle curves. God above, how he wanted to strip away each blasted too-proper garment, one by one, until she was bared to his eyes.

Her little sigh against his ear spoke of longing. Of hunger. God above, he wanted her to need his touch. Blasted shame this was neither the place nor the time.

But damned if he could stop himself from kissing her.

Lowering his head, he claimed her lips. Slowly, at first. Gently. Until Amelia moaned softly against his mouth, urging him to touch her.

Hunger surged through him. His desire for her was akin to torment. He needed her with a fierceness unlike any he'd ever experienced. He wanted her touch. Wanted to hear her whispers of desire. And more. So much more than she was ready to give.

Blasted shame he could not allow himself to taste her beyond the sweetness of her kiss.

THE MOMENT LOGAN'S lips teased hers, Amelia's heart felt whole again. Claiming her tenderly, he deepened the caress. Joy danced through her. In this moment, a pure contentment that seemed quite rare filled her. His touch mended the rips and tears inflicted by a loveless marriage, his caress binding the wounds she'd feared would never heal.

Would every kiss feel like this?

Would his nearness always inspire this feeling, this heady

sense that being in his arms was utterly right?

Holding her closer, Logan pressed her to his long, lean body. The undeniable proof of his hunger strained against his trousers, and she canted her hips in instinctive longing. Breathing in the subtle spice of shaving soap on his jaw, she curved her fingers around his arms. Beneath her fingertips, the muscles of his back flexed. Strong. Sleek. Powerful. How delightful it would be to touch his skin if he were bared to her.

If his body were hers to caress.

Hers to explore.

Hers to love.

"Ah, Amelia, ye will drive me to madness," he breathed against her lips, even as his hands skimmed the length of her back.

A jarring crash of metal against the hardwood floor in the backroom cut through Amelia's bliss. Logan's hands fell away.

"Murray's picked a blasted fine time to drop every kettle in the place," he grumbled.

As if perfectly timed to offer Amelia a reprieve from her own temporary madness, the barkeep emerged from the back room bearing a tray filled with freshly washed tumblers. Evading Logan's scowl, the barkeep carried the tray to the shelf behind the bar and efficiently went about his task.

Logan's gaze brimmed with reluctance. "We will continue this particular conversation later, lass. On that, ye have my word."

"I must admit, I found our discussion most intriguing," Amelia said in a matter-of-fact tone.

"Did ye now?" he teased.

"I'm quite certain you already know that."

"I suspected as much," he said, his voice edged with gravel.

She smiled to herself, seeing that her touch had affected him every bit as much as his had stirred her heart.

His eyes flashed with delicious challenge. My, this man was born to tempt her, wasn't he?

She didn't hold back her smile. "You are a bold one, Mr. MacLain."

"Amelia, ye only know the half of it."

The thought was thrilling, but stirred a hint of doubt deep within her core. Was she wading into waters far too deep?

His expression turned suddenly serious, his dark gaze conveying more than words could possibly say. "A woman like ye . . ." Logan's mouth curved, not quite a smile. Tracing the curve of her face with his thumb, he tucked a stray tendril of hair behind her ear, then retreated to put a respectable distance between them. "In due time, Amelia, ye will see the truth—the truth of who I am."

Chapter Twenty

S ITTING ALONE IN a well-appointed bedchamber in Logan's townhouse, Amelia absently tapped her pen against the mahogany writing desk. Glancing down at the bland entry she'd jotted in her leather-bound journal, she drew a line through one neatly penned word. *Eventful.* The adjective was far too tame to describe the experiences of the previous hours. With precise strokes, she wove in a far more fitting word. *Tumultuous.* Yes, that was a fair depiction of a day that had started with a heart-sinking view of her ransacked library, only to be capped with the thrill of Logan's kiss. Smiling to herself, she penned another phrase.

So-wicked-it-should-be-forbidden.

Perhaps even that was an understatement. Someday, long into the future, she would wish to recall each touch of his lips to hers, every delicious moment in his arms. Logan MacLain had drawn passion from her that she feared no longer existed. He'd shown her tenderness and passion, even if he had kept his hunger rather tightly leashed. She would always cherish the memory of his caress.

Pity he was to occupy an all-too-brief chapter in her life.

Closing the cover, she tucked her diary into a traveling case and mentally prepared for the evening ahead. Hours earlier, as they'd gathered up books the intruder in her library had cast about like so much refuse, she had suggested her presence at the tavern might prove useful. The man who'd attacked her had patronized the Rogue's Lair. Perhaps he'd had an accomplice, someone connected with her brother. Someone she might well recognize.

To her surprise, Logan had agreed. Of course, he'd insisted on staying close. And she'd decided to conceal her derringer in her reticule. Just in case.

Giving the matter some thought, she selected a modest ensemble from her flat for the evening, a prim, blue gown that would not stand out in Logan's tavern. She could not risk drawing attention to herself while she studied the comings and goings of the tavern's patrons.

Arranging her hair in an equally modest style, she secured her upswept tresses with a silver hairpin that had once belonged to her mother. With its two sharp, sturdy prongs, the ornament could serve as a makeshift weapon in a pinch. At the thought, a ripple of apprehension coursed through her. She braced herself with a calming breath. After all, she'd likely have no need to employ the pin in self-defense. Nor the derringer in her bag, for that matter.

After freeing a few curls to frame her face, she pinned a cameo brooch to the lace-trimmed neck of her dress. Satisfied with her rather unremarkable appearance, she shored up her resolve, and went downstairs to the parlor.

Logan waited by a polished marble-top table, the set of his shoulder muscles taut beneath his silver-gray shirt and well-tailored ebony jacket. Her breath caught. Could he deduce the wicked direction of her thoughts every time she looked at him?

He turned to the sideboard, poured a drink from a crystal decanter. As she watched him, she did silent battle with the butterflies dancing wildly in her stomach.

"Brandy?" he offered.

"Yes, thank you." Perhaps the hearty liquor would take the edge off her nerves. She drew in a breath, deep as her corset would allow, as he crossed the room.

His gaze traveled the length of her, masculine appreciation

gleaming in his eyes. "I knew ye could not do it."

"Could not do it?" She took the finely cut glass from his hand. "I don't follow your meaning."

Amusement played at his full mouth. "Ye told me ye'd dress in a manner that would make ye fade into the shadows. I knew it would prove an impossible task."

"I selected this gown with modesty in mind," she countered. "The collar reaches all the way to my throat and the sleeves scarcely reveal my wrists. Not so very scandalous."

"Do you really believe that matters? Ye could drape yerself in burlap and it would make no difference."

She enjoyed a sip of her drink. "Actually, that might attract some attention. Don't you think?"

He shook his head. "No, I do not. You see, Amelia, no amount of fabric can conceal that lovely face of yers. Or yer curves." He flashed a grin. "Good God, what a temptation for a weak-willed man like me."

She met his endearing grin with a hint of a smile. "Mr. MacLain, I see no evidence of weakness. Especially not where your will is concerned."

His eyes darkened and the amusement faded from his gaze. Slowly, he shook his head. "Ah, Amelia . . . ye've more confidence in me than I do in myself."

WITHIN MINUTES AFTER he'd escorted Amelia into the Rogue's Lair, Logan cursed himself for a fool. Why in blazes had he agreed to bring her into a lion's den? She'd made a valiant effort to dress in such a drab manner that she'd draw no attention, but her prim, unadorned gown and tightly pinned hair could not dull her natural beauty.

Her dress would've well suited a governess. Lace at the collar nearly touched her chin, while Amelia's full skirts did not display so much as a hint of her ankles. But neither the fine midnight-blue fabric nor the seemingly endless layers of petticoats could disguise her tempting curves. She'd pulled her ginger-gold hair back from her face, a simple coil of the tresses off her neck, revealing only a glimpse of her nape. Her prim appearance might have appeared bland on another woman. But Amelia's natural radiance was undimmed. Like a vibrant flower standing out amid a patch of weeds, her face drew the gaze of men.

Logan allowed his gaze to linger over the curve of her cheek, over her plump mouth. Standing protectively close, he detected the subtle aroma of lavender on her skin. Desire surged through him. Bugger it, if his body had its way, he would escort her back to his townhouse, lead her to his bed, and adore her from head to toe with his kisses.

Truth be told, if he had the sense of a billy goat, he'd be anywhere rather than here, assisting her in her plan to conduct reconnaissance in his pub, of all places.

She'd selected a table at the far corner which offered a view of the patrons entering the tavern. But if she'd thought she would attract no notice in the shadows, she had been mistaken. He saw the light in the eyes of the men who noticed her tucked away in that typically lonely corner of the pub. Their appreciative gazes lingered on the newcomer, drawn as his own was to the loveliness she simply could not disguise.

Tension ran through his body, jarring as a current of electricity. Weaving his way through the crush of men and women congregated at round tables throughout the pub, he spotted a gangly man in a dark bowler hat at the bar. Amidst the regular patrons, the man stood out. Something about his manner seemed off. Finishing his drink, he stood and turned toward Amelia. Her eyes widened as the man cut a direct path to her table.

Keeping his eye on the stranger, Logan trailed him, taking a position near the barkeep where he was nearly within arm's reach. The man said something in tones so low Logan couldn't quite make out his words, but Amelia appeared to have the situation well in hand. Her reply quickly sent the bloke on his way.

As the stranger marched out the front door, Logan turned back to the bar. He leaned an elbow against the polished wood. Near the stone fireplace, the piano player started into a lively tune. A jovial fellow who claimed to have once performed for the Queen, George Ferrell bobbed with the music as his fingers moved deftly over the keys. Logan felt a wave of tension ease from his body. With any luck, this evening would prove more dull than a night of listening to Murray reminisce about his youthful exploits fleecing highbrow lords over a round of darts.

At a nearby table, a man deep enough in his cups to not care whether or not he could carry a tune came to his feet, a stein bobbing in his hand. Notes that reminded Logan of a saw's scratch against metal erupted from his throat. Logan braced himself as the erstwhile singer threw his energy into the tone-deaf serenade.

Good God. Perhaps the piano player's wages were not money well spent after all.

Suddenly, a guttural curse cut through the noise of the crowd. An ox of a man stood within an arm's length of Amelia, bellowing epithets as he stared down at a fresh brandy-hued stain on his shirt.

Bloody hell.

Logan made short work of the distance between them. "What in Hades do ye think ye're doing?"

His face red with anger, the stranger glared at him with bleary eyes. "The little shrew—"

She rose, planting her hands on her hips. "Perhaps in the future, you will know better than to address a lady in such a manner."

"You will pay—" the man ground out the threat.

Logan clamped his hand over the man's arm and gave the limb a rough twist. "It's time for ye to be on yer way."

The oaf scowled. "She's a trollop. Nothing more."

"Watch yer mouth," Logan warned.

Understanding crept over the man's features. "She . . . she's with you?"

"She is," Logan said, keeping his tone hard as flint.

He tugged against Logan's hold. "I did not know."

"It doesn't matter who's accompanied her. She is a lady. I'd advise ye to remember that when ye speak to any woman."

"I'm . . . I am sorry," he choked out. "I meant no disrespect."

Logan loosened his grip, allowing the oaf to shrug free.

"I'll just be on my way now," the man said before beating a hasty retreat to the door.

"Do not let me see yer face here again," Logan called after him.

Amelia touched her fingers to his hand. The warmth of her touch spread through him, easing the bone-deep tension of every muscle.

"Most impressive." Her smile blended temptation with innocence. Did she have any idea of the effect she had on men?

Or on him, for that matter?

He cocked a brow. "This is what ye call staying out of sight?"

"The brute left me no choice. Why, I would not dare to repeat his rude proposition."

"Proposition, eh?"

"I've no idea what the man was thinking. Surely if I were a woman who looked to earn her coin from a man, I would have selected a more provocative ensemble."

"I told ye, Amelia—no matter what ye're wearing, ye'll still catch a man's eye."

She hiked her chin. "Is that so?"

"Believe me, it is."

"So, you would find me appealing in a gunny sack?"

"If ye donned a gown made from old feedbags, my eyes would seek ye out."

She pursed her lips. "An interesting concept. I will have to remember to present the idea to my seamstress."

"I'd wager ye'd be the first," he said, unable to resist her smile. "Do not ever fool yerself into thinking a man won't notice ye."

"I doubt another sot will trouble me now," she said, confidence flashing in her blue eyes. "Especially if I have another glass of brandy at my disposal."

"I would not be so sure."

She cocked her chin. "I intend to test my theory."

"Should I alert the poor fools to beware?"

Her eyes flashed again. "An excellent idea."

"Oh, and Amelia, I'll send over more brandy, just in case ye might be needing it."

Chapter Twenty-One

AMELIA GLANCED AT the ornate clock mounted on the wall beside the stone fireplace. Nearly midnight. A dull weariness crept over her. Other than her encounter with the drunken oaf, the night had proven rather tedious. A few men had wandered her way, though she suspected word had quickly gotten out that anyone who dared to go near her would find themselves under the watchful eye of the tavern's proprietor.

The barmaid, a sweet-natured woman whose haphazardly upswept brown curls appeared ready to tumble from their precarious perch, broke through Amelia's thoughts. With a beaming smile, she placed a piping hot cup of tea on the table.

"I thought ye might like this," Tilly said.

"Thank you. It's quite thoughtful of you."

"Ah, it's been a long night." Tilly regarded her with a look of genuine concern. "I took the liberty of adding a wee bit of spirits, just the thing to ease your weary muscles."

"Indeed." Amelia smiled. The barmaid's kindness was unexpected. And very welcome.

"I wanted to tell ye I was proud of what ye did tonight."

"What I did?"

"Putting that big oaf in his place. He had it coming."

"I certainly agree. Though causing a scene might not have been the wisest move."

"Well, I enjoyed the sight of it. I know the sot's type." Tilly glanced toward Logan. "MacLain would've tossed him out soon enough, even if ye hadn't set the oaf back on his heels."

"You think so?"

Tilly nodded. "He's there quick as lightning whenever a bloke tries to take advantage of me. Only a stranger to the Rogue's Lair would dare to harass a lady. The regulars . . . well, they know better."

"Thank you for sharing that with me."

"The truth of it is, MacLain's a good man. Truly he is. I don't care what the biddies cackle about him. They don't know him. Not at all."

Amelia's gaze settled on the man who'd declared himself her knight in tarnished armor. The choice of phrase definitely did not suit him. Logan MacLain had displayed a sense of honor that far outshone that of the so-called gentlemen she'd encountered in London. Knowing that he watched over Tilly while she was in his employ, defending her from boors and sots when he might've turned a blind eye, confirmed her instincts were right.

Logan's armor was not tarnished. In fact, it did not bear so much as a speck.

Now, as he stood near the bar, dressed in black from head to toe, save his white linen shirt and the silver-hued silk of his waistcoat, he was temptation come to life. The new growth of beard shadowing his jaw and the lean contours of his face only intensified the magnetic pull he held on her.

"Believe me, I put no stock in gossip," Amelia said. "I learned that lesson long ago."

Tilly's smile was thoughtful. Had she noticed how Amelia's gaze had lingered on him, perhaps a heartbeat or two more than was entirely proper?

"I'm glad. MacLain thinks highly of ye. If there's a villain roaming, he'll keep ye safe. Ye've no worries." The barmaid's attention turned to the patrons at a nearby table. "It looks like Barney is in need of another round."

"Thank you again for the tea. And the conversation."

"Ye're quite welcome. I can see why MacLain wants to watch over ye."

With that, Tilly scurried off to tend to her duties. Once again, Amelia was alone with her thoughts. She took a sip of tea. The barmaid's words played in her mind.

MacLain wants to watch over ye.

Quite so. Pity his determination to protect her was rather a mixed blessing.

Having Logan so near he was ready to protect her at the blink of an eye may have hampered her attempt to glean information. Some talkative gent who may have revealed some hint as to Hawk's identity might well have kept his distance rather than face MacLain. Of course, there was a fair chance her encounter with the ox-sized sot had hindered her efforts. After she'd wasted a tumbler of perfectly good brandy in response to the boor's crude proposition, no man who'd witnessed the scene wandered within a stone's throw of her table. Well, she'd had little choice in the matter, she reassured herself. She'd simply had to send the boor on his way.

The chimes at the entry jingled, a welcome distraction from her musings. *Good heavens.* Was that one of her brother's clients skulking in? She sat up at attention, taking in a better look. Even with his collar turned up and his flat leather cap pulled low, Amelia could make out the man's ginger hair and his distinctive prow of a nose. My, he certainly did resemble John Niles. But why would an industrialist's heir with a taste for fine art slip into a workman's pub, much less at this hour of the night?

As he cut a direct path to the bar, lamplight glinted off his spectacles. Behind the lenses, his pale, icy-blue eyes focused straight ahead. She knew those eyes, that ice-cold gaze. She would've wagered her last shilling the man was indeed John Niles. His plain sack coat and brimmed cap stood in stark contrast to the attire he'd worn when she'd last laid eyes on the man. On that day, he'd appeared confident, perhaps even cocky, as he stood in Paul's office, seeking an appraisal of his most recent acquisitions. Now, he walked with a stoop-shouldered uneasiness, as though he found the pub's earthy atmosphere distasteful, something to endure. John Niles was accustomed to a butler serving expensive wine in elegant crystal glasses, not a barkeep handing out ale in sturdy steins. What had brought him to this workman's pub?

Most peculiar.

Keeping to the shadows, Amelia peered over her cup of tea and observed Niles. At the bar, he'd approached a thick-necked man in a dark bowler hat. The burly man appeared to recognize him, even as he kept his features out of sight. What in blazes was the man up to?

Perhaps she should move closer. Niles was not likely to recognize her. Years had passed since she'd made his acquaintance, and the interaction had been exceedingly brief. Now, he kept his back to her, engaged in discussion with the man in the bowler. If she edged within eavesdropping range, he might not even realize she was there.

While she pondered the move, the barkeep's assistant, the amiable young man named Tim who had driven the carriage with Mrs. Langford, approached the men. Niles dismissed him with an abrupt wave of his hand.

Logan edged into her field of vision. As he'd done throughout the night, he made a point of engaging with any newcomer to the pub. His manner was amiable, but his presence nonetheless deterred any foolhardy disturbances. Amelia kept her attention on him as he approached the bar. She traced the breadth of his shoulders and the length of his long, lean body with her gaze, smiling to herself as she took in the way his body moved with power and natural confidence.

A most impressive man.

She knew better than to be so taken with a man—with any man, much less a rogue. No matter how gallant he might be. But there was no denying the way Logan MacLain's restrained power left her weak in the knees.

He approached Niles and the burly man, sidling up to them as if they were old chums. Appearing to recognize the proprietor, Niles traded his scowl for a bland expression. He exchanged a few words with Logan, meaningless banter that sounded quite forced.

The burly man in the bowler said little. His attention drifted to the corner where Amelia sat. His eyes narrowed. Hardened.

Had he recognized her?

To her relief, he turned away, lifting his glass to down a drink. Amelia let out a low breath she hadn't realized she'd been holding.

Appearing satisfied that the men were patrons and nothing more, Logan left them at the bar and headed into the back room. Minutes later, Niles glanced around the place. He was nervous. He could not disguise the way his gaze darted about, uneasy as a mouse with a cat on its heels.

When he stood to leave, he retrieved an envelope from an inner pocket of his jacket. Amelia could not decipher the words written in a cramped script above the distinctive seal. The circle of burgundy wax was nearly as large as a sovereign coin. Squinting, she could just make out the symbol which resembled an Egyptian hieroglyphic pressed into its surface. Was it a bird? Perhaps a falcon?

A hawk! A chill crept over her nape.

The man in the bowler hat tucked the envelope in his coat. In turn, he slipped Niles a small parcel wrapped in plain brown paper.

Niles turned from the bar and headed to the door. After a moment's pause, just long enough to throw Amelia a pointed stare, he left, quietly as he'd come. The man in the bowler hat placed a coin on the bar as payment for his drink and followed Niles out the door.

Amelia's mind raced. Did Niles know she'd seen the exchange? Was his cold glare meant as a warning? Or as a threat?

She drummed her fingers against the tabletop. My, she'd found more questions than answers, hadn't she?

From across the room, Logan motioned to her. When she followed him to his office, he leaned against his desk, stretching out his long legs.

"Ye know him, don't ye?" Logan scrubbed a hand against his jaw. "The lean one with the shark's eyes."

"I cannot be certain it is indeed him, but I believe the man is John Niles." She laced her fingers in a nervous knot. "I am not certain he remembers me."

"Oh, he recognized ye. I've no doubt of that." Logan met her eyes. "How do ye know him?"

"Years ago, Niles needed an appraisal of works he'd purchased at auction. When I encountered him in Paul's office, I recall thinking the man was more puffed up than a peacock."

"Yet here he is, dressed like he earns his wages by the sweat of his brow. Did ye recognize the other man?"

Amelia shook her head. "I don't recall ever seeing him. I take it he is not a regular."

"Never seen him before tonight," Logan said. "He played at being in his cups, but the bloke had little to drink. He was the more talkative of the two."

"Did he reveal anything of interest?"

"Tim caught wind of some information that might prove useful."

"And what might that be?"

"John Niles recently returned from France."

"From Paris?"

"Tim didn't hear much of the conversation, but he's clear that the tall man mentioned France."

"That may be significant. Or not." Amelia struggled against a rising sense of defeat. "Niles has ample funds at his disposal. He's known to have a fondness for the Continent."

"I thought as much." Logan plowed a hand through his hair. "This man's bones are weary. I'm of a mind to shut down for the night."

"It is getting very late," Amelia agreed.

Not quite half an hour had passed before Logan ushered the last patron from the tavern. Leaving Murray, Tilly, and Tim to their nightly tasks, he escorted Amelia through the back door to his carriage. Hazy beams from a gas lamp flickered in the night. Out of the corner of her eye, she caught a flash of movement mere steps from the building.

Concealed in the darkness of the alley, a man clutched something in his hand.

Light gleamed against metal.

"Logan!" Amelia's warning cry came a split second too late.

The man lunged from the shadows. With a quick slash of the knife, the assailant brought down the dagger in a vicious arc.

Logan dodged a lethal strike. The blade slashed down again, slicing into his shoulder with a sickening violence.

Amelia heard herself scream as Logan shoved her out of the assailant's path. The sound of her own terror echoed in her ears.

Wielding the dagger like a madman, the brute pressed his attack.

Logan dodged the blade.

Weaving with a brawler's skill.

Blocking wild, erratic slashes of the knife.

Her fear transformed to fury. Amelia tore her derringer from her bag.

She took aim.

Before she could squeeze the trigger, a deafening shot rang out.

An animal-like cry tore through the night.

She spun to face Logan. He'd planted his feet in a firing stance, his revolver steady in his hands.

His first shot had hit its mark.

Eyes glassy with shock, the cur who'd lurked in the shadows stared down at the blood streaming from his arm. A bowler hat lay on the ground. His coarse features were all too familiar.

The man at the bar.

Did the envelope he'd received from John Niles contain a

payment—a payment to kill them?

"You bloody bastard," the burly man bit off between his teeth.

"Drop the knife. Now." Logan's gaze was hard as granite. "If I pull this trigger again, I'll blow yer hand off."

"You may as well kill me now." The man's response was shockingly calm. "Hawk will see me dead."

"The only reason I have not killed ye yet is to spare the lady from the sight." Logan tapped his finger against the trigger for emphasis. "Now drop the damned knife."

Despite the misery in his eyes, the attacker scowled. Defeated, he opened his hand. The dagger clattered to the cobblestones. "Your luck will run out, MacLain. I guarantee you that much. The woman . . . she'll be the death of you."

FORCING HIMSELF TO keep a cool head, Logan stared down at the man who'd tried to kill him. God only knew what the bastard would have done to Amelia if the dagger's strikes had landed with lethal skill.

"Who sent ye here? Was it Hawk?" Logan demanded.

Murray and Tim charged out of the tavern, armed and ready for action. The men stopped in their tracks. Tim's gaze darted to the bloody knife on the pavement. "Ye should've killed him."

Logan shook his head. "A dead man cannot tell us anything."

"I won't . . . tell you . . ." The bastard who'd tried to kill him grated out the words between his moans of pain.

"Summon the constable," Logan instructed Tim. "I need to see Amelia safely home."

"Aye." Tim took off running.

"I could not help but hear the gent at the bar speaking to ye." Murray trained his gun on the attacker. "I take it ye go by Frank."

"Frank, eh?" Logan pinned the man with a cold stare. "Tell

me, Frank. Who the hell is the man called Hawk?"

"Not a bloody . . . damn . . ."

"He paid ye to come after me? Why?"

"You already know the answer."

"He'll see ye dead. Ye said as much." Logan pressed. "Ye've nothing to lose by talking, do ye?"

"Go to . . . hell."

Logan slanted Amelia a glance. Standing beneath the lamp, she'd gone uncharacteristically quiet, her features drawn.

"Dear God, you've been wounded," she said softly, her gaze settling on the blood-stained slash on Logan's coat.

"Nothing to worry over," Logan said, keeping his tone cool even as pain rippled down his arm.

A raw laugh escaped his assailant. "He's right, lass. That's nothing to worry your pretty head about. Not when Hawk is coming after you. He will see the both of you dead." His mouth contorted in pain. "Dead and in the ground."

Amelia looked away, as if she could not bear the sight of the brute. Logan summoned every ounce of control he possessed. The coward who'd dared to attack him from behind needed to give thanks that she was there. If not for that, Logan would've taught the lout a damned hard lesson.

But he couldn't subject Amelia to the sight of more violence.

He would not do that to her.

Later, he'd see to it that the detectives would compel the coward to reveal what he knew of Hawk. When Amelia was safe under his roof, he'd ensure that the bastard was interrogated. One way or another.

Chapter Twenty-Two

"GOOD HEAVENS, WHAT'S happened?" Mrs. Langford rushed to Amelia's side and took her hand between her warm fingers. "Ye look as if ye've seen the devil himself."

"It's not so bad as that," Amelia said. Her uneven voice was not convincing even to her own ears. The sight of a knife-wielding ruffian intent on cold-blooded murder had sickened her. Thank heavens for Logan's quick reflexes. If he had not dodged the worst of the strike, the coward might have driven the blade into Logan's back. Might have landed a lethal blow. The very thought of it made her tremble.

Logan joined the women in the front hall, the slightest of smiles curving his mouth as he took in Mrs. Langford's worried expression. Her gaze had settled on the gaping slash on his sleeve and the tint of blood on the wool of his coat.

"It's naught to worry yer head over." Shrugging off the jacket, he glanced at his shoulder. "God knows I've had worse."

Mrs. Langford leaned closer to look at his stained linen shirt. "Who in Hades did this?"

"That is a matter Finn and I will investigate in the morning. For now, the weasel is locked away in a cell. With any luck, he will live through the night." Logan plowed a hand through his hair. "If Finn was here, I would trust him to guard this place while I paid the cur a visit. But I will not leave you all unprotected. There's no telling who else is lurking about."

The thought of ruffians lying in wait twisted Amelia's nerves into knots. Mr. Hawk, whoever the vile man was, had her in his sights.

And now, Logan was also in danger.

How could Hawk and his accomplices be so foolish as to think she knew the whereabouts of some mysterious treasure? Why, they might as well have expected her to lead them to Merlin's wand or some other such creation of someone's imagination.

"I'll tend yer wound," Mrs. Langford volunteered, concern in her tired eyes.

Logan shook his head. "That won't be necessary. I'll pay Doc Stevenson a visit in the morning. He'll know the best course of action."

Amelia steeled herself to take another look at his bloodied shirt. When she was a girl, her father had insisted she and Paul receive training in skills he regarded as essential for survival. Proper application of a bandage had ranked high on Papa's list.

"The bleeding appears to have stopped," she observed, noting the stain had not spread. "But your wound still needs to be bandaged."

"I'll take care of it," he replied gruffly. "The best medicine for all of us now is sleep."

SITTING ON THE edge of the feather bed, Amelia brushed her bare toes against the cool floor. Her mind raced, blurring thoughts and memories and fears. Sleep would be elusive, if it came at all.

The moment the would-be assassin's dagger had sliced into Logan's arm had been seared into her mind. He'd insisted the injury was minor, but without examining it, she could not be certain. All she knew for sure was that he'd suffered harm because he had acted to protect her.

Someone had her in their sights.

And Logan was paying the price.

The stubborn man intended to tend the injury on his own. She suspected he'd wanted to spare her and the other women in his household from performing the task. Did he think she was too delicate to endure the sight of blood?

Moonlight through the curtains cast shadows against the walls. Try as she might to distract herself with the play of light and dark against the wood paneling, her thoughts kept leading back to Logan. Wrapping the wound without assistance would surely be difficult. Certainly he would benefit from her help.

Giving in to her instincts, she lit the lamp on the bedside table and donned a wrapper over her prim gown. There would be no harm in checking on his well-being. After all, he'd been injured while defending her. Any decent woman would do the same.

She retrieved a small quilted bag from her traveling case, a long-ago gift from her grandmother. In her mind's eye, she pictured the ever-efficient, ever-cheerful woman with her. Grandmother Beth had insisted one needed to be prepared for any emergency. If she could see Amelia now, shoring up her courage to enter the bedchamber of a man who was not her husband—not even her betrothed—would she be shocked at Amelia's lack of propriety? Would the smile Amelia had so cherished fade to a frown?

No, she reassured herself. Grandmother Beth would surely have understood. During her lifetime, she'd never shrunk from a challenge. She'd been bold. Rather fierce, actually. She would agree that Amelia could not allow Logan's wound to go untended. Her grandmother would expect nothing less from her. Caring for the man who'd become her defender was only right.

The fact that Amelia was drawn to Logan like a flower to sunlight was not truly a consideration.

Or was it?

Bag in hand, Amelia tiptoed along the corridor from her room to his. Somehow, the passage seemed longer than reality, with each step weighted by doubt.

As she reached the chamber, her fingers clutched the handle on her bag. She hesitated for the span of several heartbeats, praying that she would not live to regret this moment. Heaven only knew what Mrs. Garrett's or Mrs. Langford's reactions would be if they discovered her alone with Logan at this hour of the night.

Enough of that. She had no cause to be so skittish. She'd survived gossip before. Even in the worst case, she'd come through it with her head held high. She always did.

Squaring her shoulders, she willed herself to rap lightly upon his door.

"It's Amelia," she said in a near whisper.

"Is something wrong?" His tone was gruff as he opened the door.

Oh, dear.

Lamplight illuminated his body in a casual state of undress. He had stripped off his shirt and fashioned a makeshift bandage that covered his wounded arm. In place of trousers, he'd fastened a kilt in shades of green and black low on his lean hips. Her mouth went dry.

She pulled in a low breath. Perhaps it wasn't entirely proper—not even a *bit* proper, she corrected herself—to enter his room, especially given the fact he was only half-dressed. But it was not as if she were a blushing girl fresh from the schoolroom. It was not as if she had never seen a man's bare chest. Or a man's muscular legs. Not that it mattered. She'd simply focus on tending to his injury. That was why she was here.

At least, she could tell herself that. Even if the part of her that longed for his warmth knew her noble motive was not the whole truth.

"Nothing is wrong," she said quickly. "But I will not be able to rest until I know that you're well."

"Well enough. Ye've no need to worry over me."

She shored up her resolve. "I beg to disagree. May I come in?"

"Never let it be said I would turn away a lovely lass—a lovely lass wearing cotton to her chin, no less—in the middle of the night."

He stepped aside, motioning for her to enter. Perhaps too eagerly her gaze drifted over him, drinking in the masculine appeal of his lean-muscled arms and broad shoulders. Sable brown hair, even darker than that on his head, feathered over his chest, tapering over his sleekly muscled abdomen, trailing beneath the top of his kilt.

Logan's intelligent brown eyes regarded her with a blend of curiosity and a masculine hunger he could not conceal. His mouth quirked at the corner in that endearing way of his. Had he realized the direction of her gaze?

And of her thoughts?

"Ye're well aware of my reputation," he said, his voice gruff. "Ye're sure of this?"

"Quite so. After all, it's not as if you're the Big Bad Wolf," she said, infusing her voice with a lightness she did not feel.

"I wouldn't be so sure of that."

With that, he closed the door behind her. Hearing the slight creak of the hinges, she gulped another breath as if that might clear her head.

"I understand you are weary," she began, determined to keep her focus on the task ahead.

His eyes twinkled with good-hearted challenge. "A rogue is never too tired to allow a beautiful woman to—"

Heat washed over her cheeks. "I would not get your hopes up."

"Tend my injury," he said, looking rather full of himself. "Making assumptions, are ye now, Amelia?"

"In this case, it is a logical inference."

"Ah, a man can harbor hope, can he not?" Absently, he brushed a rebellious lock of dark hair from his brow. A streak of crimson marked his temple.

"You've been injured…and not just your arm."

She leaned closer for a better look. So near, faint hints of soap on his skin filled her senses. Forcing her attention to the matter at hand, she examined a small cut not far from his left ear. The laceration was narrow and, thankfully, did not appear to go deep. Had the point of the dagger grazed him during the fight?

His brow furrowed. "'Tis nothing to worry yerself over."

"My, you are a bit impatient, aren't you," she mused. "In my far-from-expert opinion, I'd wager a guess you will survive this wound. But nevertheless, it needs to be cleaned." Her gaze roamed to the strip of cloth he'd tied around his bicep. "And your arm as well."

"I've already taken care of that."

"As well as anyone could dress their own wound."

She set her bag on the bedside table and selected a bottle of antiseptic and a square of clean linen.

His brows lifted again. "Ever prepared, eh, Amelia?"

"In some respects."

In truth, she was starting to have her doubts. Though born of necessity, the intimacy of the moment unleashed butterflies flitting about wildly in her stomach. She composed her thoughts.

"My Grandmother Beth's father was an apothecary," she went on, dousing the fabric with the antiseptic. "Before her marriage, she assisted him in his shop. Later, when I was a girl, Grandmother taught me to have the proper solutions at hand. One never knows when they will be needed."

"So you just happened to bring them along?"

"Of course. Now be still," she said and dabbed the antiseptic against his temple. "This may sting."

The low hiss between his teeth confirmed the truth of her words. "By Lucifer's ghost."

Retrieving a strip of bandage from the bag, Amelia set her attention on his injured arm. "Let me take a better look."

He shot her a playful scowl. At least, she hoped it was playful.

"I presume this will entail that blasted liquid torture."

"I must say, I didn't expect so much protest from a man rumored to be an outlaw."

"Blackbeard never had to suffer yer ministrations."

"Perhaps if he had, he would have lived longer."

Logan regarded her for a long moment. "Even after he was decapitated, eh?"

She gave her head a brisk shake. "Sadly, I don't believe I could have offered much help."

"But ye'd have given it a valiant try," he quipped.

"Highly unlikely," she replied. "Now, hold out your arm. I am going to unwrap the bandage."

"There's not a blasted thing wrong with this binding."

"You've made a commendable effort, but the wound must be disinfected to reduce the chance of infection."

"More of that bloody torment in a bottle?" he grumbled as he extended his arm.

"Honestly, I had no idea you were so dramatic," she said lightly, even as her heart beat ever so slightly faster. The acceleration of her pulse had nothing to do with his protests, but everything to do with this tempting man who stood near enough to kiss.

Doing battle with her own rebellious thoughts, Amelia affected a serious demeanor and set about her task. "Fortunately, the wound is not overly deep," she observed after she peeled away the cloth. "But I predict you are not going to like what comes next—"

His gaze locked with hers. "I'd wager ye're right."

"As I told you, I need to disinfect the injury."

"I *will* make an effort to be brave," he teased.

Keeping her voice bland, she liberally applied tincture of iodine to the laceration. "I do hope so."

"Bugger it," he muttered between his teeth.

"The worst is over," she said. "Now, I will dress the wound properly."

"I had no idea I was watching over blasted Florence Nightingale."

"I consider that high praise, indeed."

As Amelia set about bandaging his arm, she noticed Logan had grown quiet. His jaw was set in a serious expression, though not one wrought by pain. Rather, he appeared deep in his thoughts.

"I do believe you will live to see another day," she said cheerfully as she finished securing the bandage.

"Well, that's a relief." Humor flavored his tone.

She could not help but smile. *Watching over blasted Florence Nightingale.* The truth washed over her. He *had* watched over her, regardless of the danger to his own life.

He had set his mind to keeping her safe. To protecting her. To helping her uncover the coward responsible for Paul's death.

"The very thought of what might have happened—what might have happened to you—twists my stomach in knots. You could have been killed." The words tumbled out in a rush.

The teasing spark in his eyes faded, replaced by a look of solemn determination. "I let my guard down. It will not happen again."

"Logan, tell me the truth. Why do you feel you owed my brother a debt? Why do you feel a duty to protect me?"

He dropped his gaze to the braided rug beneath his bare feet, seeming to mull over her questions. When he lifted his gaze, he caught her hands in his and drew her gently to him.

"Believe me when I tell ye this, Amelia. Before I knew ye, I wanted to protect ye because I made a vow. But now . . ." He brushed a kiss over the bridge of her nose. "Now, I want to keep ye safe because I cannot imagine a world without ye in it."

His words stunned her. Emotion welled in the back of her throat. "I couldn't bear it . . . if something happened to you."

Logan's smile did not reach his eyes. "Ye've no worries about me. I've come through worse than this and lived to tell the tale."

"I know you have courage. But that won't keep you alive."

"Those bastards will not get the better of me. Ye see, Amelia, I have something they don't."

She met his eyes. The irresistible spark that so tempted her flared within their depths.

"And what might that be, Mr. MacLain?"

He cupped her face in his hands. Light as a petal floating in the breeze, he brushed his lips over hers.

Tender.

Delicious.

Maddeningly seductive.

He dipped his head. Softly, he claimed the kiss she so willingly gave.

"Amelia, ye are the best reason any man could have to keep himself alive."

She drank in the heat of his body. "Is that so?"

"I do not want to leave ye. I want to learn everything . . . everything about ye."

She pressed a kiss to his lips, craving every moment of contact. "I do hope that's true."

"It's true, my sweet Amelia. Ye see, lass . . . ye're in my heart."

Chapter Twenty-Three

Y*E'RE IN MY heart.* A cascade of emotions swept over Amelia at Logan's gravel-roughened confession. His words seduced her with their honest simplicity, even as the truth crashed into her like a rogue wave.

Logan wanted her. And not for only this night.

Her stomach did a little somersault.

She had longed to hear him speak these words, words that echoed the desire in her heart and made her knees wobble.

Caressing her with a light touch, his lips brushed over hers. Gentle. Undemanding. So very, very tempting.

And then, he eased his hold, releasing her. This close, she could see the charcoal-hued hairs of new beard dusting his carved jaw. He rubbed his palm against his cheek, as if he debated a question within his own mind.

Taking a tiny step back, she pulled in a low breath. Logan's brows dipped into a frown.

"If ye think I aim to sweet talk ye into spending this night with me, ye're mistaken." His mouth curved in a rueful half-smile. "Yer bed is beckoning ye for a good night's rest."

Her heartbeat pounded in a staccato rhythm. He'd uttered the words that should send her on her way. She could simply bid Logan good night and make her way to a comfortable bed. She'd crawl beneath the covers, and sooner or later, she would fall into slumber and dream of him.

Dream of the passion she had turned away from.

Of the love that might've been hers.

No, she would not—could not—walk away. She could not allow a twinge of doubt to destroy this moment.

She wanted Logan. The hunger went bone deep. The need in his eyes, a desire he could not entirely hide, told her he longed for her with the same intensity.

Some thought Logan MacLain a rogue.

But she knew the truth. He was a good man—a man worth the risk of another scar on her heart.

She met his deep brown eyes. "I know you don't want me to leave."

"Want ye to leave?" Logan chuckled under his breath. "Lass, I am neither a fool nor a eunuch. But what I want . . . it's not what's best for ye."

Rather presumptuous of the man. Despite the quickly doused flickers of hesitation, she was a woman who knew her own mind. She would be the judge of what was right for her.

Cocking her chin, she leveled her hands on her hips. "What's best for me?"

"I shouldn't have said . . . what I said." He raked long fingers through his hair. "A woman like ye deserves more than a tumble between the sheets."

She drew nearer and reached for him. Amelia studied his features for a long moment, taking in the rugged planes of his cheeks, the subtle curves of his mouth. Slowly, she traced the contours of his hand, skimming over his slightly roughened skin with a subtle touch.

"Surely you don't believe that's all there is between us."

"Ye've been through hell, Amelia. Yer emotions are stirred up. Ye're vulnerable. I've no right—"

"Vulnerable?" She pondered the word. "Perhaps. But I am not an innocent. I am a woman. A woman who knows my own mind. My own desires. My own longings." Amelia cupped her palm against his stubble-roughened cheek. "But I have to know . . . is there nothing more between us than the prospect of a night in your bed?"

Passion glimmered in the depths of his gaze. "There has always been more between the two of us. And ye well know it."

Raw feeling tinged the words, filling Amelia with joy. Logan was not a man to seduce a woman with pretty, meaningless endearments. But if she lived to be a very old woman, she would never forget the pure emotion in his husky voice.

Her fingertips skimmed over his chest, delighting in the strength of his firm, muscular body. "I know what I want." She glided her fingers over the expanse of his collarbones, delighting in the primal response he could not disguise.

He sucked in a raw breath. "Is that so?"

"Most definitely."

He caught her hand in his, if only to still the progress of her fingers roving over his body. "What is it that ye want, Amelia?"

"You."

"Ah, darling lass," he murmured, gathering her in his arms, claiming her with a kiss that betrayed the need in his soul.

He caressed her lips, as if drinking in her essence. His lean, powerful body pressed against her. Instinctively, she canted her hips, cradling the undeniable evidence of his need against her softness.

"Ah, Amelia, I could never get enough of ye." He whispered the words against her ear, nipping playfully at her lobe, a heartbeat before his delicious mouth trailed kisses along the curve of her throat, the only area below her chin not draped in sturdy flannel and soft cotton.

With unhurried motions, he untied her dressing gown, slipping it over her shoulders until it pooled upon the floor. "I need to see ye, darling lass." Taking a step back, his brows hiked as he surveyed her from neck to toe.

Curling a lock of her hair around his fingers, he settled his gaze on the lace-trimmed collar of her modest gown. "Ye're sure of this, Amelia?" he asked. "Dressed as ye are, it's clear ye do not come to me tonight with seduction on yer mind."

"You do not find flannel alluring?" she countered playfully.

"I think I've already convinced ye that even draped in a flour sack, yer delectable body could tempt a man beyond all reason." His teasing half-smile warmed her heart. "I don't give a damn what ye're wearing. Since the moment I first laid eyes on ye, Amelia, I've seen how how beautiful ye are. In every way."

The undisguised longing in his words sent her knees to wobbling. "You do know how to make a woman feel pretty."

"I only speak the truth." He tipped up her chin with one finger and brushed a kiss over her lips. "Oh, sweetheart, I want to see ye." Desire warmed his eyes. "All of ye."

She gazed up at him. Suddenly, she no longer felt vulnerable. She felt beautiful.

And oh-so-thoroughly adored.

Her breath caught, and she stilled. "I'd like that."

Her words sounded throaty to her own ears, tinged with yearning. A delicious smile curved his mouth, and his clever hands went to the tiny buttons at her neck. One by one, he slowly unfastened each in turn, then pressed a kiss to the skin he'd bared to his gaze.

Still, the buttons had only exposed a few precious inches, scarcely to the curve of her breasts.

"Still too bloody much fabric," he mused. "And not enough of ye, Amelia."

Sliding his hands lower, he skimmed the length of her from her waist, along the length of her legs until he reached the hem. Ever so slowly, he slid the nightdress upward, his eyes intent upon her as he bared inch by inch of her body.

"So beautiful," he whispered.

And then, he tugged the dress gently over her head and let it drift from his hands to the floor.

Cool air prickled against Amelia's skin. She pulled in a breath to calm her rampaging pulse. Not so much as a linen chemise stood between her and his hungry eyes. She stood bared before him.

Without shame.

Without regret.

With only longing for this man who had swept into her life like a storm she'd never seen coming.

"My God, Amelia," he breathed the words, his raw emotion passionate as a caress. "Ye're more beautiful than I'd envisioned in my most decadent dreams."

A sudden boldness filled her. More daring than she'd ever felt in her life, she reached for him. Savoring the contact of skin to skin, her fingers slowly swept over the expanse of his uninjured shoulder. Muscle and tendon and bone, melded into a perfection of strength. Of male power. Of male beauty.

Shoring up her courage, Amelia glided her hand lower, feathering through the crisp, dark hair on his chest, drinking in the feel of hard muscle and bone beneath her touch. She smiled to herself. When she was with Logan, she felt a delicious sense of freedom. Free to express her desires. Free to savor the texture of his skin beneath her fingertips. Free to stir his need, just as he kindled the hunger deep within her. The feelings were delightfully new, an experience of pleasure she'd never dreamed would be hers.

It wasn't as if she was an innocent. Not in the most literal sense, at least. After all, she'd been a married woman. She'd been young and trusting then, and for a time, she'd believed she was in love with the man with whom she'd spoken her vows. When he'd pursued her as his bride, he'd been charming and attentive. Until their wedding night. He'd been cold then, utterly disinterested in her happiness. In Edward's eyes, a *good wife* submitted dutifully to her husband. She was to make no demands. She was to harbor no expectations of desire or pleasure or tenderness.

She'd never truly savored the sensual beauty of a man's body. Not until Logan charged into her life. Raising up on her toes, she brushed a kiss over his delectable mouth. How she wanted this time in his arms. Each moment seemed a delicious exploration of pleasure and desire. With this man, she would seek a joy that had once seemed the stuff of fantasy. She would give voice to her hungers. To those yearnings she'd once had to treat as deep secrets, known only to her heart.

"What is it ye want, Amelia?" he whispered. His husky voice warmed her.

"I want you," she said truthfully. "I want to know . . . every inch of your body."

"Do ye now?"

Nibbling her lower lip, she nodded. "I want to learn what pleases you."

"Ye're a siren, lass." Temptation and challenge glimmered in his eyes. "And what else do ye want, my sweet?"

"I want to drive you mad." She drew a fingertip over the angle of his jaw. "Mad for me."

Coiling an arm around her, he brought her closer, nesting his arousal against her softness. "Love, ye've already mastered that art."

She gave her head a little shake. "I want to know what brings you pleasure. I am only just beginning to learn."

His eyes widened. The air seemed to still around them.

"I sense a challenge I don't want to resist."

"I do hope so," she murmured, rising on her tiptoes to kiss him fervently.

Pressing her fingertips to his chest, she felt the steady beat of his heart. Ah, what she wouldn't give to snuggle by his side in bed and feel that strong rhythm. Night after night. Morning after morning.

"I am yers, Amelia." His lips feathered a caress over hers. "Tell me what ye want. What ye need."

Slowly, she skimmed her hand over his chest, over his abdomen ridged with muscle, to the line of dark hair disappearing beneath his kilt. "I want to feel you," she murmured, exploring his body with her touch. "I want to learn every inch of you."

Allowing herself a sigh, she melted against him. The ridge of his arousal pressed against her, the fabric of his tartan no disguise for his need. He dipped his head, kissing her hungrily. Mingling her tongue with his, she canted her hips, savoring the feel of his masculine body pressed to hers.

If he was a rogue, it didn't matter. Not in the least.

In that moment, all she cared about was him.

He was all she wanted.

All she needed.

She smiled to herself as he dragged in a breath, as if steadying himself against a rush of feeling, against a rush of wanting. Suddenly, her feet no longer touched the floor.

He held her in his arms and carried her to his bed. His sheets were clean and cool against her skin. He went to the lamp, but she shook her head. "I don't want darkness. I want to see . . . to see you."

"Do ye now?" A smile of pure temptation tipped the corners of his mouth as he dimmed the lamp light to a soft glow. "Yer body, my darling, is a masterpiece. But a man's body is not a work of art."

Leaning on one elbow, she rested her head on her hand while her gaze slowly roamed his body. "Allow me to be the judge of that."

His grin erased any trace of hesitation. Without a hint of shyness, he met her gaze as he peeled away his kilt. The length of plaid puddled to the floor.

Amelia's breath caught. Oh, my, he was magnificent. All sleek defined muscle and lean power.

"Touch me, sweet Amelia," he murmured as he joined her on the bed. "Take yer time, my sweet. Learn my body. Just as I will learn yers."

Suddenly, words seemed unnecessary. She wanted him. Just as he wanted her.

Slowly, softly, she swept her fingers over him, drawing a low sound of desire from deep in his throat. Each touch of her skin to his drew a response, more fevered than the last, until he dragged her to him, trailing the curve of her throat with warm, passionate kisses.

"Ye aim to drive me mad, do ye, lass?"

"It would appear I am succeeding," she whispered against his velvet mouth.

"And now, it is my turn."

His eyes flashed with wicked warning. A tiny tremor coursed through Amelia, realizing his intent. She had made him wild with hunger. And now, he would lead her to the brink of desperation with the same wanton, all-too-delicious need.

Every kiss, every feather-light touch seemed designed to thrill her senses. Amelia closed her eyes. Drinking in the pleasure. Relishing every sensation. Until her body hummed with longing and she dug her fingers into his shoulders and whispered a plea for surrender.

His clever mouth kissed her again, and then, he shifted his body, prowling over her.

"I want ye more than I've ever wanted anything in my life." His husky brogue warmed her like a caress. "Ye're beautiful, Amelia. So bloody beautiful."

"I need you, Logan." Her arms encircled him, holding him close. "Truly, I do."

Without words, he kissed her again. Harder. Deeper. His shoulders went taut beneath her fingers as his body joined hers. So very slowly. An unhurried, sensuous possession.

She gasped. Not in pain. But in delicious, nearly wanton delight as he filled her softness. Deeply. Completely.

With each wickedly sensuous movement, he drew her closer and closer to a wild melding of their desires. Sating her hunger. Satisfying her need.

Ah, she could never get enough of him. She would never tire of being held in the arms of this powerful man. Never tire of the delight of lying skin to skin in his bed. She would never tire of being *his*.

His.

The word echoed through her as elemental pleasure rushed

over her like storm-driven waves. Nibbling her lower lip, she clutched handfuls of the linen bedsheets between her fingers.

"Ah, sweet Amelia."

His low, raw moan tipped her over the edge of desire.

Her world shattered. Drawn into a swirl of pleasure, she bit back a cry of unfettered pleasure.

Floating back to reality, she drifted in a haze of richly fulfilled desire.

"Ah, my sweet," he whispered as he tensed against her. A rough-edged groan escaped his throat as he reluctantly pulled his body away from hers, mere heartbeats before shudders of primal pleasure rippled through his body.

Rolling onto his back, Logan drew her to him. She snuggled close, settling into the nook between his arm and his chest. She toyed with the lightly furred hair across his pectorals, loving the way he reacted to her slightest touch.

"I will always want ye here, at my side." He brushed a tender kiss over her mouth. "If I live a thousand lifetimes, I will never get enough of ye, my beautiful Amelia."

Chapter Twenty-Four

LOGAN STIRRED, RELUCTANTLY opening his eyes as dappled rays of sunlight filtered through the curtains. Nestled against him, Amelia sighed, her lush hair tumbling over his uninjured shoulder as she shimmied closer. God above, the feel of her soft curves pressed to his body might've tempted a dead man to life.

I will never get enough of ye.

The words he'd spoken the night before had been a confession from the heart. For as long as he lived, he would never tire of her. He knew that truth without a trace of doubt. Her body was that of a goddess come to life, damned near irresistible. But there was more. So much more. Her clever mind and quick wit stirred his interest as deeply as her beauty. For years, he'd vowed to never again involve his heart. He had sought out pleasure in a woman's arms, but little else.

Amelia's tenderness had dismantled the barriers he'd erected. Her vibrant spirit had torn down shields he never wished to rebuild.

Someday, perhaps all too soon, his time with her might well end. When she was safe—when she could go about her life without a menace shadowing her—she'd likely realize a man like Logan was not for her. Loving Amelia for a lifetime was not in the cards.

But for now, he would hold her and adore her and savor their passion.

And he would *not* fall in love with her.

He drew his fingertips over the curve of her shoulder, debating whether or not he should kiss her awake.

"Good morning," she murmured, her drowsy voice soft as a caress.

He brushed a kiss over her forehead. "Good morning, love."

Propping her head on one elbow, she squinted to see the clock on the bedside table. "My, it's rather late."

He threaded his fingers through her softly mussed hair. "I am in no hurry to leave this bed."

A little vee creased her brow. "I'd planned to rise before dawn, before Mrs. Langford and Mrs. Garrett were up and about. If I move very quickly and very quietly, I might make it to my chamber without arousing suspicion."

A chuckle escaped him. "Ye can try, but ye'd be wasting yer time. Nosy as she is, Mrs. Langford could've spied for the Crown."

Nervously, she nibbled her lip. "I hadn't intended to cause a scandal."

"Those wise ladies will not be shocked." Unable to get his fill of her beauty, Logan traced the curve of her face. "Truth be told, Mrs. Langford could see I was drawn to ye from the start. She said as much, cheeky old soul that she is."

"They will not be taken aback?"

He slowly shook his head. "Those women have lived. And they've loved."

Amelia sat up and tugged the bedsheet over her rounded bosom. Dipping her head, she kissed him softly. "If I'm not careful, I will develop a taste for spending nights in your bed."

"My sweet Amelia, it will be my pleasure to hold ye, night after night."

A hint of a frown crossed her features. "I've no doubt of that."

"What troubles ye?"

"Nothing," she said quickly.

Too quickly.

"Ye have regrets?"

"No."

Seeing the uncertainty in her eyes, he caressed her cheek as he searched for the right words. "What we did was natural, my sweet. It was right."

Her nod seemed uncertain. "In my heart, I know that truth. But I've never before felt so free in a man's arms."

He brushed a kiss over the bridge of her nose. "That's a good thing, Amelia."

A small smile touched her lips. "Your touch drives me to madness. But I know so little about you. I want to learn more. Your family. Your home. Your secrets."

"My secrets, eh?"

"I still don't know why you felt a debt to my brother."

"I've told ye the truth. He saved my life. That night, he was forced to kill a man."

Amelia veiled her gaze with her lashes. "He never spoke a word of this to me."

An invisible stone the size of his fist tumbled into Logan's gut. Bloody hell, he'd much rather be kissing her in the morning light than making confessions about a past he wanted desperately to forget. But if Amelia wanted the truth, he would blasted well give it to her.

"Taking a life changes a man," he said. "Paul would not have wanted to burden ye."

Amelia's eyes darkened to a stormy blue. Had she sensed the raw pain behind his words?

"Please, tell me what happened."

"In those days, I was a blasted fool, always looking for a quick path to line my pockets. I played cards with wealthy fools who got in over their heads. I was good. Too good, in the eyes of the man who wanted me dead."

"What happened?"

"Paul and I were at a tavern by the sea, as we did in those days. Yer brother fancied one of the singers at the place, a pretty redhead, while I set out to separate some arrogant sot from his coin. Most of the gents took their losses in stride, but one fellow . . . well, he insisted I'd cheated. I was young and hotheaded, so I hit him. I bloodied his mouth with one punch and marched out of the place. I thought that was the end of it. Until he came at me with a knife."

Color drained from her cheeks. "Dear God. How brutal."

"I was on the ground, struggling to fend off the bastard. I'd taken a couple of deep strikes, and I was losing more strength by the moment. The lout wanted me dead." The memory tightened his chest, and he pulled in an uneven breath. "By the time Paul came upon the scene, I'd nearly lost the fight. But he carried a pistol. That night, he put it to use."

"Oh, dear," Amelia said softly. "He had no choice. Paul would not have stood by and watched you die."

Another stone tumbled into his gut. "If not for my blasted greed, he never would've been forced to make that decision."

"It wasn't your fault." Gently, Amelia swept a velvet-smooth fingertip over his cheek. "You could not have known what would happen that night."

"I was arrogant. Too bloody sure of myself. I never thought about the danger."

"But now you do." Warmth flickered in her gaze. "Every time you watch over me."

"I could not forgive myself if something happened to ye."

"Because of what Paul did?"

"No, Amelia." He pressed kisses to her fingertips, one by one. "Because of you."

Drinking in her gentle smile and the light in her eyes, he wrapped her in his arms and drew her near. Hunger surged through him. With an effort to be gentle, he pulled her against his body. The feel of her canting her hips, bringing her feminine curves even closer to his hard, demanding body, pleased him beyond measure.

"Ye're so bloody beautiful," he whispered against her lips.

"Am I now?" Her eyes sparkled with decided interest.

"Ye're temptation come to life."

"Do you want me, Logan?"

Was the minx daring to tease him?

He spread his hands over her rounded bottom, bringing her so close, his erection nested against her softness.

"Can ye have any doubt, lass?"

"Not one whit. It might well prove rather scandalous." Challenge flashed in her gaze. "Making love in the light of day."

He hiked his brows. "And that concerns ye?"

Her hair shimmered as she shook her head. Her delicious smile made his cock go even harder. "As a matter of fact, I have developed a bit of a taste for scandal."

"Have ye now?"

"Indeed." Temptation danced in her lively blue eyes. "I believe I know just the rogue to sate that craving."

Ah, he'd never get enough of this woman. Not if he lived a thousand lifetimes.

He couldn't help but grin. "Amelia, ye are a siren."

"I am *your* siren," she whispered, coiling her arms around his neck. "Now, I do have one request."

"And what might that be?"

"Please, darling." She nibbled her lip in that fetching way of hers. "Stop talking and kiss me."

RELUCTANTLY LEAVING THE comfort of Logan's bed, Amelia accompanied him to the breakfast room. Mrs. Garrett's delicious meal of raspberry scones with clotted cream and cheesy baked eggs was a true treat, quite a departure from the simple soft boiled egg and crumpet she typically made for herself.

"I'm starving this morning," Finn Caldwell said good-naturedly as he joined them, plate in hand. "It's a good thing Mrs.

Garrett prepares enough food to feed a blasted regiment."

"Good God," Logan observed as he took a look at the heaping serving on Finn's plate.

"A man's got to eat," Finn said, slathering butter on a thick slice of warm bread.

"Truer words have seldom been spoken." Logan reached for a piping hot scone. "I take it ye did not return alone."

"Actually, I did."

Logan's brows hiked. "The dragon refused?"

Finn smiled and shook his head. "To the contrary, Mrs. Johnstone is eager to assist. She insisted on driving that buggy of hers—the spider, or whatever she calls it. She'll meet us here later."

"The dragon is a maniac at the reins." Logan took a bite of his scone.

"Some things do not change." Finn's expression turned darker. "I hear you ended up on the wrong end of a knife last night."

"Ye could say that. But Miss Florence Nightingale here has got me on the mend." Logan slanted Amelia a gaze that made her cheeks heat.

Finn's gaze shifted to Amelia, lingering perhaps a moment longer than proper. "I'll have to remember that if I ever encounter a villain in the night."

Logan's eyes gleamed with a blend of humor and possessiveness. "Not bloody likely, ye randy knave."

"In the event you are injured, I will be the judge as to my ability to tend your wound." Amelia kept her tone prim yet firm.

Finn flashed a cheeky grin, seeming to enjoy rankling his friend. "I do have a bit of advice for ye, Logan."

Logan shot him a scowl. "Ye do, eh?"

"Next time, avoid the blade," Finn said with an air of authority. "Ye're not a blasted cat. Ye do not have nine lives to yer name. Only one."

Chapter Twenty-Five

AMELIA PASSED A pleasant morning in Logan's study, pouring over the morning edition and savoring the quiet. Setting the newspaper aside, she refilled her cup with oolong tea from the silver pot on the sideboard, then relaxed upon a comfortable leather wing chair to take in the editorial pages.

Heathy sauntered in, arrogant as a wolf beneath a full moon, interrupting her peaceful bliss. A bootlace dangled from his mouth. Unfortunately, the leather string was attached to a shoe, the very same boot Logan had previously moved out of the dog's reach. Or so he'd thought.

Amelia bit back an unladylike word. *Drat the luck.*

Heathy plopped the boot down upon the Aubusson rug as though it was the spoils of a hunt, sprawled over the carpet, and sank his teeth into the polished leather. If it were possible for a dog to grin, Heathy was doing just that.

"Oh, Heathy, you're such a naughty boy."

Drat. Drat. And double drat.

She'd confidently insisted Logan had no worries about her dog's affinity for shoes. Heathy had certainly proven her wrong.

Ignoring the dog's whines of protest, Amelia scooped up the boot while debating her next move. Surely Logan would understand. Wouldn't he? Still, there would be no harm in placing the teeth-marked boot and the bits of well-chewed leather lace out of sight. It wasn't as if she intended to deceive Logan.

Rather, she'd simply delay the inevitable. At some point in the future—well into the future, with any luck—she would find a proper moment to inform him of her dog's newfound fondness for the taste of leather.

Yes, that's what she'd do. She would simply wait for the right time.

But before she could stash the boot, the sound of a throat clearing rather purposefully rendered her deliberations moot.

Startled, she whirled about. The shoe nearly fell from her hand when Logan marched through the doorway. A tall, strikingly attractive woman whose dark hair was laced with elegant strands of silver stood by his side. As she met Amelia's gaze, a trace of a smile danced in her vivid brown eyes.

"No liking for shoes, eh?" Logan calmly took the boot from her hands and examined it. "I'd say these are fresh teeth marks. And I'd wager you are not the one who decided to bite them."

Relieved by the good humor in his tone, Amelia felt the tension in her shoulders ease. "I am sorry. Heathy never fails to surprise me."

Logan frowned. "Somehow, the wee beast did *not* surprise me."

The brunette cast him a sneaking glance. "Such a pity the dog could not figure a way to conceal a slimy toad within the boot, isn't it?"

"Actually, it was a frog." Logan looked as if he were holding back a grin. "The creature was comfortable beneath yer quilt. I never would've taken the chance ye'd step on him."

"Ye were an incorrigible lad," she said in a tone that sounded rather fond of the memory. "I suspect ye're still cheeky as they come."

"And I suspect ye'd be right." Logan turned to Amelia. "I'd like to introduce ye to my aunt, Mrs. Elsie Johnstone."

Amelia blinked. So this was the woman Logan summoned, the *dragon* he'd rather have spent the night in the infamous Tower than call upon for help. Amelia wasn't quite sure what she had expected, but this elegant woman garbed in a lovely traveling suit was most definitely not what she'd pictured.

"Mrs. Stewart, it is a pleasure to meet you." Mrs. Johnstone reached down to pet Heathy. "And this spirited dog of yers. I'm quite sure we will get on splendidly."

"The pleasure is mine," Amelia said as a delighted Heathy basked in the attention. "And please, I do prefer my given name—Amelia."

"As you wish." Mrs. Johnstone's smile warmed her dark eyes. "The little fellow . . . what is his name?"

"Heathy. Short for Heathcliff."

Recognition settled over Mrs. Johnstone's features. "Ye admire Miss Bronte's works, do ye?"

"Despite my governess's valiant efforts to direct my focus to my needlework, I could not tear myself away from *Wuthering Heights*. I do believe my father regretted obtaining the book for me."

"Ah, after I read it the first time, I could not banish thoughts of Heathcliff from my mind." Mrs. Johnstone's words brimmed with a surprising wistfulness.

"Heathcliff," Logan commented under his breath. "Poor bastard, with a name like that."

His aunt cut him a glare. "Yer da saw no point in exposing ye or yer brother to literature. And yer ma, my dear sister, she was more interested in stories of adventure than lovelorn sonnets. But we tried our best to broaden yer minds."

"I've never had a taste for fancy words in a leather-bound tome," Logan said matter-of factly. "As for an interest in danger-filled tales, ye lived yer own for years."

"I've had my fair share of exploits. There's no denying that," Mrs. Johnstone said with a touch of pride. "Don't go putting it in Amelia's head that I was a hellion in petticoats."

Logan grinned. "Petticoats were not yer preferred attire in those days. As I recall, Ma was shocked to see ye wearing trousers."

Trousers. How very unusual. In her elegant tweed ensemble, Elsie Johnstone seemed more likely to be on her way to a society tea than to be seeking adventure in traditionally masculine attire.

"She worried so over your da's reaction." A faint smile played on her mouth. "But when we were young, your mother never wore skirts when she was galavanting about on her beloved Daisy. Why, she stitched her own riding trousers."

A look Amelia couldn't quite read fell over Logan's features. "She did not share that side of herself with her sons."

"It's a pity you did not have long with her." Caring filled his aunt's eyes. "You were quite young when the cursed fever took her. Your mother had spirit, she did."

"I do remember that much about her," Logan said, his tone more subdued than usual.

"Where do ye think ye and Ewan got your thirst for adventure? Certainly not from yer da. Now, do not misunderstand. Yer father was a good man. But he wanted a proper wife. And your ma . . . she loved him."

"Aye, that she did," Logan agreed. "After she died, he was never the same."

"After that horrible day, I never heard him laugh. Losing yer ma hit him hard." Mrs. Johnstone turned to Amelia. "Now, enough of these gloomy reminiscences. I'm interested to learn about the library you've opened. I'm told it is strictly for female patrons."

"My library is a place for women to gather, to enjoy stimulating conversation in the company of other ladies."

"Brilliant," Mrs. Johnstone said. "I cannot wait to pay a visit."

"Perhaps I might show you around this afternoon," Amelia said, pleased at the revelation of a kindred spirit. "I do need to put the place back into order. You see, an intruder vandalized the space. But, thankfully, the collection appears to have escaped significant damage."

"Mrs. Langford would enjoy driving, I'm sure." Mrs. Johnstone turned to Logan. "I presume your coach will be available."

Logan crossed his arms over his chest. "When I sent for ye, the two of ye roaming about the city was not what I had in mind."

Ah, the arrogance of the man. Amelia met his frown with an overly sweet smile. "Between the three of us, I am confident we will survive a short venture out in the light of day."

"If anyone dares to try to get to Amelia, they will regret their error." Mrs. Johnstone tapped the reticule dangling from a thick braided cord at her wrist. "Mr. Remington will see to it."

"Mr. Remington?" Amelia asked.

"My pistol, dear," she replied smoothly.

Logan plowed a hand through his hair. "Ye're sure of this?"

"Of course." Mrs. Johnstone regarded him with a serenely confident expression. "My derringer holds two bullets. If the first does not do the proper job, the second will finish the task. And ye know I am quite an efficient shot."

"Ye'll get no argument from me on that point. But do not take any chances."

Mrs. Johnstone's smile reached her eyes. Her irises were as deep and rich a brown as Logan's. "That's rich, coming from you."

"It's one thing when I'm risking my own neck. But I will not put the lass in danger." The protectiveness in his eyes stirred a comforting warmth in Amelia's heart.

Mrs. Johnstone toyed with the intricate silver brooch pinned at her throat. Her brows drew slightly together. "I must say, Logan, this is a side of you I've never seen."

Logan shifted his gaze to Amelia, a thin smile pulling at the corners of his mouth. "Some things in life are worth protecting. No matter the cost."

Chapter Twenty-Six

THE AFTERNOON SUN beamed warm rays through the high windows of the library as Amelia led Mrs. Johnstone and Mrs. Langford into the library. Amelia escorted the ladies through the main corridor, pointing out the shelves designated for various areas of interest. Her heart still sank at the sight of the disarray the vandal had left behind. But thankfully, most of the books appeared to have been left unscathed. With a bit of help, she'd soon have the collection back in order.

"Oh, I must have a better look. I do enjoy a rousing story," Mrs. Langford said with enthusiasm. She strolled among the shelves while Mrs. Johnstone browsed the collection, pausing to thumb through the pages of a leather-bound volume of Shakespeare's works.

"What a marvelous collection." Mrs. Johnstone glanced up to meet Amelia's gaze. "I shall need to visit the city more often, if only to enjoy these fascinating books."

Pausing before the art history bookcase, Mrs. Langford scanned the spines of the thick volumes. "'Tis a wonderful place. So much knowledge under one roof."

Delight bubbled within Amelia. "In truth, I cherish the good company I find in this place even more than the books within these walls."

"Indeed." Mrs. Johnstone placed the atlas back upon the shelf and surveyed the space. "Now, shall we get to work putting the shelves back into proper shape?" Instantly spotting Amelia's hesitation, she went on, "Do not regard me as a guest who shouldn't lift a finger to help. I am kin to Logan, and now I am a friend to ye. And that's what friends do."

"Ye're a wise woman," Mrs. Langford agreed. "Between the three of us, it won't take long to put the books in place. Logan and ye have already done much of the work."

The genuine helpfulness in their voices lifted Amelia's spirits. "Thank you. I do appreciate your assistance."

Mrs. Johnstone scooped up a novel the vandal had left under a chair. "Helping ye is also a chance to take a better look at the collection."

After Amelia instructed the ladies on the organization of the shelves, the trio got to work. Engaging in a robust discussion of their most cherished books, they moved from shelf to shelf, placing the collection back in order. It wasn't long before they'd arranged the books in the proper cases and were ready to enjoy fresh-brewed tea and conversation. Amelia prepared a pot of piping tea while the ladies relaxed in comfortable wing chairs. Their words flowed like those of old friends Amelia had known for years.

Amelia brought the tea on an enameled tray that had escaped the intruder's destruction. "I cannot help but be intrigued by the infamous frog in Logan's past," she said, unable to tamp down her curiosity regarding the amphibian and the lad who'd grown into the man she was coming to adore. "Care to tell me more?"

Mrs. Langford took a sip of tea and gave her head a little shake. "Ah, the lad was a rascal."

Mrs. Johnstone shot her a frown. "Polly, ye would not find it so amusing if he'd chosen yer bed for the creature's hiding place."

"He rebelled against ye because ye were the one tasked with reining him in. I was not saddled with such a challenge," Mrs. Langford replied.

"Very true," Mrs. Johnstone said. "Ye see, Amelia, when my dear sister was taken from us, the boys had no mother in their lives. Their father was too bound by grief to take another wife, so after a time, I came to live with them. By that point, Logan's brother Ewan was on his way to becoming a man, but Logan was still a mischievous boy. He rebelled against any attempt I made to teach him to be a gentleman."

"Ye knew nothing of children, much less a boy who'd lost his mum. We both know Maggie doted over him. Why, she spoiled him rotten." Emotion colored Mrs. Langford's soft tones. "Don't forget, ye weren't much more than a girl yerself. Ye went from a daring life in America to watching over two headstrong lads. But ye did well by those boys."

"As well as I could. We all did." Mrs. Johnstone cast her gaze down to her teacup. "All except for the blasted frog, that is."

Mrs. Langford chuckled. "The ugly little beast was more terrified of ye than ye were of it."

"I was *not* terrified of it." Mrs. Johnstone offered an indignant sniff. "But I certainly did not expect to find a cold, grunting companion beneath my covers."

"Cold and grunting—ah, that brings my dear departed husband to mind," Mrs. Langford reminisced, her tone a cross between wistful and cheeky. "But I'd rather talk about yer memories, Elsie. Have ye forgotten the snake?"

Mrs. Johnstone flashed a scowl. "Good heavens, no. If only I could wipe *that* memory from my mind."

"Anyone who heard ye scream that night would've thought the lad had hidden a cobra between yer sheets," Mrs. Langford said with a chuckle, clearly enjoying the memory.

"The boy was incorrigible."

"He had spirit. And he's turned out to be a fine man." Mrs. Langford turned to Amelia. "I do believe Logan's quite taken with ye."

Amelia choked down the sip of tea she'd just taken. *Oh, dear.*

"It's true," Mrs. Langford went on with a little grin. "Why, I've never seen him so besotted. Not since that calculating little—"

Mrs. Johnstone shot her a sharp glance. "I don't think Amelia needs to hear about that scrawny wench."

"Please, do go ahead. I'd like to learn more about Logan. About what's made him . . . well . . . *him*." Amelia took a little sip of tea, if only to collect her thoughts. "He crashed into my life as unexpectedly as a bolt of lightning. I take it there was a woman he once cared for."

Mrs. Johnstone nodded, holding her features taut. "Logan adored that girl. But love was not enough for the likes of her."

"She accepted his proposal, you see. But days before they were to speak their vows, Maeve broke off the engagement. After she left him to wed that pompous arse, all puffed up with his title and his fine house, Logan changed," Mrs. Langford explained. "He was bitter. And determined to make his fortune, no matter the cost. He sailed to America, then headed west to one heaven-forsaken town after another, taking risk after risk. Until finally, he returned home. His da was ailing then, but after his father's blessed recovery, Logan left the Highlands behind for another life right here, in London."

"I did not think he'd ever find it in his heart to care for another woman again." Mrs. Johnstone's gaze settled on Amelia. "Not until he met ye."

Amelia struggled for words. She'd sensed he had experienced a great loss. And now, she was learning the truth. He had loved another woman, only to suffer a crushing betrayal. The thought of his misery cut like a dull blade. Would Logan ever again truly open his heart?

The cheerful *ting* of the door chimes interrupted the suddenly uncomfortable conversation. For a heartbeat, Amelia was thankful.

Until she saw the visitor who'd strolled through the door.

Cecil Mansfield.

Years had passed since her chance meeting with Mansfield at a museum ball, but there was no mistaking the art dealer. The man displayed both his wealth and his arrogance with each tap of his gleaming silver walking stick against the wood floor. Garbed in a meticulously tailored suit with a cravat of burgundy-hued silk loosely tied at his throat, he plastered a false smile on his face as his piercing gray eyes narrowed in assessment. Why in blazes had he decided to pay her a visit? Her intuition flared into warning. She would not like the answer to her question.

Mansfield greeted her with a perfunctory tip of his hat. "You remember me, do you not, Mrs. Stewart?"

"Of course. Paul was most impressed with your collection."

Mansfield offered a solemn nod. "Your brother was a brilliant man. I valued his insights."

"He possessed an incomparable eye for art. Might I ask what brings you here today?"

"You may have heard that I plan to expand my galleries. In light of my past dealings with your brother, I am inclined to offer an arrangement you will find favorable."

Mrs. Johnstone and Mrs. Langford hiked their brows in unison.

"An arrangement? Of what sort?" Amelia questioned.

"The terms I am prepared to offer are exceedingly favorable. In truth, my solicitors believe I am offering far too much," he went on without answering her question. "I would not consider such generous terms if I had not held your brother in high esteem."

"Esteem, is it?" She did not care if he detected the skepticism in her tone.

"Why, of course." His reply was smooth. Too smooth.

Amelia let out a low breath. "What sort of arrangement do you propose?"

When Mansfield's gaze flickered to the ladies, Amelia added, "You may speak freely. Surely there's nothing in your proposal that must be held confidential."

"I suppose not. It is no secret that I am expanding my galleries. I intend to acquire this building. As you can understand, you will need you to remove your property." His critical gaze swept over the bookshelves. "The sooner, the better."

She pulled in a steadying breath. "You are asking me to relocate my library."

"You may find another space. Or you may toss the dusty books in this place into a bonfire. It makes no difference to me."

The gall of the man. Amelia squared her shoulders. "I've heard quite enough, Mr. Mansfield. I'll ask you to leave now."

"Not yet." His expression cold, he retrieved a sealed document from his pocket and presented it to her. "When you review this offer, you will see I've been most generous. But you will vacate these premises by the end of the month."

"There's no need to read this." Holding her chin high, she thrust the envelope back at Mansfield. "I am not going anywhere."

"I've offered enough to make the move, or whatever it is you end up doing, exceedingly profitable."

Amelia shook her head. "That won't do. Not at all." Glancing to Mrs. Johnstone and Mrs. Langford for moral support, she hiked her chin in defiance. "I have no intention of leaving until my right to occupy this property has come to an end."

"You must be reasonable." Mansfield toyed with the walking stick, seeming to test its weight against his hand. "I'd hoped we could come to an arrangement without delay. But I am prepared for further negotiations. If need be, I can be very persuasive."

"I am not interested in your money."

He flashed a scowl. "As I said, I can be very persuasive. In one way. Or another."

Amelia marched to the door and held it open. "Please leave."

Mansfield tapped the silver tip of the stick against his palm. The gesture was not innocent, but a thinly veiled threat.

"I will return. Another time, when I may speak more frankly." His cold eyes drilled into her. "Mark my words, Mrs. Stewart. You will come to see things my way."

He crossed the threshold, and Amelia closed the door behind his back, casting aside any care for politeness. The man's callous tone had left her far more shaken than she'd been willing to show. The *click* of the latch sliding into place offered some calm for her nerves.

"Who in blazes does the rotter think he is?" Mrs. Johnstone's tone was as fiery as the look in her eyes.

"Language, Elsie," Mrs. Langdon chided.

"I would tell the man he's a rotter to his face," Mrs. Johnstone said. "I held my tongue for Amelia's sake. Not for his."

"He deals in rare works of art. Old Masters, and such," Amelia said. "As you heard, he's set his sights on this building for another gallery."

"The man's a toad, he is." Mrs. Langford roamed to the window. Pulling back the curtain, she peeked out into the street. "That must be his carriage. Quite elegant for a reptile."

"I do believe a toad is an amphibian," Mrs. Johnstone pointed out.

Mrs. Langford shot her a glare. "Very well, then. It is an elegant coach for an *amphibian*."

Smiling despite her frayed nerves, Amelia joined Mrs. Langford at the window. A wiry man perched on the driver's bench of the elegant brougham waiting within steps of the library. Impatiently, the coach driver tapped his fingers against the seat.

"Cecil Mansfield certainly possesses the funds for such a fine carriage," Amelia said. "He's made a fortune selling works by artists who sadly saw little benefit from their talents while they were alive."

"Isn't that the way?" Mrs. Johnstone said. "Do not let the weasel trouble ye, Amelia. He will not get the better of you. Logan will set him straight. Ye can wager your last coin on that."

AS THE CLOCK in Logan's study chimed the midnight hour, the sound of boot heels in the corridor drifted to Amelia's ears. Had he returned from the Rogue's Lair? Or had Caldwell arrived with news? Tension washed over her like an icy wave. Given the nature of Logan's establishment, he'd spent many a late night at the tavern. But these were not ordinary times. His commitment to watch over her had brought danger to his door. She couldn't rest until she knew he'd returned.

Marking her place in the novel with a scrap of velvet ribbon, she set the book on the marble-top table and went to see whose footsteps she had heard.

Logan was reaching for the knob as she opened the door. His gaze locked with hers, and then, he smiled. Had he detected her quiet sigh of relief?

"Ye're up late, Amelia."

"I became engrossed in quite a riveting tale. Until the sound of a man's boots thudding against the floor distracted me."

A hint of a smile played on his full mouth. "If I didn't know better, I'd think ye were worrying about me."

"I've no cause for worry." She cupped her palm against his face, lightly drawing the pads of her fingers over the dark stubble edging his jaw. "Now do I?"

"I can take care of myself." Entering the room and closing the door behind them, he brushed a soft kiss over her cheek. "Ye've no worries about that." His expression turned darker. "I understand ye had a visitor today."

"A most unpleasant man," she said. "But I suppose you already know all about it."

"Not *all* about it. Only what Finn was able to ferret out of Mansfield's driver. The man's a talker when he's got some whisky in him."

"There's something about Cecil Mansfield—something that sets my every nerve on edge."

Logan's sable brows rose. "Did he threaten ye?"

"I cannot say that he did. Not directly. But he clearly implied a warning that I should give him what he wants."

"He's out to get his hands on the building."

Amelia nodded. "He plans to use the space to expand his

ventures."

"Do you have any idea why he's decided to acquire that particular building?"

"He did not explain his reasoning." Amelia laced her fingers together in a nervous knot. "In time, the man will get what he wants. But I won't leave until there is no choice. As you know, I made that clear to Mr. Driscoll."

"If Mansfield returns, send for me. He will soon understand he's made an error in judgment."

"He will be back." She pulled in a steadying breath. "But I am not afraid of him."

"I meant what I said, Amelia. If the bloke steps one foot in the library again, I want to know. If he gives ye any trouble, he will answer to me." Logan went to the sideboard, poured sherry into a crystal glass, and handed it to her.

"Thank you." She took a sip, warming her throat, easing the sensation that her nerves had been stretched too tightly.

Logan led her to the settee. She sank down upon the plushly upholstered piece, placed her glass on the marble-topped table, and smoothed out her skirts. He joined her there and took a drink from his glass, leaning back.

He glided his long fingers through her hair and brushed a light kiss over her lips. Searching. Asking. Tempting her to surrender her heart.

"Ah, Amelia, that pretty face of yers could bewitch a man." His gravel-edged words were a caress.

She sighed against his mouth, the sound filled with wanting she could not deny.

He claimed her lips with a kiss. Tender, yet passionate. Carnal. Nearly primal in its intensity.

"I want ye in my arms, lass. In my bed. Tonight."

And every night.

Startled by the boldness of her own thoughts, Amelia opened her eyes. Dragging in a low breath, she inhaled his scent, notes of whisky and bergamot blending with the crisp aroma of shaving soap.

Oh, she wanted him. More than she should. Much, much more than was wise.

She needed to keep her head about her. Under no circumstances could she allow herself to be swept away. Not again. But how very glorious it would be to surrender. To her own desires. To her dreams of love. To this man whose touch she craved more with each beat of her heart.

This feels so very right. But I don't know what tomorrow will bring. How dear would the price be for each delicious night she would spend in his arms?

Gazing down at her, his eyes flashed with questions. "Something is troubling ye."

"I've never been able to hide my emotions." As she spoke the words, they sounded like a confession. She glanced away, searching for words that could convey the depth of her feelings. She had shared his bed. They had shared desire and passion and pleasure.

If only the pleasure of his touch could be enough.

Deep inside, she knew passion without love would never satisfy the yearning deep within her soul. If only her heart were not so very fragile. Pity she could not build a wall around that most vulnerable part of herself.

"Tell me what's troubling ye, Amelia."

She met his gaze. He studied her. His eyes crinkled at the corners as he appeared to search her face, seeking to ferret out the emotions she could not quite disguise. Perhaps it was time she trusted him with the truth. "I am a bit afraid, I suppose."

"Afraid?" He swept the pad of his thumb over the curve of her cheek, the softest of touches. "No one will hurt ye. Trust me. I will protect ye."

"I do trust . . ." The words would not come. He would do everything in his power to protect her life. She knew that now, beyond any doubt. Logan was courageous, a man who would not run from danger. He would honor his promise to watch over her.

But protecting her heart was another story, entirely.

I did not think he'd ever find it in his heart to care for another woman again. Mrs. Johnstone's words whispered in her thoughts. Certainly, he did care for her. But could that ever be enough when every kiss swept her closer to the point of no return? Would Logan ever be able to love her, just as she was falling quite hopelessly for him?

"Don't worry yer head over that weasel," he said. "If Mansfield thinks to intimidate ye again, I will set the bloke straight."

"It's not that." She allowed herself a little sigh. "Not entirely, at least."

"I do have a solution." Logan tipped up her chin with the tip of his finger. "I've been giving this a bit of thought. I know a way to ensure ye will never have a problem with Mansfield or Driscoll again."

She met his confident gaze. "What do you propose?"

His brow furrowed. Had he noticed how she'd worried her lower lip? "Ye think I mean to threaten the fools, do ye?"

"I certainly hope that is not the case." She glanced away. "But I have no idea what else you might be planning."

A smile played on his mouth. "What I have in mind does not involve violence. Or threats."

"What are you suggesting?"

"Ye require a space for yer library." He paused, as if searching for the right words. "And I have funds to invest. I will acquire the property."

Amelia felt her eyes go wide even as the question burst from her lips. "You will do *what?*"

"I'll buy the blasted building." Logan's eyes gleamed with what looked like triumph. "Driscoll made it clear he's eager to sell. I'll have my solicitor look into the matter in the morning."

Amelia reached for her drink and downed a gulp of sherry. "You believe *that* is what I want you to do?"

"It is an obvious solution to the problem. Is it not?"

She took another sip. "You do realize that what you are proposing would make you my landlord?"

A sly grin played on his features. "To the contrary, ye will never have to answer to a landlord again. I'll see to it that the building will be yers, Amelia."

Her hand suddenly trembling, she set the glass back upon the table. "I do not possess the funds to repay such a sum."

Slowly, he shook his head. "It goes without saying that I would expect nothing of the sort."

She struggled for words. "I cannot accept such a . . . bountiful gift."

"Amelia, I want to see ye happy." Gently, he caught her hands in his. "And this . . . this will make ye happy. Will it not?"

She swallowed against a sudden lump in her throat. How could he possibly think she would want him to acquire a building—of all things—for her benefit? Surely, he did not think she would allow him to provide the flat in which she lived, much less the place which housed her library. Such an act would have been exceedingly generous had they been husband and wife. But they were nothing of the sort. They'd shared a bed, but he'd spoken no words of commitment, no words of love. She did not expect charity from this man. And she certainly would not settle for being this—or any man's, for that matter—mistress.

"Make me happy?" As she repeated his words, a spark of indignation took hold, flaring into a flame. Her incredulous words poured out before she could hold them back. "Might I ask if you have suffered a blow to the head?"

The confident smile drained from his features. A blend of confusion and indignation flickered in his eyes in its place. "What in Hades do ye mean?"

"I am struggling to understand how you could believe such an extravagant gesture would make me happy. Surely you must know I have no intention of being treated like . . . like your paramour."

For a long moment, he regarded her silently. When he spoke, his voice sounded hard as flint. "Ye think that's my intent? To set ye up as my kept woman?"

"Quite honestly, I don't know what to think." She gulped a breath, even as her heart raced. "I would like to think your motives were pure. But I am entirely certain of what everyone would say. Including my friends."

"For the record, that was not my intent." The taut set of his jaw eased, just a bit. "I want to protect ye. I want to provide whatever it takes to make ye happy, Amelia. Yer brother is not here. So now, it's up to me to watch over ye, just as he would've wanted."

Tears she didn't dare shed prickled the backs of her eyes. "So, I am to believe this idea emerged from your determination to honor a vow?" She sighed. "That it's not even about me. And you."

"Of course it's about ye. And me." He coiled his long fingers around hers and pressed his lips softly to the back of her hand.

Amelia stared down at the glass, taking in the light reflecting off each delicate cut in the crystal. "I never expected any of this. Days ago, I was living my life, and you were living yours. Our existences are so very different. For years, I've sought calm and peace and stability. And now—I feel as though I am wading into the deep."

"Ye lived a life without passion." He framed her face in his hands. "Ye cannot lie to me. Ye want me, just as I want ye. I feel it in yer kiss. I feel it in yer touch."

"I do want you." Pulling away, she blinked back against the angry tears. "But this doesn't feel right. What happens when you feel you've repaid your debt to Paul? What happens then?"

"What we have doesn't have a blasted thing to do with any vow."

Not with any vow.

Not to Paul.

Not to me.

"What precisely is it that we do have, Logan?"

"It's damned good between us." He came to his feet, went to

the sideboard, and poured whisky into his glass. Slowly, he shook his head, leaving the tumbler as he turned back to her. "I know this, Amelia—I want ye more than I've ever wanted a woman in my bloody life."

She swallowed the last of the sherry in her glass. "And what if that isn't enough?" She met his eyes. "What if there is . . . a child?"

"We both know there are precautions." He raked a hand through his hair. "But in the event a babe is meant to be, I will not turn away from my commitment. Ye can count on that, lass."

"Commitment?" She fought against the urge to hurl the elegant brandy snifter against the fireplace if only to watch it shatter into bits. Just as her heart was shattering. "How very noble of you. And what if I need more . . . more than a reassurance that you will act out of honor? What if I need love?"

"Love?" An emotion she could not quite read flickered within the depths of his eyes. Turning his gaze from her, he swept a hand through his hair. "What in blazes could I possibly know about that sentimental rubbish?"

For a moment, she could only stare at him. He'd seemed to transform before her very eyes, the warmth in his expression stripped away.

"Scoff all you wish, but I know that love is not *sentimental rubbish*." In her mind's eye, she pictured her mother and father, and a fresh wave of emotion washed over her. Their bond had been deep and rich and enduring, unbroken until their last breaths. "I know love is quite real."

"So, is that what ye want from me, lass? My blasted heart? Or is it a band of gold on yer finger that ye're after?" Logan kept his voice low, his words under tight control. He marched to the window, pulling back a drape to stare into the night. "I cannot do anything about the heart, lass. But the ring can be arranged. That is, if ye truly wish to tie yerself to a man like me for the rest of yer life. What would ye say if I asked ye to marry me?"

She folded her arms and glared at his back. "An hour ago, I might have believed the answer to that question to be 'Yes.'"

He turned to her, the set of his features unreadable. If her words surprised him, he didn't betray it. "Did ye, now, Amelia?"

She steeled her spine even as she swallowed her hurt. "Fortunately, you have done an excellent job of ridding me of such foolish notions. Rest assured, I have no intention of becoming your—or any man's—mistress."

An icy hardness fell over his features. "In that case, ye can thank me for clearing yer head. Now ye can bide yer time and wait for some high-and-mighty bloke to whisk ye away to his country manor. A beauty like ye should have no trouble enticing some chinless fop to bend down on one knee."

A hot tear streamed down her cheek. It felt as though it had seared her flesh. "What has made you so cold?"

"A woman like ye doesn't want to settle for a man who earned his fortune rather than inheriting it. I learned that lesson a very long time ago, Amelia."

She gulped against the sudden burning in her throat. "I know that someone hurt you."

Understanding flared in his midnight dark eyes. "Ah, I see. My aunt has seen fit to inform ye about the lass who hardened my heart. She's warmed to ye. It makes sense she would want to warn ye."

Amelia shook her head. "It was nothing like that. Quite the opposite, really."

"Is that so?" He crossed the room, standing near enough to touch her, but he held his hands very still. "Ye're right that a woman hurt me. At the time, it seemed a betrayal. But now, I see she was right. I could not have given her what she wanted."

"But I am not her." She blinked hard, struggling to hold back rebellious tears.

"No, ye're not, lass." The faintest hint of a smile curved his mouth. "Ye cannot hide yer feelings. Ye're not one to make promises to one man while enticing another. The lass I was going to marry found herself a more prosperous match. She returned my ring via a blasted courier. She did not even have enough regard to tell me to my face."

The lingering pain in his eyes tore at Amelia's heart. "I am so sorry that happened to you."

He shrugged. "Looking back, she did me a favor. A cruel turn of fate often turns out for the best." He grazed his fingers over her cheek, brushing away a teardrop. "Ye're nothing like her, Amelia. Yer heart is kind. But ye don't know how to trust a man . . . a man like me who puts no stock in the stuff of myths and lonely poets and blasted fairy tales."

With that, he turned and went to the door The stout panel closed softly behind him, leaving Amelia alone with her thoughts and her bitter tears.

Chapter Twenty-Seven

*P*ROMISES. *VOWS. RINGS.*

Ugly memories of the night before played in Amelia's thoughts. Even as the barbed words she and Logan had hurled at each other seemed to echo in her ears, she forced herself to carry on with the work at hand. Mrs. Johnstone and Mrs. Langford had insisted on joining her at the library, and with their eager assistance, they had made short work of cleaning what remained of the vandal's dismal handiwork. The enjoyable tasks and the women's light banter had served as merciful distractions from the dull throbbing in her chest. In the company of the women who'd become newfound friends, she had better things to do than to mope about like a lovesick maiden.

Lovesick. The very idea of it was ridiculous. She'd taken a chance. She had never expected permanence. From the start, she'd known better than to risk her heart, much less on a rogue like Logan MacLain. Sharing his bed and his passion and his tenderness had been a sweet folly. Nothing more. Pity that for a time, she would pay a heavy price until her heart fully healed.

Someday, she might happen upon a lover who was true, a man who wanted her to the depths of his heart and soul.

Logan was not that man.

His kiss was so very delicious. So very tempting.

If only it was enough.

He had not lied to her. Truth be told, Logan had been honest from the first. He had crashed into her life in the name of honoring a vow.

He was undeniably handsome. Undeniably charming. Undeniably tender. Logan desired her touch. Her kiss. And when they'd made love, his every caress held passion and heat and delicious delight.

But he had walled off his heart.

Logan was not willing to give her the thing she craved most of all.

He would not offer his love.

Perhaps he'd believed she was like him. Did he think she was capable of keeping her own heart so well guarded, even while she warmed his bed and savored the pleasures of his touch?

No, she would not settle for less than love.

"In all my years, I cannot recall a spring so cold and damp," Mrs. Langford said as she swept a broom along a low shelf near Amelia's legs, pulling her from her thoughts. Setting the tool aside, she rubbed her arms as if to ward off a chill.

"It is rather cool and gloomy today, isn't it?" Just like her mood. "You're welcome to borrow my cardigan jacket. It's quite warm."

"I'll not take the clothes off yer back and have ye come down with a chill." Mrs. Langford flashed a cheeky grin. "I'm going to take a bit of time to warm these old bones by the fire and finish my tea. And if Elsie thinks I'm lazing about, she can jolly well—"

"I could do with another cup myself. I do think I'll brew another pot," Mrs. Johnstone cut in with a smile. Crossing the room to head to the stove in the back room, she stumbled over the edge of a small, braided carpet. "Good heavens, I nearly took a tumble." She kicked the offending rug out of her way. "The floorboard's come loose. Amelia, do you have something we can use to tap the nail back in?"

"Of course." Amelia went to the back room to fetch a small hammer, then began to slip the board into place.

"No, Amelia. Don't move it." Mrs. Johnstone leaned closer to examine the plank. "There . . . do ye see it? Something's here, under the floor." Sweeping her skirts to the side, she crouched low and jostled the board loose. "Polly, please bring the lamp here."

While Mrs. Langford held the lamp over the spot in the floor where the plank had been, Amelia peered into the hollow. A plain cotton bag not much larger than Amelia's hand lay between the joists. Crude, black stitches closed the pouch at one end. Mrs. Johnstone reached down to take hold of it.

"Do be careful," Amelia urged. "There's no telling what could be in there."

"I so enjoy a hunt for hidden treasure." A touch of excitement colored Mrs. Langford's voice.

Mrs. Johnstone slid her an incredulous glance. "When in blazes have you ever hunted for treasure?"

"I haven't," Mrs. Langford said, unflaggingly cheerful. "Until now."

As Mrs. Johnstone gingerly retrieved the object from its hiding place, her mouth thinned. "Polly, close the curtains."

After the windows were secured, Mrs. Johnstone yanked apart the stitches that held the sack closed. Lamplight glimmered against what had once been a gilded frame surrounding a crudely painted image of a garden gate.

"Well, well, what do we have here?" Mrs. Johnstone examined the painting rendered in unskilled strokes on canvas. "Do you recognize this?"

Amelia studied the landscape which seemed a poorly done imitation of Monet's technique. "My brother dabbled in oils. But I do not believe this is his work."

"It may be valuable," Mrs. Langford said hopefully.

"That's rather unlikely," Amelia said. "Why, I don't even see an artist's signature."

Suddenly, Helen Tanner's words came back to her in a rush.

He entrusted the treasure to you.

Tingles crept along Amelia's nape. Surely this crudely

wrought painting in a battered frame was not the bribe Hawk had offered in exchange for his silence.

Unless . . .

Unless the painting was merely a ruse.

Dragging in a breath to steady her racing pulse, she turned the frame to take a look at the back. "Mrs. Langford, please hold the lamp closer."

Under the light, she studied the frame, then the canvas. Had this image been painted over an artist's original?

She sighed. Her expertise in such matters was minimal. But she had no doubt that Paul would've known what to do. He'd have known how to hide a valuable work.

"I don't know what we're looking at. Or for," she admitted. "I don't know if this work has any true value."

"Why would someone place it here, beneath the floor?" Mrs. Langford asked, shifting to hold the lamp at a different angle.

With the sudden tilt of the light's rays, Amelia's gaze was drawn to a scarcely noticeable flaw. The painting rested unevenly against the worn edges of the frame. How very peculiar.

Was something else there, behind the canvas?

Slowly, hesitantly, she pried an edge of the painting from the wood.

The heavy canvas frayed, revealing another layer beneath it.

Her suspicion was correct.

Another layer of canvas lay within the frame. This piece bore no sign of color. Perhaps it was merely a backing for the landscape.

Still, she had to be sure.

Carefully, she peeled away the canvas.

Good heavens.

A folded piece of parchment lay behind the landscape. Carefully, Amelia unfolded the square.

An artist had rendered an intriguing sketch of a very beautiful woman. Amelia lifted it to the light. Each stroke of its creator's pencil was sure and brilliant. An intricately drawn jewel at the beauty's throat actually appeared to twinkle.

She spotted a signature in the lower left corner.

Antonio Caravelli.

And beneath the name, a date. *1575.*

Amelia's pulse raced. Her brother had spoken of the Renaissance artist with great enthusiasm. He'd been convinced that Caravelli's genius would finally be recognized. Not long before he died, Paul had collaborated with an anonymous collector to assemble a gallery show of the artist's finest works.

Including this one.

Juliet's Diamond.

Amelia's mind raced. *The treasure.* Was *this* the jewel the intruder had hunted? The diamond he'd would have killed to claim?

Mrs. Johnstone gasped. "Are my eyes deceiving me, or is this scrap of paper more than three centuries old?"

The floor seemed to shift beneath her feet. Amelia drew in rapid breaths to steady herself. "I do believe that is the case."

Mrs. Langford leaned closer, taking a better look. "That pretty little drawing must be worth a fortune."

Mrs. Johnstone's brow furrowed. "Ye may be right."

A sudden pounding on the door jolted all three women in unison. Irritation replaced Amelia's sense of alarm as she peeked through a side window. "Oh, dear, not *him.*"

"Who is it, dear?" Mrs. Langford asked in a low voice.

"Mr. Driscoll," Amelia said as she tucked their discovery back into the bag. "The owner of this building."

"I know you are in there, Mrs. Stewart," he called through the door. "I must speak with you. It is a matter of great importance."

"I will be right there," Amelia replied, stashing the pouch out of sight in the cabinet drawer.

"The bloke has impeccable timing." Mrs. Johnstone calmly retrieved the reticule she'd placed on a high shelf and took hold of her double-shot pistol by its pearl-handled grips. "It's quite lovely, isn't it?" Quietly confident, she concealed the weapon within the folds of her skirt.

As Amelia slid the floorboard and rug back into place, Mr. Driscoll pounded on the wood with renewed vigor.

"I demand you open this door. I am here to inspect my property," he bellowed.

Satisfied their find was hidden from the dolt's view, Amelia motioned to Mrs. Langford to allow him entry.

"There, there, no need to be so impatient." Mrs. Langford met the man's scowl with a plastered-on smile.

His bushy brows knit into one dark slash. "I have a right to enter my own building. Who in thunder are you?"

Amelia marched up to him. "I'll ask you not to speak to my guests in such an impolite manner. What brings you here today?"

"I believe you already know the answer to your question."

"Do enlighten me, Mr. Driscoll."

His eyes hardened. "I understand you were not willing to consider Mr. Mansfield's generous offer. You will find he is not inclined to be as patient as I am."

Amelia held her ground. "Your patience is not my concern."

His gaze lit upon the wrinkled carpet. "What've your hooligans done to my floor?"

"Recently, I have noticed that the board has worked loose. I had not wished to trouble you with the matter, but perhaps now that you're aware of it, you will send someone to make the necessary repair."

"I will do no such thing." His scowl intensifying, he marched to the spot on the floor, kicked the rug aside, and lifted a corner of the unmoored plank. "When you leave, I will expect compensation for the damage. How in thunder did you—"

The tap of a walking stick against the floor cut through the landlord's tirade.

Good heavens, not now. Amelia whirled around.

Cecil Mansfield strolled toward them. *Blast it. Why had the infernal man returned?*

A wiry, sharp-featured man in a well-tailored suit followed Mansfield into the room. Had he brought his solicitor to pressure her to accept his offer?

Mansfield coolly took in the scene. "In view of this unsightly damage, perhaps I shall have to adjust my offer."

"I was not expecting you." Appearing ill at ease, Mr. Driscoll set the board back in its place. "I will see to the repair."

"Obviously." Mansfield's mouth shifted into a serpent's smile. "It appears it is rather fortunate for me that you had not anticipated my arrival."

"Pay no mind to this," Driscoll said, seeming to picture the sum he'd counted on from his deal with Mansfield evaporate into thin air. "I'll fix up the place. You'll see—"

"Yes," Mansfield said, leaning heavily on the silver cane. His attention fixed on the crumpled rug. "I can see what has happened here. It's quite clear, isn't it, Mr. Smith?"

"Without a doubt," the wiry man replied.

"I will see Mrs. Stewart and her companions on the street before the ruffians who frequent this place do more damage," Driscoll went on.

"Ruffians, eh?" Mansfield toyed with his walking stick.

Driscoll offered a solemn nod. "Unsavory sorts of the worst—"

A wolf's smile curved Mansfield's mouth. Light flashed against the metal cane. Without warning, he whipped the rod around in a brutal arc.

The walking stick crashed into Mr. Driscoll's temple.

He sank to the floor. Eyes wide and uncomprehending, his mouth moved weakly. "Help me," he choked out.

Amelia's scream echoed in her ears as Mansfield met the man's helpless plea with another ruthless blow. This time, Driscoll's eyes went shut.

Betraying no sign of emotion, Mansfield wiped the walking stick against the landlord's coat and began to search the pockets of the unconscious man's jacket. "This one's always so bloody nervous. Makes me wonder what the fool has been hiding from me. Wouldn't you agree, Mr. Smith?"

"Indeed." The tall, lean man nodded as he eyed Driscoll with distaste. Stepping past the unconscious man, he turned his attention to Amelia. "It's high time we had a talk." His tone was as coolly threatening as the dagger in his hand.

Instinctive fear surged through her. She could not surrender to it. She had to stay calm. There was no choice.

Out of the corner of her eye, she saw Mrs. Johnstone raise her weapon. Amelia's pulse thundered in her ears. She needed to keep the men's focus on her.

"Don't . . . do not come any closer," she said, deliberately infusing her words with a pleading tone.

Smith continued his advance. The look in his eyes told her he enjoyed the sight of her fear. "You'll do what we tell—"

Mrs. Johnstone squeezed the trigger.

The bullet slammed into Mr. Smith.

He froze in mid-stride. For a moment, it seemed he did not comprehend what had taken place. He stared blankly at the ugly red stain spreading over the formerly pristine wool of his coat, a hand's breadth beneath his right shoulder.

"Bugger it," he murmured. Slowly, he turned to Mrs. Johnstone. He took a lumbering step toward her. "You've only one shot. You think that will stop me?"

"Sadly—for ye, that is—ye're mistaken." Mrs. Johnstone said calmly, even as her gaze darted from Mr. Smith and Mansfield, who was at that moment still rummaging through the unfortunate landlord's inside pockets. "If ye stay quite still, perhaps I won't have to pull this trigger again."

Smith took another step toward her, then another. "I'll make you pay—"

Another shot roared in Amelia's ears. She felt herself gasp as Smith clutched his chest. The knife he'd brandished in his now-limp hand clattered to the floor.

Knees buckling, he collapsed. Staring at the ceiling, he murmured what sounded like a plea for help. And then, he went silent, his shark-like eyes still open, yet now without sight. Without life.

"That was rather unwise," Mansfield said as he rose to his full height. Lightly tapping his walking stick against his palm, he regarded Mrs. Johnstone with an icy gaze. "Using both of your bullets on my associate . . . I do appreciate that you did not save one for me."

"Amelia, leave now," Mrs. Johnstone said, her voice steady with courage.

Mansfield shrugged. "She has no place to go. No place where I won't find her."

Tap. Tap. Tap. The rhythm of the walking stick against the wood punctuated his every step. "I must say, I'm rather impressed with you," he said, coming closer to Mrs. Johnstone with each movement. "I'd wager that if you had another weapon, you would have retrieved it by now."

"Run, Amelia," Mrs. Johnstone said, low and steady. "Leave!"

"Your concern for your friend is admirable." Mansfield regarded Mrs. Johnstone with an icy contempt that contradicted his words. "But sadly misplaced."

Quick as a snake, he whipped around, cane in hand. The stick crashed into Mrs. Johnstone's head with a sickening thud. A heartbeat later, her eyes went wide, dazed with pain.

The gun tumbled to the floor.

Dear God! No!

"Amelia," Mrs. Johnstone murmured. Her lids fluttered, not quite shut, while her knees buckled.

As she sank to the floor, Mansfield wiped a red streak from the walking stick.

Mrs. Johnstone's blood.

Terrible understanding pulsed through Amelia. She felt Mansfield's piercing stare cut through her as she darted to Mrs. Johnstone's side. Seeing the rise and fall of the woman's chest, relief coursed through her. Mrs. Johnstone still had breath. She was still alive.

"That was a very foolish thing to do." Icy rage simmered in Mansfield's gaze. He pulled Mrs. Langford to him, holding her in an iron grip, a pistol pressed to her jaw. "I would suggest you do not anger me. You will not like the result."

"Run. Now, Amelia." Mrs. Langford's words were a mere whisper. "Please."

"Don't hurt her," she pleaded.

"Do as I say, and no more blood will need to be shed." Mansfield's cruel eyes contradicted his words.

"Don't listen . . . to the bastard," Mrs. Langford choked out, even as he dug the barrel into the tender flesh beneath her chin. "Run!"

Chapter Twenty-Eight

L OGAN HUDDLED AROUND a table in the tavern office with Murray, mapping out strategies to protect Amelia from further threats. The assailant who'd come after him with a knife was behind bars, but he'd refused to cooperate with the investigators. The bastard made no secret that he would take whatever fate awaited him at a judge's hands over the retribution Hawk would mete out if he talked. At this point, the only thing Logan could be sure of was that the man had not acted on his own. Someone had sent the oaf on his foul task, someone who wanted to see Logan dead and Amelia at their mercy.

"Ye've been making yer way around town," he said as Finn joined them. "Have ye turned up anything on the bastard who calls himself Hawk?"

"He might as well be a phantom." Finn shoved a hand through his hair. "No one will speak of him. But I did hear something ye're not going to like."

"And what might that be?"

"There's talk of a smug bloke looking to buy the building where Amelia has her library."

"So I've heard," Logan said. "An art dealer named Mansfield."

Finn rocked back in his chair and stretched out his legs. "That's not all he deals in."

Murray leaned closer. "What are ye saying?"

"The cur pretends he's a bloody aristocrat, but he's worse

than a common thief," Finn said. "For years, Mansfield has honed his talent for deceit. He peddles forgeries to gullible collectors. But he's moved on to more lucrative and violent ventures. Word on the street is that he deals in stolen gems, jewels taken from the people he's swindled."

A dire suspicion kindled in Logan's brain. "Stolen gems, eh?"

"It's said he leads a gang of thieves. In bloody Paris, if ye can believe it," Finn went on. "Diamonds, rubies, a king's ransom in gems has been taken."

An unseen fist plowed into Logan's gut. Paul's mistress had claimed a robbery had gone wrong. She'd spoken of a murdered man. And a bribe intended to buy Paul's silence.

A king's ransom in gems.

The intruder in Amelia's library had been hunting a diamond, a stone he thought she possessed.

Bloody hell.

The door creaked open. Tilly stood in the entryway, her features pale and drawn. "I don't mean to interrupt ye, but I'm afraid this cannot wait."

The worry on the barmaid's features drove the fist deeper into his stomach. "What is it, Tilly?"

"I left the boarding house early today. Mrs. Langford had asked if I might stop by the library on my way to the pub to lend a hand. But when I arrived, the door would not open. I knocked, but no one answered. Then, I heard Amelia's voice. And a cry."

Good God.

A fear unlike any Logan had ever felt coursed through him.

Amelia was in danger.

He couldn't lose her.

When he bolted to the door, Finn followed close behind.

"Stay here with Tilly," he called back to Murray.

Lord, let me get to Amelia in time.

FIGHTING TERROR THAT threatened to paralyze her, Amelia met Cecil Mansfield's cold gaze. The bastard pressed his pistol to Mrs. Langford's jaw, relishing their fear. One wrong move, and the dear woman would die.

A terrible understanding filled her. "You're the one they call Hawk."

"A fitting name, indeed." Icy pride glimmered in his eyes. "Now, give me what I want, and that will be the end of it."

A chill grazed Amelia's nape. *The end of me.*

"I've no patience for further delays," he went on. "I know the Caravelli sketch is here. If you lie to me, I will kill the lot of you and tear this place apart until I find it."

You will kill us in any case. The predatory glint in his gaze betrayed the truth. He had no intention of letting them live. Her mind raced. If she could get to her gun, she could disable the cur.

But first, she would have to convince him to release his hostage.

"I will give you the drawing," she choked out the words. "But only after you've let her go."

"Setting terms? Rather bold, I'd say." He eyed her with contempt. "I must say, you've shown more backbone than your brother did."

Bastard. Amelia bit back the ugly retort. She couldn't take the bait. She would not give him an excuse to hurt Mrs. Langford. "You're the one—the one who murdered Paul."

"I did not send him to his grave. But I am the one who ordered him dead. He knew too much. And the fool had a conscience. Quite a troublesome combination."

Amelia's knees threatened to go weak. "And Helen . . . you had her killed?"

"I took care of that troublesome loose end with my own hands." Mansfield's half-smile chilled her blood. "I could have eliminated her some time ago, but I suspected she could lead me to the Caravelli sketch. Mr. Smith gained her trust. Rather ironic, really. The fortune teller could not foresee that her benefactor meant only to betray her."

The Lovers. Suddenly, the tarot card made sense. Amelia's pulse thundered in her ears. "You had no reason to kill her."

"She left me no choice. I couldn't chance her carrying tales."

Amelia gulped a breath, bracing herself against the horror of Mansfield's cold-blooded confession. But she could not give in to her shock and her fear. "If I give you the drawing, how can I be certain we will not share her fate?"

"Life offers no guarantees," he said. "But if you make me wait much longer, I will put a bullet in this woman's brain. Won't that be a pretty sight?"

Amelia's stomach knotted. "Very well," she said. "But please, lower the gun."

"Get me the bloody sketch."

"I'll give you the drawing. It's here." She went to the cabinet, angling her body to conceal her actions. "I have it . . . it's in here." Slowly, she opened the drawer. Her derringer lay beneath the pouch that contained the sketch. Her heart hammered wildly. She was a good shot, but with Mrs. Langford in such a vulnerable position, she could not take the chance. Not yet. Not until she'd convinced him to free her.

Careful to conceal her weapon with the pouch, she lifted both from the drawer. With one subtle motion, she slipped the small gun inside the pocket of her jacket.

Holding the bag close to cover any telltale lump in the coat, she turned back to him.

"Let her go. And it will be yours."

"Show me the blasted thing. Before I lose patience." He ground out the words.

Summoning every ounce of courage she possessed, she edged toward the fireplace. "I propose a bargain."

"Bargain?" Mansfield's voice was raw with scorn. "The time for that has passed."

"A simple negotiation." She stood close by the hearth now, near enough to feel the heat of the crackling flames. "Something you need, in exchange for something I need."

"What in hell's name would that be?"

"Release Mrs. Langford. Empty the chambers of your weapon. Then, and only then, will I give you the sketch."

"And if I refuse?"

"If you will not honor this simple request, I'll know your intentions. In that case, there will be nothing to lose if I toss this drawing—I presume you know its worth—into the fire."

"You are playing a risky game." His voice was low, his anger tightly controlled.

"Am I, now?" She fought to hold her voice steady. "The way I see it, the moment I give you what you want, you will have no reason to let us live. But if you let her go, we may be able to come to an agreement."

He regarded her with cold, impassive eyes. "I was right. You do have far more backbone than Paul ever did."

She swallowed hard against a sudden surge of fury. He was trying to goad her. If she lost control of her emotions, he would win.

"Do you really think it wise to taunt me?" She dangled the parchment closer to the hearth. "We both know what will happen the moment these flames touch this old, dry paper."

He scowled. "Very well. We will play the game your way. For now."

He lowered his weapon and gave Mrs. Langford a vicious shove. Stumbling over her skirts, she rushed to Mrs. Johnstone's side and knelt beside her friend.

A silent prayer for strength whispered in Amelia's thoughts. Never had she imagined she would be forced into such a dangerous standoff.

Her heart raced, but she held her focus on Mansfield. "Remove the bullets. Toss the gun away. Now."

"I think not," Mansfield said with a chilling absence of emotion. "I've come up with a better plan."

A shiver washed over Amelia despite the heat of the fire. "Do as I say. Or I will destroy the sketch."

An ugly smile pulled his mouth taut. "Perhaps I should thank you. It occurs to me that if you destroy that little drawing, you will eliminate the evidence which ties me to several crimes."

"You're bluffing." Amelia met his cold-eyed smirk. "It is worth a fortune."

"In any venture, one must be prepared to make sacrifices." Mansfield raised the gun and leveled it at Amelia. "I have no intention of going to prison. Or worse."

Fear and shock crashed over her. Her desperate gambit had not succeeded.

And now, the women would join her in paying the horrible price.

A sudden sound—a violent splintering of wood—tore Amelia from her terror. *My God, what was happening?*

The door crashed open.

Mansfield whipped around. He leveled his weapon at the man who'd charged through the door.

At Logan.

"No!" Amelia screamed.

Desperation surged through her. No time to think. No time to reason. Driven by instinctive fury, she grabbed her gun. Took aim. Pulled the trigger.

Too late. As she shuddered against the gun's recoil, Mansfield's shot roared against her ears.

Logan jerked against the violent impact. He staggered back. A look of shock filled his eyes. Amelia heard herself cry out. It felt as though she were a witness to her own terror.

The pain of Mansfield's fingers digging into her arm shattered her horrified daze. "You little witch." Gritting out the words between his teeth, he shoved her to the floor.

She landed hard on the wood planks. Shockwaves rippled through her body, even as her gaze darted to Logan, desperate to reassure herself that he'd survived.

Mansfield stood over her, a crimson stain spreading over his upper chest. He stared down at her, his actions deliberate. Cruel. His finger rested on the trigger of the gun aimed at her heart.

Her pulse pounding wildly, she searched for Logan. He was on his feet. *Still alive. Thank heaven!* Mansfield's shot had not taken him down. If she was going to die, she would take comfort in this final image of him.

But now, she had hope.

His hand closed around the revolver holstered at his hip. Cold fury flashed in his gaze.

He drew. With a sure aim, he fired.

Mansfield's body shuddered violently. His gaze shot to Logan. Fixed on the gun he held in a steady grip.

Struggling to stand, Mansfield took a step back. Then another. He stared wild-eyed at Logan. The man he'd thought he had killed was still very much alive. And still very dangerous.

"Bloody hell." The cur's voice was like a low growl.

"Throw down your weapon." Logan's command was softly spoken but clad in iron.

His features contorted in pain, Mansfield dropped his gaze to the crimson stain seeping onto his coat. He lifted his pistol in quivering hands. "You will not win, MacLain."

"Put down the gun," Logan commanded. "You don't have to die. Not this way."

Mansfield slowly shook his head. He leveled his weapon at Logan. "I will destroy—"

Logan fired.

His aim was true.

Mansfield clutched at his chest, his expression strangely calm. And then, his gaze went blank as his mouth moved in a soundless cry.

The man who'd ordered Paul's murder crumpled to the floor, lifeless as a discarded puppet.

Kicking Mansfield's weapon aside, Logan cut a straight path to Amelia. He cupped her cheeks between his hands and gazed down at her. He searched her face. "Did the bastard hurt you, love?"

"No." Tears streamed down her cheeks.

"Thank God." His voice sounded rough, tinged with feelings he did not disguise. "Ah, *mo chridhe*."

My heart.

Amelia rose on her toes to kiss him, a fleeting brush of her lips against his. If only she could savor this moment. But the sight of blood slowly spreading over his upper arm was a far more pressing matter. "You need a doctor."

Logan glanced at the spread of blood over his upper arm. "In due time," he agreed. "Believe me, I'll survive this. I've had far worse."

"I tried to stop him," she murmured.

"Ye threw off his aim." He brushed a kiss to her forehead. "Ye saved my life, love."

"Thank God," she whispered, a simple prayer of the heart.

Amelia glanced toward Mrs. Langford. The sight of the old woman on the floor cradling Mrs. Johnstone's head tore at Amelia's heart.

The thud of footsteps outside the entry drifted to her ears. Finn strode through what remained of the door, brandishing a long gun. "What in thunder—"

"Mrs. Johnstone—she needs help," Amelia cried out.

Finn cut a straight path to her side. Mrs. Johnstone's eyes fluttered open.

Groaning softly, she struggled to sit up as Logan rushed to kneel at his aunt's side. "Lay still," he urged.

"Do not worry yer head over me," she said, her voice surprisingly strong.

Amelia turned to Finn. "She's suffered a blow to the head."

"I'll fetch Doc Stevenson." Finn bolted to the door. "He'll know what to do."

Mrs. Johnstone set her gaze on Logan. "Ye killed the bastard?"

His expression was grim. "I had no choice."

"Ye saved the lass." Mrs. Johnstone reached out, pressing her hands over his. "I knew ye would."

"Thank God." Logan turned to Amelia, raw emotion darkening his irises to the color of midnight. "I made it in time."

Chapter Twenty-Nine

BY SUNSET, THE physician had tended Logan's wound and examined his aunt, even as she insisted they were making too much of a fuss. Despite her protests, Logan had seen the clear look of relief on her face after the physician pronounced her in good health. Following ample rest, she would soon return to her energetic self. After Doc Stevenson went on his way, Aunt Elsie lay on her brass bed, comfortably propped up with pillows, a novel in hand. He chuckled at her tone of aggravation as Mrs. Langford interrupted her reading as she doted over her old friend like a mother hen.

With Amelia by his side, Logan went to his study. She relaxed in a well-upholstered wing chair while he eased into the Orkney chair he'd acquired during his travels and stretched out his legs. The whisky in his tumbler took the edge off the throbbing in his arm. He was a damned lucky man. The bullet had caught flesh, not bone. The wound had been a small price to pay for Amelia's safety. God only knew he would have willingly taken a slug to the heart to protect her.

Allowing himself a moment of pure contemplation, he drank in Amelia's unpainted beauty. Despite the dull ache in his shoulder, he smiled to himself. Thank God he had women like Mrs. Langford and Aunt Elsie in his life. Good-hearted and courageous, they'd stepped in to help raise him after his own mum died far too young. And now, the valiant women, unwilling to surrender to a brutal bastard, had defended his sweet Amelia. They had resisted Mansfield and his hired thug, and in the process, they'd bought much needed time. Suspecting Mansfield would return to threaten Amelia, Logan had raced to the library like a madman. But without the women's efforts, he might have been too late.

Too late. The mere thought that he could have failed to protect Amelia seemed a bare-knuckled blow.

"Come, I've prepared a light supper," Mrs. Garrett said, her face worn with care. "Ye both need to eat."

In the dining room, he and Amelia dined in near silence. She'd been through so much. Her features were drawn, her reserved demeanor very much unlike her usually vibrant manner. At the moment, it seemed best to keep to his own thoughts. There would time later to discuss what had happened that night. And what he wanted to see happen in the future.

Shortly after they'd finished the last of their meal, Tim arrived from the tavern with a message from Finn, an uneasy look on his face. After reading the brief missive, Logan understood the younger man's misgivings. Blast it, the detective who'd taken charge of the investigation had requested a meeting with Amelia. What in Hades was Finn thinking, sending for her at this hour? And after the hellish day she'd had?

"Tell him the inspector will have to wait."

Tim shifted on his feet. "Finn said ye'd say that. He did not think that would be a wise move."

"And if I don't give a damn—"

"I'll go," Amelia spoke up, a steely tone to her words. "I need to I know whatever it is the detective has learned."

The courage in her eyes touched him. But he had to watch out for her. "It can wait until morning."

"I must disagree," she said. "I simply won't rest until I've heard the truth. All of it."

"Ye're sure?"

Her expression was weary. But determined. "I still have so

many questions. Perhaps tonight, I will get some answers."

"I'll stay with the ladies," Tim offered. "You've no worries. I've brought my pistol, and I'm a good shot."

"Good enough," he said, confident he could trust the barkeep's capable assistant.

Keeping Amelia's well-being in mind, Finn had wisely suggested that the detective meet with them away from the dismal setting of the jail. Inspector Herrin had agreed, and as Logan escorted Amelia into his office at the Rogue's Lair, they found the men engaged in an animated discussion. Their conversation came to an abrupt halt as they laid eyes on Amelia.

After informal greetings were exchanged, Logan quickly got to the point. "I understand ye have news on Mansfield."

Exuding nervous energy, Inspector Herrin paced the floor. "Cecil Mansfield deceived many in his path. His gallery served as a front for his criminal activities. We have evidence he ordered the killing of Jack Turner, the man who attacked you, as well as several other murders."

As the detective laid out his findings, Logan observed Amelia as she took it all in. Her brother had crossed paths with an evil man whose greed had run unchecked until Logan sent him to hell.

"Inspector, it's logical to conclude that Mansfield had Turner killed after he was in police custody to prevent him from telling what he knew." Amelia was direct. "But the intruder seemed desperate, perhaps even frightened, when he accosted me in the library. Can you explain why he was in such a state?"

"As we understand it, Jack Turner was not acting on Mansfield's orders that night." Inspector Herrin's expression was solemn. "This will be painful for you to hear, but you deserve the truth. Your brother became entangled in Mansfield's criminal dealings. As a result, Turner and another ruffian were sent to silence him. They were also ordered to retrieve the art Mansfield had offered as a bribe." The detective paused, rubbing the back of his neck as if to ease a sudden ache. "When they failed to recover the drawing, Mansfield suspected a double-cross. Turner's accomplice met a rather ugly fate. When he realized he was next, Turner became desperate to find the sketch. And then, he came after you."

Her complexion paled. Logan restrained the urge to mutter an epithet. Damn the brutes who'd dragged her through this ordeal.

Composing her features, Amelia spoke in a quiet, calm voice. "But why did Mansfield wait until after my brother's death to come after the drawing?"

"He prided himself on his cunning and stealth. Often, his victims weren't even aware they'd been robbed. When the Paris burglary led to murder, he blamed Turner and his two accomplices. One of them was stabbed to death the night before Turner came after you."

Logan mulled the detective's words. "And the other accomplice killed Turner to ensure he wouldn't talk."

Herrin nodded. "Frank Fincham had worked as a guard at the jail and killed Turner in his cell. Now the rotter won't stop running his mouth. He thinks incriminating a dead man in his crimes will save him from the hangman."

"He'll be joining Mansfield in hell soon enough," Logan said coolly.

"Indeed," the detective agreed.

Finn turned to Amelia. "Do ye know a man who goes by the name of John Niles?"

Even more color drained from her face. "He was one of my brother's associates."

"The name is an alias. He was born John Stanton. The man's an art thief wanted in London and Dublin for his crimes. He was working with Mansfield to retrieve the Caravelli sketch," the detective explained. "He knew your brother had hidden the drawing. They searched his residence, then went after Miss Talbot with no success. So they concluded he had hidden it in either your library or your flat."

Amelia went to the window and pulled back the curtain, taking in the cool night air. Her shoulders were taut with tension. "Are there others . . . who might come after me?"

Inspector Herrin did not hesitate with his response. "At this time, we believe Mansfield's conspirators are dead or behind bars. But you would be wise not to let down your guard. Not yet."

"Not to worry." Logan joined her by the window, clasping her hand within his. "Yer brother trusted me to keep ye safe. Ye're mine to watch over. As long as it takes."

SEATED ON THE garden terrace beneath the light of the full moon, Amelia studied Logan behind the veil of her lashes. His words played in her thoughts. Again and again.

Mine to watch over . . .

In Logan's eyes, he was her protector. He would defend her, whatever the cost.

Pity she wanted more.

Ever so much more.

She should have known better than to heed her foolish heart. Now she'd fallen for a rogue, a charming, handsome man who could stir her hunger with his tenderness.

With his desire.

She had understood the risk she was taking when she kissed him that very first time. Logan knew how to be a lover. Knew how to be a protector who would do whatever it took to keep her safe.

If only she'd listened to the instinct deep within, warning her against her heart's desire. If only she had not fallen in love with him. Logan had given her his passion. His courage. He'd adored her body with a tenderness she had never before imagined.

And still, he spoke of watching over her, as if his debt to her brother would never be paid.

Yer brother trusted me to keep ye safe.

Did he see himself as a guardian, willing to sacrifice even his own life to fulfill his obligation?

Seated in a wicker chair, he stretched out his long legs. "This has taken a toll on ye. We should've waited until the morning to meet with the detective."

"No," she countered softly. "It's a relief to have it out of the way. To know the truth . . . at least in part."

"Ye've nothing to concern yerself about, Amelia. I meant what I said. I intend to watch over ye."

She took a sip of wine from a cut crystal glass. "I don't believe that will be necessary."

He shook his head. "I will not take any chances with yer safety."

"The Caravelli sketch is now out of my possession. Before long, it will be returned to France, to its rightful owner. I am confident the threat has passed."

"Ye cannot take any chances."

Amelia pushed her back against the chair, steeling herself against her doubts. She couldn't go on like this. She needed more than a lover. More than a bodyguard.

She couldn't stay here for much longer. Heaven knew she wanted Logan more with every passing moment. With every breath, she craved a place in his heart.

No, she had to leave. She had to protect herself. The pain of leaving him behind would cut to the bone. But now, she could endure it. It wouldn't be long before she'd be at the point of no return. She would be hopelessly in love. And then, the misery when they went their separate ways would be far too much to bear.

"I have an aunt in America, my mum's sister. She's a widow. Quite well off, with a lovely, rambling home. When Paul died, she invited me to come to live with her." The words tasted bitter on her tongue. "Now, doing so might be for the best."

"America." His brow furrowed, as if he weren't convinced he'd heard correctly.

"I have not seen Aunt Jane in more than a year. This seems an opportune time."

Lines creased on his forehead. "And what of yer library?"

"I cannot go back there and simply carry on as if nothing happened. I must start over."

Slowly, he shook his head. "I cannot let ye do that, Amelia. The risk is too high."

"I do not require your approval." Softening her tone, she forced herself to meet his eyes.

A muscle in his jaw tensed. "I cannot stand by and see ye take such a chance."

If his eyes had not betrayed a true sense of shock, his forceful words might've left her indignant. After all, it was not as if they had spoken any vows. Or made any promises.

They had never even uttered a single syllable of commitment.

Not a single word of love.

But she supposed he had a right to be surprised. Days earlier, she could not have anticipated she'd consider leaving the city that had long been her home. Let alone cross an ocean in the hopes of starting again. She might not find love in America.

But at least, she could still harbor that hope.

Amazing how very much could change in such a short time.

She reached out, drawing the tips of her fingers along the hard edge of his jaw. "You've settled your debt, Logan. You've protected me. Now, you will be able to return to your life."

"And ye to yers, eh?"

She fought back tears. "Everything I thought I wanted in my life—it is no longer enough. I need to begin anew."

He stilled, regarding her as if he'd discovered something quite new and rather fascinating. "What is it that ye do want, Amelia?" His question was raw, rough-edged with emotion.

"I'm not quite sure," she said truthfully. "I only know that what I have—what I have with you—isn't enough."

He stared down at his hands. "The two of us . . . we are not so different, Amelia."

"I beg to disagree, Mr. MacLain."

"Mr. MacLain?" His brows quirked. "Rather formal coming from the lips of a woman who's warmed my bed."

She lifted a brow. "A gentleman would not speak of such things."

"Ye knew I was no proper gentleman from the first time I laid eyes on ye."

"Quite true."

"And yet, ye wanted me." His husky voice seemed a caress. "From the first time I kissed ye. Just as I wanted ye."

She laced her fingers together, determined to project a sense of calm she did not feel. "Danger has a way of heightening passion, or so I've been told."

His eyes darkened with emotion. "So ye've been told, eh?"

"Perhaps I read that . . . somewhere."

His tempting mouth curved at one corner, as if he was not quite sure what to make of her. "Or deep inside, ye know the truth—yer body and yer heart can recognize a man who wants ye more than the air he breathes, even if that oh-so-practical head of yers cannot."

For a heartbeat, perhaps two, Amelia could only look at him. He'd left her momentarily speechless.

Wants ye more than the air he breathes.

"And if wanting isn't enough? If I need more . . . if I need love?" The words tumbled out in a rush.

"Then, lass, ye'll have to make a choice."

Without another word, he rose and crossed the room. The door to the terrace swung shut behind him.

He'd left her. Just as he had walked away that night in his study.

Tears she had willed herself not to shed burned her throat.

Ah, her heart had been stubborn. So wistful. And so foolish. But now she knew the truth. She knew better.

She would make a new life for herself. And in time, Logan MacLain would be nothing more than a memory. A tempting, infuriating, confounding memory at that.

Chapter Thirty

TWO MISERABLE WEEKS passed before Logan received the message he'd dreaded, the message he'd known would come. A blasted fortnight wasted in a haze of drink and denial, and all the while, he'd struggled to convince himself that he had not made the biggest mistake of his life.

Amelia had not wanted riches. Nor jewels.

She'd wanted the one thing he did not think he could give.

Blasted fool that he was, he'd walked away. He'd turned his back and closed the door behind him.

She'd bared her soul to him. And like a harebrained dolt, he'd left her there, her lower lip quivering as she valiantly fought back tears she was too proud to shed.

All because he couldn't find the courage to speak the words she needed to hear.

Even though he knew the truth. He'd thought he could wall off his heart. But it was too damned late. He loved Amelia. More than he'd ever loved anything or anyone in his life.

And now, he'd lost her.

Within hours, she would be on a steamship heading away from England. Away from him.

But far more than an ocean would keep them apart. He had hurt her. At the moment when he'd last looked into her eyes, she had struggled not to weep. Now, she'd never forgive him. Not that he could blame her. Bloody hell, he couldn't even forgive himself.

Why hadn't he spoken the words she'd longed to hear? Why hadn't he told her the truth?

When the courier arrived not long after dawn, Finn's hastily scrawled message had seemed a blow to the gut. Logan had read the note not once, but twice, then crushed the paper into a ball and tossed it into the fireplace. At this point, it didn't matter. Amelia would depart London that day. Soon, he'd be little more than a memory to her, the dolt who'd let her slip through his fingers.

So why in Hades had he come to the building where Amelia had housed her cherished library, the very place he expected to find her?

He wanted to offer a proper farewell. Or so he tried to convince himself. She deserved that, and so much more.

But that wasn't the half of it. He wanted to see her again.

No, not wanted. Needed.

If only to burn the image of her coral-rose smile and sapphire eyes into his memory.

Now, standing before the place where he'd first laid eyes on Amelia, he saw Finn emerge from the building, hauling a large steamer trunk down the steps. Spotting Logan, Finn threw him a scowl.

"Logan MacLain, I'd always known ye were a stubborn arse. But I had never taken ye for a blasted fool."

"Fool, is it?" Logan folded his arms and returned Finn's glower. "The way I see it, ye're the one breaking yer back."

Finn made it to the pavement and deposited the trunk in his spacious coach. "Funny that you mention it—my back, that is." He stood away from the carriage and rubbed his sides for effect. "It would be better for all of us if ye convinced Amelia to stay. My sore muscles would be most grateful."

"Ah, it's good for ye to put them to use for something other than chasing skirts." A peculiar lump settled in Logan's gut. "Where is she?"

"She's gone off with Mrs. Langford for something or other she needs for the voyage. I expect them back within the hour."

An unfamiliar emotion coursed through Logan, like a poison in his veins. "I see she's got ye wrapped around her finger."

"Amelia needed assistance. She couldn't very well turn to ye, now could she?"

"Not wasting any time, are ye?" Logan gave voice to the peculiar bitterness that had suddenly infused his thoughts.

"If I had the energy, I'd set ye straight on yer arse for saying such a thing."

"If I find ye've any thought of taking advantage of the lass, ye will answer to me."

Anger flashed in Finn's eyes. He stalked toward Logan. "Has a blasted horse kicked ye in the head? The lass has eyes for ye and ye alone."

"It's not *her* motives I am questioning."

"Ye know damned well I would not do such a thing . . . not to Amelia. She deserves better than a man like me." Finn scrubbed his hand against his jaw. "Besides, she doesn't want me. Or any other man, for that matter." He glared at Logan. "For some confounding reason, the lass wants you."

"She's got some blasted fairy tale in her head. The lass wants a bloody poet who will spout sonnets and declarations of love."

Finn cocked a skeptical brow. "Sonnets? Blast it, MacLain. I'll be damned if ye're not the most dunderheaded mule I've ever known. Ye're going to let her leave? Ye're going to stand here and let her put an ocean between the two of ye?"

"What choice do I have? I can't give her what she wants. What she deserves."

"The hell ye can't."

"Amelia is a lady. She deserves a gentleman. Not a bloke like me."

Finn slowly shook his head. "Ye will regret this 'til the end of yer days. The lass loves ye."

"And I love her." Logan raked his fingers through his hair.

"Which is why I am letting her go."

Finn stared at him as if he'd sprouted horns. "Don't try to convince me ye're being noble. I know better."

The words plowed into him, but Logan met his cousin's eyes. Damned if he'd show the bastard he had hit his mark.

"She deserves a better man than me."

Finn's scowl eased. "She deserves a man who loves her, ye bloody dolt."

"In time, she'll find a respectable gent who can give her the life she wants." Logan stared down at the ground. "It's for the best."

"Ye're a blasted fool."

With the words echoing in his ears, Logan turned and marched away. Finn was right. He was a fool. He never should've come here. How could he have believed he could simply bid farewell to Amelia, as though the lass had been little more than an acquaintance? When she left, she would take a piece of his heart.

But he'd meant what he had said.

It *was* for the best.

He stormed through the doors of the Rogue's Lair, marching straight up to the bar. Murray regarded him silently, his weary eyes saying enough.

"Do not start on me," Logan said, keeping his tone low and even despite the emotion coursing through him. "Finn said enough."

Murray shook his head as he wiped down the bar. "Evidently, *not* enough. If he had, ye wouldn't still be standing here. Ye'd be doing everything in yer power to stop the lass from sailing off to America."

"Ye know bloody well why I can't stop her."

Murray's bushy brows knit together. "I know why ye think ye should let her go. I also know ye're dead wrong."

"We both know I'm not the man for her." The words tasted bitter in Logan's mouth.

"I know someone did ye wrong. But that was a long time ago. Ye need to remember—the lass is nothing like the woman ye'd planned to marry. I've seen how Amelia looks at ye. She's not eyeing a title. Or a fortune. She's looking at a man—a man who's a blasted idiot if he stands back and lets her sail out of his life."

The words slammed into Logan like a blow. "We both know I cannot give Amelia what she needs."

"And what in blazes is that?" Murray regarded him for a long moment. "Do ye love her?"

Logan knew lying to the man who'd known him since he was a lad was pointless. He'd speak the truth, no matter how it clawed at his chest.

"Yes."

Murray nodded, confirming he'd already known. "And the lass . . . she loves ye?"

"I believe she did. Until I walked away."

The barkeep leaned his elbows on the counter and pinned Logan with his gaze. "Then I'll ask ye, MacLain—what in hell are ye doing here?"

LOGAN HAD ALWAYS believed himself a determined man. When he set his mind to something, he'd see it through, come hell or high water. But now, as he walked through the doors of his townhouse, the quiet of the home assailed him. His housekeeper and his aunt had both gone to see Amelia off on her journey. How oddly silent the house seemed without the pleasant sound of their banter. Each room felt strangely barren. Strangely empty.

Just like his heart.

Without Amelia.

He headed directly to his study and retrieved the velvet-covered box he had stored in his desk. Stashing it in the pocket of his jacket, he turned on his heel and left the house.

By hellfire, he'd been an arse.

But he would set it to rights. He would fix the mess he'd made of things. Her home was not in America. She belonged with a man who loved her more than life itself. Amelia belonged here.

With *him*.

And now, he'd convince her to stay.

Chapter Thirty-One

NAVIGATING HIS PHAETON through the congested street, Logan tensed his fingers around the leather reins. As he approached Amelia's library, he was struck by one indisputable fact.

Caldwell's carriage was nowhere in sight.

Amelia was gone.

Damn the luck. An invisible fist plowed into his gut.

He needed to get to her. He had to tell her the truth—the truth he should've spoken days earlier.

He loved her.

Bollocks, he'd been a pig-headed dolt. Like a fool, he had hurt her deeply and allowed the wound in her heart to ache. Could she forgive him?

Or would she board a steamship for New York and sail out of his life?

Forever.

The fist twisted in his gut.

Suddenly, his attention was drawn to the glint of sunlight against metal. What in blazes was lying on the steps, nearly at the landing?

He slowed the carriage to a stop and bolted up the stairs. Light gleamed against a thin length of silver.

Heathy's collar.

He lifted it up to examine it. He'd never questioned why

steadfastly practical Amelia had chosen a decidedly impractical silver collar for her little mop of a mutt. Now, seeing the engraving on the band, he understood. The outer surface bore the dog's name in ornate script. But the inside of the band was marked with an endearment that brought Paul's hearty chuckle to mind.

A bell . . . for my dear Pixie's beloved little beast.

Again, the fist twisted into Logan's belly, deeper and more unforgiving. Tucking the collar inside his pocket, he headed to the carriage. If he managed to find Amelia at the dock, she would be delighted to see he'd found the collar. At least he could count on that. Her response to seeing *him* was very much more in doubt.

Returning to his phaeton, he spotted Finn's coach. Evidently, they'd been returning to the library. Mired in the congestion on the avenue, he'd stopped the brougham a few blocks away. Logan watched as Finn let down the steps. Amelia hiked her skirts past her ankles, navigated the ornate metal treads, and rushed down the street.

He knew the moment when she first spotted him standing there, in front of what had been her home. Her brows quirked and her head tilted slightly, as though she wasn't entirely certain her eyes were not deceiving her.

As she drew closer, her mouth settled into a line, not quite a frown, as though she were making a great effort to maintain a semblance of composure.

Just as he was.

"Looking for something?" Meeting her eyes, he forced a casualness into his voice he did not feel.

The tension in her mouth eased by a fraction. "I believe you know the answer to that question."

Taking the collar from his pocket, he handed it to her. "I came upon this on the steps."

As she gazed down at the silver band, her perfect mouth curved into the most subtle of smiles. She drew her fingertip over the engraving. "Thank you. This means a great deal to me." Her smile broadened. "I don't know how the little rascal wiggled his way out of it."

"The wee beast has a strong will. And a sense of mischief."

"Quite so." Amelia tucked the collar into her reticule. "If I had known you were coming to wish me well, I would have waited."

Rays of sunlight danced over the lush red-gold hair she'd piled atop her head and topped with an elegant little black hat. For a long moment, as he took in the rebellious strands framing her face, Logan could think of nothing other than releasing the tresses from the pins which held them properly in place, freeing the waves to tumble unbound around her shoulders.

God above, she was lovelier than a man like him could express.

Amelia's vibrant spirit was a light in the darkness that had shrouded his heart.

He met her gaze, seeing the questions she could not hide, no matter how resolutely she squared her shoulders and tried to pretend she was simply preparing to say goodbye to a man who'd come into her life for a purpose that was now over and done.

Just as she believed *they* were over and done.

She still had not puzzled out the elemental truth between them, a truth as clear as the stars in the sky.

He loved Amelia. Beyond all doubt, he knew that elemental truth.

When he held her in his arms, he wanted for nothing else in the universe. And he prayed she felt the same. He had seen love in her eyes. True and enduring, unlike any he'd ever known.

Amelia was meant for him.

And he, for her.

He had never been more certain of anything in his life.

Now, he had to convince her.

"Amelia, there is one thing ye haven't yet figured out. When yer brother sent for me—when he asked me to watch over ye—

he gave me a gift."

Her eyes flashed with a gentle challenge. "Did he now?"

"He led me to a treasure. To a gift more precious than riches could buy. Yer spirit will keep me intrigued until I am an old man."

Her top teeth grazed her plump lower lip. "An old man?"

"A very old man." Reaching for her, he caught her hand in his and brushed a kiss over her satin skin. "An old man whose bones creak as he trudges up the stairs every night to share a bed with his enchanting wife."

"An old man with creaky bones." Mischief lit her eyes. "Rather a tempting prospect, I suppose."

A fierce yearning coursed through him. Amelia was his treasure, infinitely more valuable than the gems in a monarch's crown.

He wanted her in his arms. In his bed. In his heart.

Tonight.

And every night.

"Ye'll still be a beauty then. Waiting for me there with your hair lying loose over the pillow."

She blinked and took a step closer. "By then, my hair will be more silver than ginger."

The sounds of familiar voices cut over the clatter of a carriage rumbling along the street. Logan glanced up. Finn and Mrs. Langford sat on the driver's bench of the carriage. The coach slowed to a stop, and Finn offered both a tip of his hat and a word of advice.

"Be a man, ye dolt," he grinned. "Tell her."

Cocking her chin in that fetching way of hers, she regarded him for a long moment. "And what might it be . . . that you need to tell me?"

Steps from the place where he had spent his first night with her, a night during which he'd slept on a torture-rack of a chair while a cheerful dust-mop of a dog licked his hand rather than leave her unguarded, Logan met her keen-eyed gaze. Blast it, he should've brought his whisky flask. He had never been a coward.

But at a moment like this, a man could surely use a gulp or two of emotional fortification.

Finn was right. It was high time he spoke the truth in his heart.

"No matter if we're both old and gray and creaky, I will never be able to take my eyes off ye, *mo chridhe*."

Had he ever spoken truer words?

Her eyes softened with emotion. "My heart."

"Amelia, my sweet, I'll want ye until I take my last breath."

"But . . ." Her plump lower lip quivered. "Do you love me?"

He couldn't help but grin. "Aye. How could ye doubt it, lass?"

Her eyes widened, seeming to drink him in. Glimmers of pure joy danced in her gaze as a smile played on her tempting mouth. "I must say, I've never heard the words directly from your lips."

"Amelia, I was a fool." He searched her eyes, as if in their depths he would find the answer to the question he desperately needed to ask. In his life, he'd faced down cheats and killers. He had not cowered in the face of danger. Yet now, looking at the beautiful face of the woman he would cherish until his last breath, he felt tongue-tied. At a bloody loss for words.

"Tell me again, Logan." Amelia's eyes glistened with tears.

"If ye will have me, I want ye by my side for the rest of my days. For the rest of my nights." He caught her hands in his. "With every breath . . . with every beat of my heart, I love ye, Amelia."

I LOVE YE, Amelia.

Waves of emotion crashed over Amelia. Her pulse raced, and she struggled to find her voice. The man she adored had spoken with raw feeling and honesty. Logan was not a man accustomed to flowery words. He was not a man who crafted smoothly spoken seductions.

His gravel-edged declaration had come from the heart. From his soul.

How she'd longed for this moment. Her love for him would hold strong for every moment she had breath. And beyond.

She drank in Logan's warm gaze. Was that a trace of uncertainty in his eyes? Could it be he truly did not know the depth of her love?

Slowly, he drew the pad of his thumb over her hand, tracing small circles against her skin. "I do not expect ye to make any promises. Not just yet,"

She edged closer. Smiling with all the joy in her heart, Amelia wove her fingers through his sable-brown hair. She didn't care a whit that curious onlookers had stopped in their tracks, eager to take in the scene.

She didn't care that Finn and the ladies were hanging on their every word.

At this moment in time, all she cared about was the man who'd spoken the words that made her heart sing.

She cupped her palm against his jaw, delighting in the feel of his skin against hers. "I am not inclined to utter any promises. Or any vows. Truth be told, I don't really want to *say* anything."

Understanding flashed in his eyes. Had her smile given away the truth?

"Is that a fact, lass?"

"It is." She whispered against his mouth. "All I really want to do is this."

And then, she kissed him.

Perhaps it was her imagination, but through the haze of her joy, she heard the crowd emit a collective sigh.

And then she kissed him again.

Slowly, reluctantly, they parted.

He caught her hand in his and pressed it to his heart. His gaze seemed to see into her soul. Had he read the uncertainty in her heart?

"Every beat is for ye, Amelia."

"I do hope this is not all a dream," she said with a lightness she did not feel.

"A dream?" His smile was by equal parts seductive and adoring and amused. "I am very real, and ye're very much awake. I do love ye, my sweet lass. More than ye can imagine. Now the question is, do ye love me, too, my sweet Amelia?"

She pulled in a draught of air, willing the words to come. Why was it so hard to tell this man, this man she adored with every fiber of her being, the truth in her heart?

"Oh, Logan." She glided her fingertips over the curve of his face, over the stubble of new beard on his chin and jaw.

"Say ye love me, lass."

Swallowing against the emotion welling in her throat, she met his eyes. "I do love you, Logan. Truly, I do."

He stilled, seeming to take it in. "And ye want to be with me . . . for a very long time?"

"Yes," she whispered. "A very long time."

"'Til death do us part?"

Slowly, she nodded. "'Til death do us part. And perhaps beyond."

Behind her, the crowd sighed, as if in unison. He grinned, genuine joy lighting his dark eyes.

"So now, Amelia, there's only one thing left to do."

"And what might that be?" she whispered.

He retrieved a small velvet-covered box from his pocket. "I'd planned to give this to ye at a more romantic time," he confessed.

Anticipation swept over Amelia. "I cannot imagine a more perfect moment."

As he opened the lid, sunlight gleamed off an intricately cut diamond surrounded by tiny emeralds. Her breath caught at the beauty of the ring. If this was indeed a dream, she didn't want to wake up.

Logan dropped to one knee. His smile warmed her very heart and soul as the adoration in his dark eyes entranced her.

Good heavens. Her heart thrummed with emotion. *This is*

happening . . . it is truly happening.

When he spoke, Logan's voice was rough with emotion and an unfamiliar note of uncertainty.

"Amelia, my love, I have a question for ye."

"Do you now?" she teased, prolonging his misery.

"Aye, I do. Will ye travel to the Highlands with me, my love?"

"I do believe I would enjoy that," she said, feigning a nonchalant tone.

"And there is one more thing we need to do, my sweet Amelia."

She blinked against the hot, happy tears in her eyes. "Tell me, Logan."

He slipped the ring upon the third finger of her left hand. "A Highland wedding."

Chapter Thirty-Two

Three Months Later

BASKING IN THE warmth of rose hips scented water, Amelia stretched out her legs, her body not quite filling the length of the oversized clawfoot tub. The bath seemed a tonic for her weary limbs. After a morning spent walking the grounds of her husband's family estate, taking in the rugged terrain and drinking in the pure, fresh air, her soul felt an instinctive exhilaration. Sadly, her feet had not experienced the same level of joy. Her toes had felt pinched within her shoes—she'd see to obtaining some proper walking boots quite soon—while her legs had protested against the unfamiliar hills. Now, she savored the calm of this elegantly appointed bath chamber in the MacLain family home.

She propped her head against a small pillow, resisting the urge to close her eyes. At least, for the moment. She wanted to take in every detail of this beautiful room. Separated from their bedchamber by a heavy oak door, the bathing suite was an ingenious luxury, designed with comfort in mind. Above her head, the intricate swirls of the ceiling caught her interest, each pattern lovely in its uniqueness. The mosaic tile floor surrounding the tub had been laid by a skilled craftsman, the pattern in dark and ivory hues betraying an artist's creative eye, while the intricate details in the wood cabinetry had been constructed in a manner that was both functional and beautiful.

Relaxing against the tub, she sighed and allowed her eyes to flutter closed. She wiggled her toes in the warm water in delight. Ah, she could become accustomed to this. Visiting the place and family that had helped to shape her husband into the man he was would be a pleasure.

She'd traveled to Scotland years earlier, but now, experiencing the sights and sounds and smells with Logan by her side, she'd relished every moment. Logan's family had welcomed her into the fold, and she treasured the sense of belonging.

The soft protest of the door hinges interrupted her bliss. She opened her eyes to the sight of her husband filling the doorway, a sly smile lifting the corners of his full mouth.

"A more tempting sight I've seldom seen." Logan closed the door behind him and came to her with long, steady strides. Bare to the waist, he'd loosely tied his plaid around his hips. Dappled sunlight streaming through the glazed window over the tub danced over his flat, muscled abdomen, over the light feathering of sable-brown hair on his chest. So very delicious—ah, she would never tire of the sight of her husband's powerful body.

Amelia's mouth went dry with longing. She smiled, attempting to play coy, though she knew she'd failed rather miserably. She simply could not conceal her desire for the man who'd stormed into her life and captured her heart.

"I might say the same," she said, beckoning him to come closer.

"Ye're a beautiful bride, Mrs. MacLain." He grinned. "I do like the sound of that—Mrs. MacLain."

"As do I, Mr. MacLain."

The diamond and emerald ring Logan had given to her after he dropped to one knee on a London street glimmered as the sun's rays fell upon it, brilliant as the diamond band Logan had placed on her finger on their wedding day. So very beautiful, a cherished symbol of their love. And their passion.

He took a cloth from a basket near the tub and came to her. His hungry eyes swept over her, from the upswept curls on her head to the peaks of her breasts, skimming over her legs. The rose-scented water concealed little from his gaze, and Amelia relished the way he drank her in. She felt no shyness. No need to hide herself from him. Not when he made her feel as beautiful as any goddess a sculptor ever carved.

Without words, he dipped the square of soft cotton in the water. His expression intent, he drew the cloth over her back and along her nape, setting off tingles of pleasure through her body. Inch by inch, he swept the cotton over her body, his attention to her body tender, almost reverent. Each touch was a seduction.

"Ah, that's so very nice," she whispered against his mouth. "I want you to kiss me, Logan."

"Do ye now?" His eyes gleamed with wicked promise.

She responded in kind, making no attempt to disguise the longing in her tone. "Could you have any doubt, husband of mine?"

"Never."

He brushed his mouth over hers, a light, teasing caress. Meeting her eyes, he dipped the cloth in the water again, then slowly, deliciously swept it lightly over her breasts. With a tender touch, he caressed each in turn before anointing each peak with a delicious kiss.

Continuing his sensuous ministrations, he made small, light circles with the cloth over her belly. And then lower, between her thighs, stirring her delicious ache for him to a blazing fever.

He kissed her again. Deeply, this time. So very carnal. So very possessive. So very hungry for her.

"Ah, I love you, Logan." She encircled her arms around his back, pulling him close. His skin was smooth against hers, and she drank in the masculine feel of the man she'd married. The man she loved. With a low sound of need, his mouth claimed hers in a kiss that seared her soul.

And then, she was in his arms. Anticipation rippled through her as he carried her to the bedchamber.

"Ye're mine, love." A low fire burned in his eyes as he gently placed her on their bed. "And I am yers. Forever."

A BRIEF TIME after their delicious midday interlude, Amelia and Logan strolled through the gardens of his family home. She swept him a lingering glance. He had donned a white linen shirt and kilt in shades of green against black. As the breeze blew against the soft wool, she took in the delicious power of his muscular legs and his strong, lean form. Keeping a leisurely pace, he led her to a magnificent old tree, gnarled in spots by centuries of existence, yet breathtaking in its beauty. Smiling, he pointed to a low-hanging branch.

"I'll have ye know this tree was the cause of the silver in my aunt's hair. Or so she says"

"The tree?" She smiled at the man she adored, picturing him as a mischievous boy. "Or the lad drawn to scale it?"

He grinned. "It was not the climbing that turned her hair gray. But the tumbles I took."

"It is a miracle you're still in one piece."

"I was a hardy lad. Each time I fell, I wanted to scale the tree again. If only to prove I was not afraid."

"To yourself?" She studied him for a long moment. "Or to others?"

"To myself. Later, when I grew into a man, I still tried to prove that I was fearless. Again. And again." He caught her hand in his, his hold possessive and gentle and tender. "Until I met ye."

Emotion welled in her throat as she saw the adoration in his dark eyes. "You don't have to prove anything to me."

"Ye've taught me that lesson, my sweet Amelia. And more." With a sensuous touch, he brushed a kiss over the back of her hand. "There are times when we're in bed at night, just before I fall asleep . . . when I look at ye, I can scarcely believe my luck."

She met his smoky gaze. "I also watch you when sleep is near.

When we're relaxed. And warm. I treasure those moments."

"Just as I treasure you, Mrs. MacLain."

Amelia's pulse sped. Would the sensuous notes in her husband's gravel-edged voice ever cease to set her heart racing?

His lips brushed hers and gently, he drew her closer. The crisp aroma of his shaving soap and the clean scent of Highland air delighted her senses.

A well-timed clearing of a male throat jerked her from her bliss. Logan bit off a curse as he turned to look over his shoulder.

"Tell me ye're not looking to give poor Aunt Elsie another gray hair?" Ewan MacLain's smooth voice carried to Amelia's ears as he made short work of the distance between the manor house and the tree. Long and broad shouldered, Logan's brother shared his carved features and lean, powerful build and dark hair, but his eyes were green as a forest.

Logan flashed a scowl. "Yer timing leaves a lot to be desired."

Ewan's robust chuckle declared his affection for his younger brother. "Ye're a married man now. Ye've no need to be sneaking off for a rendezvous with yer lady."

"I'd think ye would want me to share my Highland home with my bride," Logan countered.

"From the looks of it, she wasn't getting to take in much of the scenery." Ewan grinned, his expression softening as he met Amelia's gaze. "My brother's a lucky man, he is. He had to waste no time putting a ring on yer finger before ye came to yer senses and changed yer mind."

Glancing at Logan, she couldn't help but smile. "I count saying 'I do' as the wisest words I've ever spoken."

"I meant what I said, Amelia. Logan's a lucky man to have a woman like ye at his side."

"I am a fortunate man." Logan coiled his arm around Amelia and held her close. "Now, what's brought ye here, brother?"

"Cara and Bonnie have requested Amelia's presence for afternoon tea." Ewan looked like he wanted to sigh as he mentioned his spirited young twins. "The girls fancy themselves to be proper young ladies and want to show off their fine manners. Our oldest daughter, Lily, is also eager to spend time with you, Amelia. She's a young woman now, intrigued by life in the city. She wants to learn all she can about it."

"It will be my pleasure," Amelia said, smiling with happiness. "At what time will the tea begin?"

"Cara's setting up for it now," Ewan said. "The young lass would not be this excited if Queen Victoria herself had arrived."

"Somehow, I do think that would be a far more momentous occasion," Amelia said.

Ewan slowly shook his head. "The girls are thoroughly impressed that ye've civilized their uncle."

Amelia cocked a brow. "Civilized?"

"Suffice it to say that before he met ye, my brother was not above taking part in a brawl in town."

"Or two," Logan offered with a cheeky grin.

"Somehow, I've no trouble imagining that," Amelia admitted.

"Ye knew I was a rogue when ye said yes to my proposal."

"Quite so." Amelia brushed a kiss against his cheek. "And I am entirely confident of one truth in my life."

"What might that be, wife of mine?"

She grinned with all the joy in her heart. "You will always be *my* rogue."

Epilogue

December 1893

DECKED OUT WITH a festive plaid bow attached to his silver collar, Heathy trotted about the library, becoming acquainted with the library's new patrons with a hearty sniff or two. Amelia's old friends Beatrice and Edith lounged in comfortably overstuffed wing chairs as sunlight streamed through the stained glass windows, casting colorful shapes against the far wall.

"I never would've believed it," Bea gushed as Amelia joined them. "You've utterly reformed him."

"Reformed?" Edith scoffed with a little shrug of her shoulders before Amelia could reply. "But Mr. MacLair does make you happy, doesn't he, Amelia?"

"Happier than I'd ever dreamed possible," Amelia said.

"They do say that rogues make splendid husbands once they've sown enough wild . . . well, you know what I mean," Edith added with an air of authority.

"Truly, they do," Bea said a bit wistfully.

"You may be right," Amelia agreed.

"I must say, I am impressed at your husband's efforts in assisting you to establish your new library," Beatrice went on.

"As am I," Amelia said, taking in the large, well-appointed rooms of the building her husband had converted to a permanent home for her collection. She hadn't been able to bring herself to consider reopening the library in the place that had been the scene of violence and fear. Her former landlord, recovered from his injury, had tried to convince her to purchase the building, but Logan's blunt response had sent Mr. Driscoll away in a sulk. Days later, upon learning of a café whose owner planned to retire to the countryside, Amelia and Logan had offered the gentleman a generous sum and acquired the building that now served as the ladies' lending library.

"Mr. MacLain and I were set on purchasing this building. The location is ideal," she said at the precise moment that Heathy took an unfortunate fancy to a new patron's ribbon bedecked muff. "If you'll excuse me," she murmured, then dashed off to keep Heathy out of trouble.

She scooped up the dog and spun on her heel, nearly bumping into her husband's broad back. He turned and flashed a grin she couldn't resist.

"Ye have visitors," he said as he ushered his sister-in-law and nieces through the door.

"Ah, Amelia, you are looking lovely." His brother's wife, Hannah, spoke in a tone as warm as an embrace.

"Hello, Aunt Amelia," his nieces greeted in unison. Holding her twin's hand, Bonnie went wide-eyed when she spied Heathy while her older sister surveyed the room, taking in the large collection.

"I predict I will spend many an enjoyable hour here," Lily, a willow-thin beauty, said. "You see, I've taken a position as a teacher in the city."

"How splendid," Amelia said. "I suspect you will come to love this place. Just as I have."

Heathy squirmed just enough to reach Cara and licked her face with enthusiasm. A joyful giggle bubbled from her mouth.

"He wants to be my friend," the young girl said with delight.

"Oh, he's definitely taken a liking to you." Amelia held the dog a bit more snugly as she caught him once again eying up her patron's ribbons.

Hours later, after Amelia and Logan had returned home to share a grand meal with Ewan, Hannah, and their daughters, their visitors retired to the guest quarters. With a grin Amelia could not resist, Logan lured his bride up the stairs to their bedchamber with the promise of a tempting kiss.

Or two.

Or many, many more.

He latched the door behind them and enfolded her in his arms. His tender caress stirred her heart. And her desires.

"Ah, Amelia. I do wonder if yer brother knew he had given me a precious gift," he whispered against her lips. "If he suspected I'd fall in love with ye."

Relishing the warmth of her husband's lean body, she melted against him. "I do believe he might have hoped for that outcome."

His fingers went to work on the fastenings of her dress. "I've been waiting all night for this moment."

"I adore your family, but I must confess, there were moments when I couldn't keep my eyes off you . . . couldn't stop thinking about what I wanted . . . when we were alone."

He nipped playfully at her earlobe. "So many delicious ways I want to touch you—and taste you."

Wishing her husband would finish with the tiny buttons at the back of her dress, Amelia sighed.

"Impatient, are we?" he teased.

"Dreadfully so, I'm afraid," she whispered as he slid the last button through its loop.

"Anticipation makes it all the sweeter," he murmured before kissing her deeply.

Tenderly.

Passionately.

She drank in the desire in his dark eyes. "There are no words to convey just how much I love you."

"We don't need words. We only need this." He traced the pad of his thumb over her lip, then kissed her again. And again. "I will always love ye, my sweet Amelia. You will always be my greatest gift."

THE END

About the Author

Award-winning author Tara Kingston writes historical romance laced with suspense and intrigue. She lives her own happily-ever-after in a cozy Victorian with her real-life hero and a pair of deceptively innocent-looking cats. When she's not writing, reading, or burning dinner, Tara enjoys movie nights, cycling, hiking, DIY projects, and cheering on her favorite football team.

Visit Tara at her webpage, www.tarakingston.com. If you'd like updates on new releases, historical romance news, excerpts, and more, please sign-up for Tara's newsletter at www.tara kingston.com/newsletter-signup.

9 781965 539828